A DREAM OF SILVER

A DREAM OF SILVER

J. Laughton Johnston

The Shetland Times Ltd.
Lerwick
2006

A Dream of Silver

ISBN-10   1-904746-20-9
ISBN-13   978-1-904746-20-1

Cover designed by Maggie Riegler

First published by The Shetland Times Ltd., 2006

A catalogue record for this book is available from the British Library.

Printed and published by
The Shetland Times Ltd., Gremista, Lerwick,
Shetland ZE1 0PX, Scotland.

To my father.

$\mathcal{A}$CKNOWLEDGEMENTS

Thanks to various members of the family who read this as an early draft, particularly to Sorley, to David and Gudrun for their helpful and professional comments, to Nigel for medical notes and to Wendy for editing.

My thanks also to Laurence Graham for casting a critical eye over my Shetland dialect and to Maggie Riegler for the cover.

CHAPTER 1

'Eventually I fell asleep, secure that while I slept
the light would continue to pulse over me until the dawn.'

"This is the beginning." The old man said to the boy who sat beside him on the bench.

> *Every now and then, be it summer or winter, a boisterous wind blows through the broad streets of Edinburgh. It races up Leith Walk and Inverleith Row and through the New Town, to swirl and eddy in the open spaces of Princes Street and the gardens below the castle. When the rain accompanies the wind the good citizens fly for shelter, for on days such as these it is as impossible to hold an umbrella as fly a kite in a gale. Such invigorating days are a reminder to them that their city overlooks the Firth of Forth and the cold North Sea.*
>
> *Not so very long ago, down by the shores of the Forth, the small fishing villages of Granton and Newhaven and the large trading port of Leith were discrete communities. Now they are just a part of their illustrious neighbour that burgeoned from the 18th century, northwards to the sea and southwards to the foot of the bare green Pentland Hills.*
>
> *Ten miles west of Edinburgh, also on the southern shore of the Forth, lies Queensferry, the old ferry crossing from the Lothians to Fife. The ferry is no more and now two great bridges span the estuary. Immediately to seaward of the bridges are several islets and opposite the port of Leith, is the island of Inchkeith. Finally, where the Forth meets the North Sea, are two more tiny islands clinging to either shore like eye-teeth in a gaping and otherwise toothless mouth.*

A Dream of Silver

On the south side, just off the Lothian shore, is the solid, cliff-bound sentinel of the Bass Rock, stained white from the guano of thousands of gannets. Once, it was a prison for the politically most dangerous. Opposite, on the north side, off the Fife shore, lies the Isle of May or Maas, or gulls. This was once a place of holy pilgrimage for Scotland's kings and queens, was the location of a disastrous naval exercise in the First World War and today, like the Bass Rock, it is a seabird reserve. The Isle of May, as it happens, is also the site of the oldest continuously operating lighthouse in Scotland.

On a clear day the whole sweep of the city, its coastal satellites and the Firth of Forth from the Queensferry to the Isle of May – the scene of the first part of my story – is visible from Edinburgh Castle's ramparts high above the city. Almost everything in this entire scene has, in one way or another, been woven into the novels of many of Scotland's writers.

If you look down from the castle ramparts, you will see, towards the eastern end of Princes Street, a tall, soot-stained, gothic monument within which winds a narrow and seemingly never-ending stone staircase to a tiny balcony near its summit. Sheltered at its base, within its four sturdy legs, sits a white, marble statue of the novelist and instigator of the great Scottish romantic myth, Sir Walter Scott: a writer still held in particularly high regard by Scots.

Until very recently, nowhere in Edinburgh was there a monument to Scotland's other great novelist of the 19th century, Robert Louis Stevenson, who was born fifteen years after Scott's death. Like his predecessor, Stevenson made imaginative use of the bloody history of Edinburgh and the intimate landscape of Scotland's countryside. However, his creations were infinitely more subtle and dangerous than Scott's. Today, at last, just below the castle ramparts in the West Princes Street Gardens, a small and graceful circle of young silver birch trees can be seen, in remembrance of Stevenson.

Among Scots themselves, opinion is divided on their relative merits. The story that follows is the account of my part in this great debate and my coincidental discovery of a curious link between them that was to bind them forever in my imagination. Although, looking back, it is also the story of my brief and troublesome relationship with Stevenson's ambiguous fellow ... Long John Silver.

The old man was dressed in an old pair of jeans and wore two pullovers over his shirt. Both were of hand-knit Fair Isle pattern. The inner was of browns, greens and greys and had a roll neck. The sleeve ends were frayed and there were holes in both elbows. The outer was sleeveless and patterned in bright mauve and red: the colours of both were as faded as his once bright-blue eyes. On his head he wore a yellow woolly hat pulled down over his ears and on his feet a well-worn pair of wellies whose tops were folded down to make for easier walking and to prevent chafing of the back of his knees when rowing.

He regarded the boy who sat beside him.

"Do you really need to say all that?"

"D'you think it's a bit pretentious?"

"What?"

"Over the top."

"Well … you said you were going to tell me a story about when you were a boy, like me." He indicated the papers in his grandfather's hands, "That doesn't sound like that."

The man reached under his woolly hat and scratched his head where some grey curls made a bid to escape. "You can't just tell a story without a beginning."

The boy made a face.

"Look, you have to have an introduction." He folded the manuscript sheets and put them in his back pocket. "The action will start soon enough."

"Yes … but …"

"You must have patience, Thomas."

"Tom."

"Sorry … Tom." He raised a hand over the boy's shoulder, but then withdrew it. "Story-telling is not always simple, there is often much more to a thing than just the obvious."

"What d'you mean?"

"Well, there's the rub. I can't explain it without doing it. If you see what I mean."

"Grandad, I can't understand you." Tom got up off the bench and returned half-heartedly to raking up the last of the autumn leaves on the front lawn.

Maybe Bill couldn't tell Tom everything the way he wanted. Maybe he shouldn't. He took out his pipe. As he filled it from the plastic tobacco pouch he was reminded, as always, of the leather one he used to use. When he had first inherited it there had been a painting of a tsar's head on it, but that had gradually worn off until only the smudge of white that had been the face remained. Finally it had fallen apart and, very reluctantly, he had had to discard it. He lit up and watched Tom carrying out his punishment for not having done his homework the previous evening. He shook his head slowly. Tom stopped raking and leant against the shaft. It was longer than he, large as he was for his age. Bill waited.

"I'm always getting into trouble."

He was at an awkward age, his limbs and torso outgrowing his control so that at times he was clumsy. A self-conscious nature only added to the problem.

He had his grandfather's curly hair and build, but the shape of his face came from his mother. Bill tried to reassure him. "It's all relative."

"There you go again."

"Sorry. I mean sometimes things can seem much worse than they really are."

"So?"

"Well, if you can keep that in your head when things go wrong … if you can think of much worse things, then the things that are happening at the moment won't seem so bad."

"Seems to me that I would just have two things to be fed up with."

"No, it's a matter of perspective."

Tom banged the rake on the grass in exasperation and it bounced out of his hands. "Grandad!"

"Sorry, I deserved that." He got up, picked up the rake and handed it back to Tom. "But you've kind of made my point about the story." They stood side by side both holding the rake. "It is sometimes easier to illustrate something than try and explain it verbally. In a story the sense doesn't exactly only come from the words; it also comes from the plot, characters, events, and emotions. In a story you try and explain something using words but the message is in some ways in the un-said, it's as if it is in the atmosphere of the story … in the texture of the pages." The wool tickled his scalp and he scratched his head again. "Sorry, I'm not explaining that very well. It's strange really."

"You're the one that's strange!"

Bill looked down at his grandson and smiled, saw his own son *and* himself at that age – old enough to know some things but not old enough to understand them. Yes, he must seem strange. "How old are you, Tom?"

"Ten. I will be 11 in March. How old are you, grandad?"

"Oh … hmm … 70 something … good gracious, yes."

"When's your birthday?"

"Em … September …" He glanced around. "Is there a wheelbarrow?"

Tom pointed to the shed at the side of the house and resumed raking up the leaves into heaps. Bill fetched the wheelbarrow from the shed and began stuffing it by the armful. The damp leaves clung to his sweater and he brushed them off. Tom regarded him questioningly. Bill shrugged his shoulders.

"You're doing what your dad told you, I'm wheel-barrowing. Alistair didn't say I couldn't do that."

They looked at each other for a brief moment. Bill wondered if Tom's almost yellow hair would darken like his father's or remain yellow like Alice's, Tom's grandmother and *his* long-dead wife.

He gazed absently at the garden. The weak and hazy sun that had struggled only halfway up the sky seemed to have given up. It had just enough warmth where its rays fell to thaw the overnight frost, but in the shadows of the hedge the fallen leaves were stuck together, stiff and white. The clematis on the front of the house was just beginning to turn to bronze and the late blooms of the roses were drooping on their savagely pruned stalks. Bill found that he wanted to get on with the story. He liked his beginning. He looked around at his son's comfortable suburban home set in its tree-lined street on the south side of the city, into which he had just moved. He wondered if he was ever going to get used to seeing the castle from this angle. It didn't look right. It was … the wrong side of the castle … wrong side of the tracks. He missed the sight and smell of the sea.

"Tell you what."

"Uh hu," Tom mumbled as he raked.

"Why don't I take you to where *I* was brought up and we can start the story properly from there?"

Tom paused and pondered. "I'll have to ask mum."

"Yes, of course you will." Over his shoulder through the large living room windows he thought he caught sight of someone moving away from the curtains. "Let's finish the leaves first, eh?" He looked around at the thin covering on the large lawn. Alistair could have swept the leaves up with his ridiculous little tractor … but, Bill thought, there's probably a principle at stake here. He felt an old pang of guilt. Maybe he should not have given Tom a hand … oh dear.

They piled the leaves up on the compost heap behind the screen of Leyland cypresses and put away the rake and wheelbarrow in the shed. Bill pushed a brick in front of the door.

"You have to snib it too."

"Oh, okay."

At the back door Tom took off his shoes and Bill his boots. The old man watched Tom put on his slippers and then followed him in his thick-ribbed boot socks through the utility room, where the washing machine hummed and the freezer throbbed, into the kitchen.

"Mum."

Cat turned from the cooker. "Well, are you finished?" She glanced briefly in acknowledgment at Bill, trying not to look at his pullovers, then back to Tom. "Put the rake away?"

"Yes, yes, but mum, can grandad take me out this afternoon?"

"You must not bother your grandad. Anyway, wherever to?" She raised her eyebrows and looked at Bill who indicated with a shrug that it was no bother. But his heart sank a little. Tom looked at him too. If he said he was taking Tom to where he used to live, Catriona – he always found it difficult to think of her as Cat – and Alistair, might wonder why. He did not want them to know that he had promised to tell Tom a story about his childhood. It sounded rather pathetic.

"I thought we might go to a pitch and putt course. There used to be a nice one on Leith Links."

Cat turned to Tom. "That's very good of Grandpa. What do you say, Thomas?" She turned to Bill as Tom raised his eyebrows. "But is the Braids golf course not closer, or the Meadows?"

"Yes, but the Links used to be a longer course," and in a stage whisper behind his hand, "it'll tire him out." He attempted a conspiratorial wink over Tom's head.

"I doubt," muttered Cat.

Out of the corner of the other eye Bill thought he saw Tom sigh and give an infinitesimal shake of his head.

Cat turned and ruffled Tom's hair. "Sounds a nice idea to me. Do you need to take some clubs?"

"No, no, they supply a ball, putter and something like a six iron."

After lunch, to Tom's initial annoyance, they set off walking to the bus stop. To Cat's relief, Bill had discarded his garden wear for a slightly more presentable pair of trousers, jacket, raincoat and shoes: the woolly hat was in his pocket.

"Why can't we take mum's car?"

"I haven't driven a car for a long while." He looked up at the chestnut trees above them and down at the split and empty mace-like heads littering the pavement. The freshly exposed insides looked as smooth and green as an avocado. His mouth watered.

"So?"

"Now, don't be cheeky."

"Don't you sort of pick it up again quickly, like riding a bike?"

"The answer to that question is both yes and no. For the moment take it as a no."

On the bus Bill struggled to find the right change and ended up over-paying. He looked at the driver who pointed his finger at the 'No Change Given' notice above his head. Tom led the way upstairs towards the front.

"Are we going to Leith Links, to play pitch and putt?"

"Yes, that's the intention," Bill muttered doubtfully, "but the pitch and putt may not be open this time of year."

"Are you going to show me the house where you grew up?"

"Questions, questions, questions! Patience … let's just wait and see, eh?"

Over the seventy years he had known the city remarkably little of it had changed. Sure, there were a few grand redevelopments – all looking a little cheap and brash against Edinburgh's New Town and the natural grandeur of the castle, but the streets still ran in the same directions and the skylines, by and large, were little altered. The old anticipations of what lay around a corner, over a hill or up a side street, were still rewarded with much the same views, the same associations. At the foot of the Bridges he could not help saying to Tom, "Our tram crashed here once."

"Tram?"

"Yes, tramcar. I used to go to school on a tramcar."

"Were you hurt in the crash?"

"No, but we were late for school *and* we had a great excuse."

"What was it like in a tram?"

He thought back. "It rattled a lot and the noise of the electric motor was quite different from the diesel engine of a bus. No gears for a start, so the note of the motor rose and fell steadily without interruption. One thing I remember very clearly about a tram was the way it cornered. It wasn't smooth. It was as if the wheels could only point straight ahead, so that it went round corners in a series of jerks." He turned to Tom. "D'you know why I remember that?" Tom shook his head. "Because sometimes *I* didn't do *my* homework when I should have … like some people I will not mention … and I had to try and do it on the way to school in the tram. My handwriting is bad enough, even when I try very hard, so when I wrote on the tram, every so often the jerk on a corner flung my pen nib across the page. If I did not get a punishment for not doing my homework I certainly got one for doing it messily!" and he laughed ruefully.

"Ah ha," said Tom.

They had passed through the centre of town and were heading down the mile-long length of Leith Walk, one of the widest, longest and most striking streets in Edinburgh, or Leith, depending on one's allegiance. Bill pointed to a side street as they passed, "That's where my dad, your great grandfather, was born. D'you know, *my* grandfather once told me that he remembered coming up Leith Walk on the back of a hansom cab!" Tom looked at him blankly. "A roofed cab pulled by a horse."

"Wow!"

"There are people living who were alive when the Wright brothers flew for the first time at Kitty Hawk in 1903 *and* when the Neil Armstrong stepped on the moon in 1969!"

"Cool."

"Pardon?"

"I said that's cool."

"Right … "

At the foot of Leith Walk the bus swung off towards the links. The sunshine became even hazier, perhaps because it was nearer the sea or maybe it had just sunk a little lower in the sky, for when they alighted the cold hit them sharply. Bill tucked Tom's scarf around his neck, put on his own gloves and pulled his woolly hat over his ears. He stood for a moment getting his bearings. "C'mon, this way," and he set off towards a road that ran uphill at right angles to the links.

"What about the pitch and putt?"

Bill stopped and they scanned the flat grassy links. "D'you know, I think Mary Queen of Scots played golf around here." He looked wistfully across the links. In a far corner he could see a round, wooden hut whose doors were closed. Then he noticed that there were no flags sticking out of the ground. "Can't be open. Ah well, can't be helped. C'mon." They took the road up the hill and came to four small late-Georgian houses trapped between a tenement building and a row of modern terraced houses. They stopped at one. "That's where I lived until I was about seven or eight. But I don't really have any memories of the place. Then we ... I ... moved a few miles to Newhaven."

Tom looked at the adjacent terraced houses, hunched shoulder to shoulder, their cramped front gardens hardly large enough for shrubs. Each had little squares of grass and narrow borders imprisoned behind low walls or hedges, as neat and dull as graves. Several borders still had the last fading flowers of this year's annuals and they seemed to Tom to be dying slow and miserable deaths. It was depressing compared with his home. They stood on the edge of the pavement to let people pass, Bill's gloved hands hung at his sides. Tom blew on his fingers and then stuffed his hands into his pockets.

"Why did you move?"

Involuntarily, Bill took a deep breath. He put a hand on Tom's shoulder and gently turned him so that they faced back down the hill. "Let's walk across the links, get a bus to Newhaven and I'll tell you."

They returned down the hill in silence, Bill deep in thoughts of the past and Tom absorbed for a moment by the local gang of kids on their bicycles, circling idly, their loud, sharp cries tossed like hot coals between them. They shouted over the tops of passing cars, through buses and around pedestrians trying to cross the road, as if nobody else was there, all the while playing wheelies and tricks. One caught Tom's eye and in the briefest of glances measured him, took in his elderly companion, and judged him not worth a further thought.

They crossed the busy road to the links by the traffic lights and took a tarmacadamed track that split the links in a long diagonal towards Leith Docks. Even on this cold day people were walking dogs or throwing sticks or frisbies and there were the inevitable joggers, including one pushing a large wheeled tricycle with its sleeping bairn. Bill turned as they passed, shaking his head and embarrassing Tom. A group of men and boys played football, their laughter cutting through the still air, their warm breaths forming tiny evanescent clouds above them. Once off the links they made their way through grey streets with exotic and foreign sounding names like Salamander Street, Elbe Street and Baltic Street: reminders of the port of Leith's historic and fruitful link with the ports of Europe. They passed an imposing entrance to the docks and entered Bernard Street with its broad square and elegant buildings, mostly ex-shipping and customs offices.

"How much further, grandad? My feet are hurting."

Bill looked round just as a bus came into view. "Quick, this one will take us to Newhaven in just a few minutes." They ran the few steps to the stop and jumped on board. Bill, hiding a little weariness, followed his grandson up the stairs.

The bus route took them along the main thoroughfare parallel to the docks. First, they crossed the Water of Leith where it met the sea after its long and winding journey through Edinburgh from the Pentland Hills. Once over the bridge they passed by great blocks of old bonded warehouses with tiny, square, prison-like, iron-barred windows. These once marked the boundary of the docks but now were converted into expensive flats. As they came up to the old harbour at Newhaven Bill got up.

"We're here."

"Already?"

"Yup."

Standing on the pavement Tom saw they were clear of the docks and that they could now see a broad stretch of the Forth, and even Fife, five miles away across the choppy and leaden-coloured water. Bill pointed obliquely ahead to an almost vertical stretch of a municipal park comprised mainly of grass and flower arrangements that faced directly across the road to the sea. The largest arrangement of flowers, in the centre, was an eight-pointed star. "Mari, star of the sea," Bill whispered under his breath, and then aloud to Tom, "Starbank Park."

"Not much good for football."

"But great for Easter eggs!"

Bill bent and extended his arm in front of Tom. A woolly finger homed in on a two-storey terraced house with a yellow wooden gate, halfway up the steep and narrow road that ran up the side of the park. In contrast to the black-looking stone of the houses where Bill had first lived, these were built of a pinky-red sandstone. Tom also noticed how the steep angle of the street meant that each house stood successively a little higher than its lower neighbour, as if they were leaning on each other for support. They were narrow too and the front gardens were open and bright. The whole effect was one of intimacy and warmth, even friendliness. At the foot of the hill Tom noticed the street's nameplate on the wall: Laverockbank.

"D'you know your Scots … what that means?"

"We had it in a poem once I think … wait a minute," he bit his lip in concentration, "… no, I can't remember."

"The lark's bank," Bill said and recited:

> *"The lav'rock lo'es the grass*
> *The muirhen lo'es the heather;*
> *But gi'e me a braw moonlight*
> *And me and my love together."*

"That's Burns by the way." He put his arm around Tom's shoulder and they looked at the manicured park. "I wonder how many years it has been since a lark sang here. I doubt even my grandfather would have heard one had he been here as an infant." After a pause he glanced at Tom and began, "Well, this is where I grew up and … " He saw that Tom's mind was elsewhere. "Something the matter?"

"I'm hungry."

Bill looked at his grandson. Of course the lad was hungry, and maybe a bit cold and bored too. It was beginning to get dark and although it was not yet late afternoon the streetlights were on. He looked around. There was the Starbank Inn at the foot of the road and the Old Chain Pier bar across the road. He was tempted but neither looked right for Tom. Then he remembered the new fish restaurant at Newhaven. "I know a good place."

"Not another bus ride!"

Bill laughed. "No. It's a chip shop and it's just across there," and he indicated the old harbour with a nod of his head. "I'll tell you a bit about this place when we get something warm inside us."

Bill bought chips for Tom and a mug of tea and a sandwich for himself. They sat by a window overlooking the tiny fishing harbour, now cleaned up and a berth for private yachts. On the slip someone was renovating a 1900s fishing smack that lay on its side, round and black-bellied, like a stranded whale. Tom sat absorbed, slowly and deliberately sampling one chip after another, hot, salted, vinegared and dipped in ketchup. Bill's yellow hat and gloves and Tom's striped red and white school scarf lay in a small heap on the table between them. They luxuriated in the heat and the smell of cooked fish and chips. Bill tapped his feet rhythmically on the floor beneath the table to bring back the circulation to his toes. He sipped his tea and looked around, remembering the building as the fishmarket shed when he was a child. It had been cold and wet, the floor covered in packed wooden boxes of grey fish with gaping jaws and bulging eyes. He had never handled live fish but somehow knew they were never warm. Men in gloves and boots, and yellow aprons sequined with fish scales, slid the heavy boxes around with casual twists of long and murderously hooked lengths of metal. The older men had worn caps and the younger men either jaunty woolly hats or none at all. Only one man had worn a trilby and he was the auctioneer. Bill recalled that he had stood on an upturned box and spoke so fast that he had not understood a word he had said. He had been tall and extremely thin, with a large bony nose like a beak. His hands had always been in his jacket pockets, elbows sticking out like bony wings, only emerging to wipe drips from the end of his nose with a neatly folded handkerchief, acknowledging bids with savage little nods of his head. He had looked like a great hungry bird stalking from one fish box to the next. And then there had been his officious looking assistant who had scribbled things on a dirty pad of paper, tearing off pages and laying them like postcards on top of the sold fish boxes; his scrawl as indecipherable as the auctioneer's call.

There was something about the harbour that had drawn him as a child, part the busy cheerfulness and part the strange breed of men. They had mended great tents of black nets with large, shuttle-like wooden needles, as if darning a giant's string vest; swung boxes brimming with fish that moved like liquid, from holds to quayside; or leaned out the little cabin windows, like hermit crabs, smoking stubby black pipes. Then there were the fishwives, who had lived in the old fishing village that still overlooked the harbour, who had sold their fish door to door, dressed in their traditional shawls and striped skirts. They had carried fish creels on their backs, whose weight was taken on their heads by a broad strap that passed around their foreheads. They had strained forward like beasts of burden. It was many years before he had understood why the sight of their toil had made him feel so uncomfortable. The smell of fish had permeated the very material of the place and clung like a kind of wet vapour to his clothes. His grandparents had always known when he had been to the harbour, almost before he had crossed their polished red threshold.

I suppose the story really begins with that threshold in Leith in the early 1940s. I was seven or eight. Someone was dressing me in my coat and having difficulty threading the belt through the buckle. Others were talking in subdued voices. There was a ride in the back of a strange car with my grandfather. It was dark and at this front door my grandmother was waiting. She put her arms around me. She fussed and talked quietly and continuously, but I was not aware of the words that were spoken around and possibly to me. I was confused and probably in a state of shock. It was not until my grandmother left me in the attic bedroom, the door ajar and the landing light casting a narrow swathe of blue carpet into the darkness that I began to understand what had happened. That is when the tears came; when I was alone. And they came in a silent torrent and grief took ownership of me.

A voice was addressing him. He looked at Tom across the table, sucking a chip dipped in ketchup and speaking to him at the same time. At first he did not register his words. "What?"

"I said you were going to tell me about the house ... the one we've just seen."

"Ah yes ... well ... " He pulled himself together. Where to begin? "You won't remember the last war?" Tom frowned in concentration then shook his head. "Of course not, stupid of me." He looked down and was suddenly conscious that his fingers were wrapped tightly around his mug of tea. It still hurt to talk about it after all those years. Then he began. "I was born not so long before the beginning of the last world war ... in the 1930s. We lived in the house I showed you above Leith Links." Bill scratched his head and tried to think of a way into the events of the early part of the war. "Have you seen pictures on the television of aeroplanes bombing cities?" Tom nodded his head. "Well, during the war, German ... the people we were fighting against ... bombers came over Leith ... around about where we are right this minute ... and they dropped their bombs."

"Why?" Tom said, wiping his plate with his last chip.

Bill started at the casualness of Tom's question. He almost laughed and it eased the tension that was gripping him.

"The very short answer is that I suppose they were trying to destroy the docks and the railway lines ... to disrupt the war effort ... make our side weaker? Anyway, my mum and dad had been out seeing friends and when the siren came they had just set out on their way home." He looked at Tom to see that he had his attention, and then glanced out the window. It was now almost dark and getting foggy. "There had been several false warnings ... "

"Wolf."

"What?"

"Cry wolf ... we had it in school. Peter and the Wolf?"

"Quite possibly."

"No ... we did!"

"Okay. Well, apparently, they didn't think this warning was any different and decided to continue walking home." Bill leaned across the table towards his grandson as if he wanted to tell him a secret. Tom reciprocated. "They never got home."

"What happened? Were they bombed?"

"Yes ... they were." They both sat back in their chairs.

"What were they like ... your parents?"

"You know, it's a terrible thing, but I remember so little about them." Absentmindedly, he rubbed a circle of condensation off the window. "I have a picture in my mind of a laughing, mild mannered man, clean shaven, severely cut curly hair, wearing a thick overcoat and … a yellow scarf, bending down to push me on a sledge. I think that memory is genuine, the others I'm not so sure of." He looked at Tom, squinting as if trying to recognise someone behind him, so that Tom nearly turned around. "My mother … you would think I would have stronger memories of her, but I don't have one that I'm sure of. From the few photographs of them, mostly of their wedding or posing with me as an infant, she looked to be a severe lady, or maybe she was just nervous. I don't know." His stare returned to Tom. "I suppose I could have found out more about them, but apart from asking my grandparents the usual sort of questions – what was my dad like when he was my age and what did he do for a living – I never enquired."

"Was that when you went to stay with *your* grandparents … after your parents were killed?"

"You knew that?" Bill said, somewhat surprised.

"Yes, dad told me."

"Well, that's quite right. I had no uncles or aunts in Leith and my mother's people were down in London, so that's when I came to live here."

"Grandad?"

"Yes, Tom?"

Tom bit his lip, "Could I have some more chips?"

Bill put his elbows on the table, cupped his chin in his hands and frowned threateningly. "Look, if you don't eat your tea when we get home I could get into big trouble. No, I think it's time we were going. C'mon."

For a second Tom did not know whether or not his grandad was serious. They rose from the table. Bill smiled and Tom grinned in reply.

Much later in the evening, when Tom came into his grandad's sitting room to say goodnight and, under instruction, to thank him for taking him out, he found him writing at his desk. The sweet smell of tobacco smoke hung thickly in the air.

"Homework?" he joked from the doorway.

Taking his pipe from his mouth, Bill turned from the desk, "Touché."

"What?"

"Forget it. Goodnight, Tom."

"Night, grandad."

Left alone Bill returned to his writing.

> *I don't know for how long I had been crying but eventually I fell asleep. In the middle of the night I awoke and my eyes were dry and sore. For a few moments I didn't know where I was. There were no familiar traffic noises, nor the bright light of streetlamps as there had been at home. Instead, there was the distant sound of empty railway*

wagons shunting and one wagon after another banging noisily against its neighbour in seemingly endless repetition.

Then it all came back to me. I stared at the ceiling and couldn't cry anymore. I felt empty and numb, and not so much alone, as abandoned. I didn't know what had happened, only that there had been an accident and they were never coming back. What had I done that they had left me? I turned towards the wall and pulled the slipping eiderdown quilt closer around my neck. The events of the last few hours dragged so heavily on me that I couldn't begin to imagine what lay ahead.

I was just closing my eyes again when I became aware of the briefest flash of light. It seemed to have swept across the wall immediately above me and then was gone. I looked at the wall in the dark and there was nothing. Then, there it was again, this time followed closely by another flash. They were very short, but in their brief existence I was sure that the light swept from one side of the room to the other. I waited. After a short interval the flashes came again and after another similar interval, yet again. I began to count the seconds and found that the blinks of light occurred regularly, about every minute. I turned over on my left side towards the window and from far away, through an opening in the curtains and through the black panes, came the light. The room was not entirely dark as the landing light had been left on. I slipped out from under the blankets and eiderdown and padded across the strange room to the window. Pressing my head against the cold pane I caught sight of the beam. Its source was far away, almost on the horizon. From there, it swept horizontally across the sea, faintly at first and then as it crossed Leith Docks – for I recognised them – and Newhaven, it grew brighter until, as it passed over my face, it blinked sharply twice and then faded as it moved on out of sight towards Granton. I waited until it passed again and then was aware of the many other pinpricks of light that shone on the sea and from Fife across the Forth. Most were still but some moved ever so slowly. I shivered with the cold and went back to the warm bed. I lay there facing the window and even when I closed my eyes I could sense the light as it brushed my face. Eventually I fell asleep, secure that while I slept the light would continue to pulse over me until the dawn.

CHAPTER 2

'I wouldn't be here and neither would you.'

*I*t seemed to them both that they had discussed the possibility of making a home for Bill almost endlessly over the past few weeks. In fact, ever since he had scribbled on a postcard – of the burning Viking galley from the Up-Helly-A' celebrations – that he too was going to burn his boats; in other words, leave his cottage and move into some kind of residential care. It had become the first subject at breakfast, at least when Tom was not there, and the last thing at night before Cat picked up her latest Ian Rankin. Bill was such a self-sufficient character that the proposed move had surprised them. Bill had not lived in Edinburgh since long before they had married and it was unsaid between them that they probably would not have seen a great deal more of him, even had he stayed.

Alistair and Cat lived on the south side of the city in a large Victorian house, at the back of which was a small extension that had once been the maid's quarters. Cat had a fantasy that one day they might have an au pair and that she would live there. The au pair would be French, from whom Tom would learn the language and when he was sixteen he would go to a Lycée in Paris. Alistair, meanwhile, had thought that one day he might work from home and the flat might be his office. Both were reluctant therefore to take on Bill and make the old maid's quarters into a kind of granny flat.

Alistair had never got on with his father and they had become even more distant since Alice, his mother, had died, almost on the eve of his wedding to Catriona. It was not that they had fallen out over a specific issue. It was just that Alistair was naturally conservative while his father, if Alistair had had to describe his political position, was a woolly liberal. So that, whenever they had a discussion they quickly found themselves at odds. Bill found it quite strange that Alistair had inherited so many physical attributes of his mother, such as her colour and build, even her ever-so-slightly-crooked smile … that always distracted Bill when Alistair did it quite unconsciously in argument … and even her politics, but not her talent, nor even her interest, in art.

Because of this distance between them, Alistair was therefore more reluctant than Cat to even consider having him stay with them permanently. On the other hand, he did acknowledge that Bill *was* his responsibility and both knew Bill well enough to know that he would not be leaving the cottage unless he really had to. They agreed that it must be a money problem. They surmised, wrongly, that faced with a choice, Bill would find it as hard to go into sheltered housing in the islands as leave and move to Edinburgh to be with them. The islands were where his grandparents came from. He had known them since childhood and had lived there himself for the past ten years or so. It was Cat who pointed out the ultimate inevitability of it all: there *was* no alternative. Bill would have to come and live with them. The logistics and expense of travelling regularly to visit *him* in a home in Shetland ruled that option out.

Reluctantly, Alistair took a few days off work and flew north in the late summer with instructions from Cat to bring Bill back with him. He did not have a love for the islands like his father. He found them cold. There was never a summer to speak of, the landscape was bleak and there was only one semi-decent 18-hole golf course … and of course, as he knew would happen, his flight was delayed overnight in Aberdeen because of fog in Shetland. Nevertheless, he did his filial duty and faced up to the prospect of spending a long, ill-tempered day and an equally long evening of too much whisky, arguing with his father in his claustrophobic cottage that was not much more than two rooms and an attic. As he had foreseen and dreaded, there was no escape from his father and his pipe other than outside. To cap it all, after the fog cleared, it blew a gale, so that when, in desperation, he did have to get out for a walk in the early evening, wrapped in his city raincoat, he was soon soaked and chilled. Reluctantly forced back indoors, his temper was not improved by having to accept an ancient woolly jersey of his father's that smelled strongly of his tobacco.

Bill gave Alistair a whisky. It was a fine, single malt, grudgingly acknowledged. They sat on either side of the stove each waiting for the other to speak: both better at repartee than attack. Eventually Alistair had given in: he only had one night after all.

"Dad."

Bill lifted his gaze from his glass with all the enthusiasm of a patient awaiting a bad prognosis from his doctor.

"Dad." He hesitated again. If he said "I", his father would say what about Cat, and if he said "we", he would say what about you? "I … that is, we … Cat and I … want you to come and stay with us."

Bill absorbed the word "want" into his curmudgeonly mood and it resulted in an outbreak of stubbornness.

"You know I would rather stay here."

"Yes, of course. But we would hardly see you … you wouldn't see your grandson … we wouldn't be able to look after you."

"D'you *want* to see me?"

"Oh dad, don't be so difficult. Of course we all want to see you." Alistair swallowed a generous mouthful of whisky, nearly choking on it in his frustration.

"Where would I stay? I would be under your feet. I wouldn't want that and I don't suppose you would either."

"Dad, listen … we've planned for quite a while now to redecorate the old servants' quarters at the back of the house. It's semi-independent. As well as a bedroom, there is a sitting room, a bathroom and a kitchenette … and it's all heated."

"Don't you want it for anything else?"

Alistair put his empty glass on the floor, leaned forward towards his father and lied very convincingly. "No … we have no other plans for it."

"I don't know how I'd get all my things packed."

"We can arrange to have all that done professionally, dad."

"I'd want to keep on the cottage."

"What for, dad? Really, you'd be better selling it."

"I would like to think it was still there for me … you might not understand."

"Dad, why are you making this so difficult for us all?"

He had not expected Alistair and Cat to want to have him and he had only just reconciled himself to the idea of leaving the cottage and living in a local sheltered housing scheme, and *that* after many days agonising over the options. To seek a solution he had gone for a long walk on the hill, but if the weather had been better he would have taken his boat out. The silence of the lochs and the moor, broken only by the thin calls of high-flying migrant waders and the sight of the last yellow flowers of the tormentil desperately trying to brighten the sopping earth, reminded him that he too could not escape life's seasons. In Shetland at least, he had thought, he would still have his few friends and relatives around him, distant though the latter were. With a bit of luck he might even have a view of the sea from the window of his room and the opportunity on a fine day of filling his lungs with that so familiar salty tang. But now here was Alistair saying that they *wanted* him.

By the end of that long evening with Alistair, Bill was tired out, mentally and physically. With a fine sandpaper of guilt his son gradually wore down his resistance. Ironically, Bill thought that had they got on better, Alistair would probably have given way to his wish to stay in Shetland and *he* would not have felt this guilt in trying to deny Alistair the moral high ground. Either way, Bill rationalised, they were probably not going to be a problem for each other for as long as Alistair imagined. In the end he gave way, rather ungraciously and with the proviso that he did not part with the cottage immediately. It was such a big, possibly final, step that he just had to feel it was still there for him, at least for a little while.

A relieved Alistair returned south with his father's promise that he would follow him as soon as he could arrange for the transport of his things and the care of the cottage. Bill also needed to dispose of the boat and outboard. Neither was particularly valuable and the former was now a rather ugly and battered piece of fibreglass, but it was the principle of disposing of them that was the difficulty, for never again would he be able to look forward to summer evening fishing trips, or beachcombing and driftwood-collecting expeditions to remote beaches. The bike, he lied about, not selling it but leaving it in the care of a friend. The hoard of ropes, fish boxes, various pieces of hardwood and useful plastic containers from ten years of beachcombing, plus rusting tools, tins of paint, garden implements and some objects whose use he had forgotten or never fathomed, all cluttering up the old byre attached to the cottage, were all to remain in place. Some of them anyway, through years of degradation, were almost part of the building.

In Edinburgh, Cat hastily arranged a redecoration of the flat including a wall of bookshelves, a new carpet in the sitting room and a new bedroom suite. The little fireplace was blocked up, much to Bill's disappointment when he arrived, and new fittings were put in the bathroom and kitchen. Bill offered to pay although they, and he, knew that without selling the cottage he could not afford it. After a brief telephone conversation with Alistair he was persuaded that his contribution was not necessary. He was also told not to bother bringing any crockery, pots and pans etc., as Cat had already bought these. For that he was grateful as he was quite glad to leave behind his rather battered and cooking-oil stained pots.

It was almost a month later when Bill completed his packing up and left. The cottage was small so he had relatively little furniture or personal belongings to bring. He left behind his bed, an armchair, the kitchen table and chairs and the long wooden resting chair that fitted so naturally and comfortably between the window and the stove, taking only his desk, a pianola with matching music cabinet and his favourite little couch on which he liked to put his feet up. He also left many other bits and pieces and instructions with his neighbour to leave on some low-level heating, just in case.

The most precious personal items he brought were his hi-fi equipment, tapes and records, his books – of which he had many – Alice's colourful miscellany of Scottish hand-painted pottery that they had habitually used and, of course, her paintings. The first items were important as music had always played a central part in his life and was rarely far from his ears or absent from his head. Coincidentally, it was to be through the music, or at least its reproduction, that his relationship with Tom would become established. His books were his hobby *and* business and took a long and tedious day to pack into thirty cardboard boxes. The third and fourth items he just could not imagine living without.

Leaving the islands, on the overnight boat from the capital, Lerwick, was one of the most emotional experiences of Bill's life. The customary blast on the ship's whistle as it passed by the town and out into the North Sea had always brought a smile to his lips, now they were compressed in a grim struggle to stifle embarrassing tears. Wrapped up in his overcoat on the deck he stood long into the evening as the islands imperceptibly merged into the dark of the night. Later, he was grateful for the womb-like throbbing of the engines and gentle rocking movement of the ship as he fell asleep in his bunk.

Tom was reluctant to enter Bill's flat, but his mother sent him up with a cup of coffee only the day after Bill arrived. When he first saw them – the record and tape collection, the turntable and the two enormous speakers – they were an immediate source of fascination. Bill explained the delicate nature of the recording mechanisms, the importance of good needles and correct arm balance. Tom ran off and returned with his Walkman. He put the ear pieces on his grandad. Bill listened respectfully to a pop tune and in response stood Tom close to one of the big speakers, putting on an organ concerto at three-quarters volume. Tom was blown by the depth of sound, rather than the music, and learned that 'obsolescence', a word of his father's, was a relative term. He also learned the meaning of 'relative'.

So it was that Tom and Bill began to get to know each other that autumn. For each it was a new experience and they trod warily. For Bill it was a relationship that he could not politely hold at a distance, as he did with Alistair and Cat. For Tom, the novelty drove him to break through the barrier of his grandfather's reserve.

The door that separated Bill's flat from the main house gave off from the kitchen from where a short uncarpeted staircase led to Bill's sitting room. Off that were his kitchenette, bedroom and bathroom. Below the sitting room, at ground level, were the old washhouse and the garage. Once Bill, with the help of Alistair, had got everything in place, which did not take long, he wondered what he would do apart from his second-hand book business. Back in the cottage much of his time had been taken up with the mundane chores of running the place and feeding himself. He had no central heating, only a couple of electric radiators and a stove that had to be fed continuously with peat or driftwood. Much of his time in the summer, therefore, had been taken up with raising and transporting the peat his neighbour cut for him, or beachcombing: his favourite pursuit. He had never minded all the necessary physical activity to keep himself warm, in fact he had found it rather satisfying and fulfilling. Shopping or posting involved a trip of three miles to the village store or a day's bus trip to and from the superstore in Lerwick, thirty miles away. His time had also been taken up with his duties as secretary of the local history society, involving the taking of the minutes and editing the reports for the monthly newsletter.

Bill had expected Alistair or Cat to come up with a list of sources of activities or clubs he could contact and he was indebted to them that they had decided to leave him to his own devices, at least to start with. He was not interested in gardening and there was therefore nothing he could contribute there or around the house. He had thought briefly that he might develop his business. Maybe expand it from its relatively narrow base of Shetland books only, but quickly dismissed the idea when he realised how much effort that might take.

The last thing he had expected was that he would find a kind of companion in Tom and that this would result in him writing. It all began on Tom's second visit to his flat. Tom was gazing round the room taking in the collection of records, the speakers and Bill's desk that resembled his father's, except that the latter's surface was only occupied by a computer while this one was cluttered with paper and books that were almost burying Bill's old Remington typewriter. He gestured towards the desk and nudged a pile of books on the floor with his foot.

"What are all these for, grandad?"

Bill regarded him from his chair by the desk. "I buy and sell them."

Tom could not hide his disdain for old books. "Who wants them?"

Bill bristled. "Collectors, researchers, libraries … sometimes people who simply want to read them."

"Did you always do that?"

"Casually … "

"Pardon?"

"I mean I did other work mainly and sold books for fun, but then when I retired this became a sort of full time hobby."

Tom picked up a book from the desk, turned it over, glanced at it and put it back as if it had no interest to him whatsoever. "What did you do then?"

"I was a journalist."

"What does a journalist do?"

"A journalist writes articles for newspapers and magazines."

"That was stupid of me not doing my homework, wasn't it?"

Tom's ability to skip lightly from one subject to another entirely unconnected left Bill floundering. When he had regained his foothold he found to his surprise that it was rather exhilarating. In fact he was rather charmed.

"It *was* rather."

Tom's face fell.

"But it was a minor misdemeanour. I wouldn't get too upset about it if I were you."

Tom fiddled with the bits of paper on the desk. "Did you get into trouble when you were small?"

"Oh yes."

"Did you get punished?"

"Oh yes."

Bill gently took the sheets of paper out of Tom's hands and those he had dropped randomly back on the desk and returned them to an order that Tom could not discern.

Tom leaned towards him conspiratorially. "What did you do?"

"Well … I," and then he thought … where do I begin?

"Yeh?"

It was at that moment that Bill found himself suggesting that he write down the story of his childhood for Tom, and so it was that he began to pass his time by typing it on his old Remington; that is, after politely declining the offer of lessons on Tom's PC. He placed the desk opposite the only window in his sitting room so that his back was towards it and he could sit facing his favourite watercolour of Alice's – the cottage and its setting – with the light upon it.

Passing through the kitchen on his way to collecting his bike from the garage, a week after their visit to Newhaven, Tom paused briefly by the flat door. In the quieter moments of some music he heard the distinctive rattle of the typewriter. He knocked, but Bill was so absorbed he never heard him. Opening the door and putting his head around it he saw the back of his grandfather sitting at his desk. He was kind of stooped and his unruly, grey and curly hair spilled over the collar of his opened and rumpled shirt whose sleeves he had also rucked up to his elbows. It was a state of sartorial untidiness that Tom could only envy and marvel at as he watched Bill pounding away with one finger of each hand literally beating the words out of the machine.

"Hi, grandpa."

Bill swung around and greeted Tom. "Well, what are you up to today?"

Tom crossed the room and leaned on the desk with his hip. "Not a lot this morning. I have to go to town with mum in the afternoon though." He toyed with one of the pieces of stone that Bill used as paperweights then leaned over the desk to peer at a soapstone carving that lay at the back. "Need new rugby boots." He picked it up, "What's this?"

"A beluga."

"What's that when it's at home?"

"It's a small white whale that the Inuit sometimes hunt." He took the whale gently from Tom, turned it over in his palm and pointed out the initials carved on the base. "I got it from a native Inuit in Greenland who took me hunting … many years ago."

"What were you doing there?" He held his hand out to take the carving back but Bill replaced it on the desk.

"I was a naturalist on a student expedition. Don't know why. I wasn't particularly knowledgeable in that field at the time."

Beside the typewriter, among piles of paper, was a collection of half-a-dozen black and white photographs that Bill had obviously been referring to in his writing. Tom picked them up. "Can I look at these?"

Once again Bill gently took the objects out of Tom's hands. "Tell you what … you make me a cup of coffee and I'll show some to you."

"How do I do that?"

"You can't make coffee?"

"Ehhhhh … no."

"Goodness me, what *do* they teach you?" He got up and led Tom into the kitchen where he demonstrated coffee making à lá cafetière. He offered some to Tom who grimaced in reply. Back at the desk he selected a black and white photograph and held it up. It was of an old couple posed in a garden. He showed it to Tom. The man in the photograph stood slightly behind the woman, with his left hand on her shoulder while she sat in a wicker chair. His right arm was bent, the jacket of his suit pulled aside and his thumb tucked into the exposed waistcoat pocket. A chain ran from the pocket across his lower chest to the other pocket that obviously held a fob watch. His expression was a little severe, but a trick of the light suggested a hint of humour in the eyes. On the other side of the woman, a walking stick hung by its crook over the arm of her chair. She appeared to be rather more nervous, sitting with her hands clasped, or clenched, on her lap, leaning almost imperceptibly against him. Her attention, however, was on the camera holder and she was smiling. She wore a long, dark skirt and a ruffled white blouse with a high collar closed at the throat by a silver brooch. The clothes were loose fitting but she was obviously quite slight. Her hair was black and wiry and her eyes dark and large. If her eyebrows had not been quite so thick and her nose perhaps a shade smaller she would have been a striking beauty. As it was, the slight imbalance of her features gave her an intriguing look and just the hint of an intensity and intelligence. The man was slim and like Bill his hair was thick and curly, but unlike Bill, snow white.

The feature of the man that caught Tom's attention was his luxurious walrus moustache.

"Who are they?" Tom asked.

Bill put down his cup of coffee. "They are your great great grandparents … my grandparents on my father's side."

"Gosh."

He pointed with the stem of his pipe at the man and then at the woman. "That's James Manson and that's Annie Manson, née Bairnson."

"Nay?"

"Her maiden name … her surname before she married."

Tom held the photograph. "That must be a long time ago?"

Bill smiled. "Not so long ago really. Let's see … " he puffed on his pipe and Tom fanned the smoke with the photograph, "… it was May … " He took the photograph from Tom, "see the cherry blossom on the tree behind them … May 1951."

"How d'you know that?"

"I took it."

"Wow! How old were they?"

Bill put his pipe to his lips and Tom backed away. "They were very close in age, must have been eighty-one or two."

"How old were you?"

"About the same age as you."

"Then I should take one of you now and I could show it to my grandson. That would be cool, eh?"

"That *would* be cool," Bill agreed.

"Did you stay with them at Newhaven then?"

Bill nodded as he stared at the faces of the two people who effectively became his parents at the age of seven. How did they cope with him? They were as old then as he was now! He looked at Tom and could not imagine trying to raise him.

"What were they like?"

"Luckily for me they were rather unusual people." He shuffled the remaining photographs and extracted two. "This one is James as a young man." The picture was a studio portrait of a clean-shaven James as a merchant navy officer.

"Was he a lieutenant or a captain?"

"This is him as a second mate, see the two rings on the sleeve. Later he did become a captain, both in sail and steam. This one," picking up the second, "is my grandmother about the same age." Annie stood in all the promise of youth by the side of a grand piano.

"She looks beautiful," said Tom quietly.

"Doesn't she just."

"Why is she standing beside a piano?"

"Because she played well." Bill leaned back in his chair and studied the picture at arms length.

"Did she play at concerts?"

"No, I don't think she was quite good enough for that, but she couldn't, or wouldn't have anyway."

"Why not?"

Bill picked up the garden portrait again. "D'you see the stick beside her?" Tom nodded. "Her right leg was damaged in an accident when she was a child. It was never strong and latterly quite withered. Part weakness, part vanity, I suppose, prevented her from performing in public."

"What happened to her?"

"Oh ... it was a big horse. You know ... used for ploughing. I was told that she was leading it out of a byre and it spooked at something, threw her against the wall, then in panic trampled on her."

"That's awful, grandad."

Bill put his arm around Tom and squeezed him gently. "She could have been killed. She was very lucky ... and so were we."

"You wouldn't have known her, for example?"

"I wouldn't be here and neither would you!"

Tom took it in slowly. "Scary."

"Very."

They thought about it, each relative to themselves. Then Tom indicated James in the later picture. "Did he sail to America?"

Bill got up and pulled an old atlas off the bookshelf. The pages were loose and discoloured. He returned to the desk, pushed back the typewriter and papers and set the photographs aside. Flipping through the pages of the atlas he found a world map.

"The company's main trading destination was the Far East via the Suez Canal – Malaya, Singapore, Philippines, Borneo, Thailand, Japan and occasionally China. They took out machinery and finished goods from here and Europe and brought home things like rubber, copra, timber and tea. Under sail the trips took about six months, under steam about four months. Not long after John, my father, was born, my grandfather switched companies and joined the Home Trade so that he was no longer away for so long. The ship's homeport was Leith and trips were only to Europe and back, mainly to Antwerp, Hamburg, Rotterdam and the Baltic ports."

Bill turned the pages of the atlas until he found northern Europe. He pointed to the east side of the Baltic. "At the outbreak of the First World War with Germany, in 1914, your great great grandfather's ship was trapped at the

Latvian port of Riga." His finger tip traced the coast of Germany that dominated the south coast of the Baltic. "If they had tried to come out through the Kattegat and the Skagerrack there is little doubt they would have been picked off by the German navy."

Tom peered at the map. "What did they do?"

"They abandoned their ship at Riga. Can you imagine that? Having to just walk away from something as valuable as a ship?" He shook his head in disbelief as Tom considered the matter. "Then they set off north to go around the Baltic … overland … quite a trek." He indicated the route. "First, they went through Finland in the back of lorries. They hired them with the local currency they made from selling off everything in the ship they could, even many of their personal belongings as they knew they would not be able to carry them all the way home … though grandfather did keep the essential tools of his trade like his sextant and log tables. They didn't get much for what they sold because everyone there knew they would have to leave nearly everything behind anyway."

Bill took his pipe out of the corner of his mouth and with his free hand pointed at it. "Being the man he was, my grandfather swapped some of his clothes with the foreman of the stevedores for this – he waggled the pipe – and a tobacco pouch. They couldn't get clothing like his in Latvia then." He tapped the yellow stem of the pipe. "This is amber. D'you know what that is?"

Tom shook his head.

"Have you ever touched a cut Xmas tree. Yes? It weeps a very sticky resin that is difficult to get off your skin. He tapped the stem again. *This* is fossilised resin from the great coniferous forests of the Baltic." Then he held the pipe by the amber stem and indicated the grey-brown bowl. "This part is made of meerschaum, a rare kind of clay. You can't get pipes like these nowadays."

"If you wanted them," said Tom, screwing up his nose.

Bill shrugged and smiled. "If you wanted them," and as if to indicate his preference he took out a match and relit his pipe. "Years later, when ribbing my grandmother one night, grandfather told us about the Riga Balsam that he had also brought back." He leaned back in his chair as Tom leaned against the desk. "My grandmother's upbringing was rather sheltered. She was so teetotal she even drank tea reluctantly. She was sweet, but she was very stubborn about some things. Funnily enough she had a weakness for popular songs, but she only listened to them on the wireless in the kitchen when she was working. It was a Presbyterian guilt thing; she pretended she was somehow not actually enjoying them. Anyhow … grandfather told her that the balsam was medicinal. So, when either of them had a cold, they took a teaspoonful of this stuff, apparently it was even given to my father too when he was a child. My grandmother didn't like it, but she took it. Well, that night I remember my grandfather admitting to her that it was really a form of alcohol! When my grandmother realised she had been tricked into taking alcohol for all those years she was so upset and confused she burst into tears, threw down her knitting and rushed out of the parlour, banging her stick on the stairs all the way up to their bedroom. Grandfather went after her and it was a long time before he could persuade her to forgive him and come downstairs again. She was so ashamed she wouldn't even look *me* in the face for a day or two!"

"Did he drink?"

"My grandfather? Not much really, he was a very upright man. He would not have approved of the casual way people drink alcohol today, especially the young."

"What else did they take with them when they escaped?"

"They took a good supply of food but not much clothing … it was late summer. Even so, they were just south of the Arctic Circle as they crossed into Sweden. He said it was miles and miles of nothing but forests and lakes until they reached the tundra at the very north end of the Baltic, then it was just nothing. Then they had to make their way south again, down the Swedish side of the Baltic, this time by train, until they could cross over to Stavanger in Norway. There, a ship was provided to take them all home along with a number of other seamen who were similarly trapped." He sat back in his chair and turned to Tom. "That was a journey of about 1500 miles!"

"Wow!"

"Granny told me that she had no idea what had happened to him. She thought that he might have been captured and imprisoned in Germany, or his ship sunk and he drowned, for all she knew. Apparently … somehow … word got ahead of the imminent arrival at Leith of a ship with British seamen from Norway. She was down at the dock with a large crowd when the ship tied up. All of those waiting were in a terrible state of anguish. Would there be word of their loved ones? Would they be there? She told me that she saw him on the deck, cool as could be, and when their eyes met he gave her a cheery wave just as if he had been away on a day-trip! Granny had been clutching the front of her blouse as she looked up at the boat and the first thing grandfather did, after kissing and hugging her, was to ask how she had come to meet him in such a blouse. What had happened to the buttons? She looked down to find that she had twisted half of them off!"

"Thomas!" They heard his mother calling from the foot of the stairs. "Come and get your lunch, we'll be going soon."

Tom shouted in reply, "Coming!" then he ran out the door without hearing his grandad say:

"Bye, son."

For a few moments Bill stared at the photographs. Then he poured some more coffee into his cup. It was cold and he put it aside, with the atlas, on the floor. He re-positioned his chair, pulling it in to the desk, dragged the typewriter towards him, straightened the paper and began to read what he had written:

> *I learned something about them, a year or two after I came to live with them. If I remember rightly, it was after they had been telling me about my dad, their son. My memory of my parents is very hazy. I'm not sure I really remember them at all. Perhaps all the images I have in my head are from photographs and stories. Anyhow, we were sitting round the fire in the parlour, granny never ever called it the sitting room, and I asked them how they came to live in Newhaven. It was a tiny room really and quite overcrowded with her upright piano, their two armchairs, grandpa's desk and, between a small table and the fire, a chaise longue upholstered in a green brushed fabric, like the pelt of an animal, over which I habitually ran my finger tips. That chaise longue became mine, so to speak. I could pile books and comics on it, take off my shoes and curl up snug and warm in front of the fire on a winter's evening.*
>
> *Well, that particular evening when I asked my question of them, I remember that they looked at each other to decide who should begin. It was really a little game between them because granny always deferred to grandpa. That was the first time I learned about the family connection with Shetland and realised that the accents I had come to accept as normal were not those of Newhaven. Grandpa explained that both he and granny came from Shetland, although they did not meet until they had come south. The middle and late 19th century was a very difficult time for ordinary Shetlanders like them. Their parents were crofters without any security over their land, at a time of the potato famines and the clearances – one day I will explain that. Grandpa, as Shetlanders had done for generations, went to sea. Many went to the fishing and some to the whaling, where he went first, and then many, like him, ended up in the merchant navy. This way they were able to send money home to help their families. Grandma came south to live with wealthy relatives of her mother. I think in the hope of treatment for her leg. They took advantage of her at first, using her like a maid, but when they discovered that she had a natural musical aptitude, impressed their guests at their soirées and won them many plaudits and compliments, they got her the best tuition available. That is how she came to take lessons from one of the great Scottish pianists of the late*

19th century, Frederic Lamond. And she must have been good or he would not have taken her on. He himself had taken lessons from Liszt and he was an international concert pianist. Grandpa used to joke that she had shaken the hand of a man, who had shaken the hand of a man, who had shaken the hand of Beethoven! But I am wandering off the point.

Both granny and grandpa were living in Leith – known in those days as Little Shetland as so many Shetlanders had emigrated there. It was almost inevitable therefore that at some point they would come together. It happened at a soirée to which grandpa had been invited. He told me, looking across the hearth to grandma, that he had been transfixed by her the instant he saw her in the doorway, and when he saw that she hirpled towards the piano with her stick, he wondered if it was only pity that he felt. But when she played the opening bars from a Schubert Piano Impromptu he knew it was love and lost his heart to her completely. The way she played, he said, her hands riffled over the notes like sparkling water over river pebbles.

When my grandfather – a man who had faced down the toughest seamen and survived the wildest tempests around the Horn – was introduced to her later that evening, he admitted that he found himself stumbling over his words like a wee boy. Grandma said she fell in love that evening too, with the handsome and modest sailor whose face and hands were brown and weathered and whose eyes were so fierce and passionate. He was a man from another world compared to the Leith and Edinburgh worthies who were her suitors until they noticed her stick.

They married soon after that meeting, raised a son ... my father, and had lived at the house in Newhaven for fifty years and were in their early seventies, before they unexpectedly lost their first son and gained a second in me. They must have wondered how they would cope with such a young child and one who had just lost both his parents.

I didn't help ... right from the very beginning. It was not as if they did not give me love in their own way, but it could never be the love of a parent. At the time, of course, I did not know why I came to misbehave in the way I did.

CHAPTER 3

'... listening to grandma play Paderewski's Minuet as they discussed me in low tones way above my head.'

*I*t was early December. Bill had been in Edinburgh for nearly three months and was finding that he no longer took much cognisance of which particular day he was living in. His routine had used to be to rise at eight, have breakfast and beachcomb one or two miles along the shore near the cottage, returning to a hot bath and coffee. After that he had spent the rest of the morning at his book business. The afternoons had been taken up with domestic chores, the post and shopping.

At first he had forced himself to take a similar early walk around the suburban streets but he soon found the exercise very irritating, as there was nothing to look at but hedges and pavements. He was also beginning to find the walk a little tiring, as he had been forewarned. So now he took to having an early bath and then breakfast, before going for a much shorter walk.

Today, the post brought new orders, it being the beginning of the pre-Christmas present buying season and Bill found himself busy on the phone to book dealers in Glasgow and Lewes, chasing early descriptions of Shetland, including a rarity, *A View of the Ancient and Present State of the Zetland Islands* (1809) by Arthur Edmondston, who had been a doctor and member of a local landowning family. Also wanted, by a retired academic in Northumberland for a study on the history of geological exploration and mapping in Scotland, was a *Description of the Shetland Islands* (1822) by the geologist and traveller Samuel Hibbert. Hibbert was one of Bill's favourite writers on Shetland in the 19th century. He had been a great shambling man of six feet who had perambulated all over the islands in the worst and best conditions the climate could throw at him, sleeping in his damp and weathered clothes in the roughest of accommodation or at the Laird's if he was lucky, often staggering in of a night weighed down by pocketfuls of rocks. He had been curious about everything around him and his eye had missed nothing so that the pages of his accounts of the country were full of literal and metaphorical gems.

Bill ran a permanent advertisement for books in the local Shetland paper and occasionally in one or two journals. They only just paid for themselves, but that was not the point. He loved handling books, the business of satisfying his customers and the distant contact with them. He imagined his fellow bibliophiles, secluded like heretics in a media-filled world, in book-filled rooms like his, scattered anonymously throughout the country. He would not have admitted it, to anyone else that is, but he also hugely enjoyed opening the small parcels and packets that regularly arrived in the morning post. What he did not enjoy anymore, however, was transporting and posting the outgoing mail. From his cottage it had been a ten-minute journey by bike to Magnus and Maisie at the shop-cum-post-office in the village. Muckle Magnus' was the hub of the community and Bill had encouraged him and Maisie, at a very late age, to break the mould and serve coffee to their customers. The outgoing post-run in the afternoon had become the highlight of Bill's day when he had spent a very pleasant hour in the shop drinking coffee, chatting and gossiping. Here, in Edinburgh, it was very different, no longer enjoyable: neither the journey to the post office nor the inevitable queuing at the counter. He had enquired to see if the post could be picked up from the house, but that would have been far too expensive.

The great hole in his life that he had seen approaching and which he had feared to face, was the afternoon, from lunch until six-thirty, but, providentially, thanks to Tom, this had become filled with writing. After that he joined Alistair and Cat for pre-dinner drinks. Unfortunately, drinks were usually with Cat alone as Alistair rarely got home before seven. At seven-thirty they dined and he had to admit to himself that it was pleasant to have a good meal once a day. Although his appetite was not great he enjoyed what little he ate. Cat was a good cook. The only thing that had annoyed him, at least at first, was having to change into respectable clothes. He had been aware of something amiss at their first joint dinner, but had only understood what it might be through Alistair's unconscious irritation with his open-necked shirt and frayed cuffs.

Tonight, Bill stood with his back to the fireplace, warming his legs at the mock-coal gas fire. Cat leaned back in the corner of the large oatmeal-coloured settee, twiddling the stem of her glass as she balanced it on the onyx-topped table beside her. It was not yet seven and they awaited Alistair and Tom. Bill could not get used to calling her Cat. It seemed too intimate a contraction of

Catriona. He felt ill at ease alone in her company. They had nothing in common except Alistair.

It was unexpected when it came, but Bill realised afterwards that Cat had probably been working up to the discussion for some time.

"Bill, tell me about Alice. I never really knew her."

Absentmindedly, he put his glass of beer on the mantelpiece alongside the coaster. Cat fidgeted involuntarily.

"Alice … no, of course not … you wouldn't have."

She uncrossed and re-crossed her legs, adjusting the hem of her dress over her knees. "Alistair said that she had quite a strong personality."

Bill looked at her. "You could say that!"

Cat laughed nervously. "In what way? Did she have very strong views on things?"

Bill took his glass to Alistair's armchair and sat down. "It may surprise you …" then he recalled – how could he have forgotten – how alike Alistair was to Alice. "But … on the other hand it may not … how different her politics were to mine. But in other things, in art and literature, we shared a lot in common."

"She was not a socialist?"

Bill couldn't decide the angle she was coming from.

"No, I would say she was a conservative with a small 'c'. I always found it very strange that one could be an artist … and she was a good one … *and* be conservative." He smiled at the memory. "But she didn't."

Cat inclined her head questioningly.

"We just agreed to differ." He picked up his glass and Cat followed suit. "We had other things that more than compensated for our political differences. Bless her though, she wasn't a very good mother, never really interested in children until they could fend for themselves." Bill held up his glass and looked at the light filtering darkly through the depth of the beer. "But then, I wasn't a very good father either." He looked across to Cat who got up to replenish her glass from the trolley of bottles behind the settee. "I suppose we were both rather selfish in our ways."

Cat turned from the trolley and put the question that Bill realised she had been leading up to. "D'you think … " and mid-sentence glanced down as she set her drink back on the trolley as if the question was entirely casual, "that had any effect on Alistair?"

"Undoubtedly, but then what parents do not have an unintended influence on their children?"

Cat opened her mouth but Bill held up his hand.

"Yes … I wish we had done it better and I do regret I did not give Alistair all the time I should have."

"Maybe, if you had just given him quality time … "

Bill spluttered.

Cat resumed her position on the settee with her legs crossed. "Alistair and I make sure that during the week I give Tom at least an hour of quality time and at the weekend Alistair tries to fit in a couple of hours."

In his mind's eye Bill imagined Alistair and Cat switching on and off over Tom like a couple of ultra-violet lights on a seedling. He managed, as near as he could muster, a noncommittal, "Hmmm."

"We think it is very important."

"I'm sure you do."

"Don't patronise me, Bill."

The gloves were off … well. He swallowed the last quarter of the glass in one go and sat forward in the armchair. "Don't you think that there's no one patent on how to raise a child?"

"We think this is the right way."

"But … surely you would agree … that there's more than one way to skin … " he bit his lip, cutting off an expletive, "I mean … I think every generation invents its own way of raising children and not one of them is perfect."

"Surely some are better than others?"

Bill leaned back. "Yes, I suppose they are, but none are probably as good as we think."

Cat uncrossed her legs and sat up defensively.

Bill hastily intervened. There was no point in upsetting Cat. "I'm not criticising you and Alistair. I think you're doing a wonderful job with Tom … he's a super wee boy."

There was silence for a few moments as they both gazed at the fire and collected their thoughts. Bill was first to recover the ground and spoke to the fire.

"I'm sorry Alistair and I don't get on as well as we should. I do love him as my son … we're just very different … that's all."

Cat accepted the gesture and sought for another subject.

"What was that piece of music you were playing on your hi-fi earlier? I couldn't help but hear it from the kitchen?"

"The piano piece?"

"Yes."

"Liszt's Hungarian Rhapsody No 2."

"You must like it." She looked at him over the rim of the glass as she sipped.

"How's that?"

"You've played it a couple of times since you have been here."

He wondered if she didn't like it. Maybe she didn't like any music. "Does it annoy you. I'm sorry, I'll turn it down."

"No, no," she reassured him. "I do like it. I just didn't know what it was … familiar you know, but I couldn't put my finger on it."

Relieved, he said, "Do you know why I play it?"

She shook her head, put down her glass and waited.

"You won't remember … it's before your time, but there used to be a popular song just after the war. I can't remember the title, but it went something like … *put another nickel in, in the nickelodeon and all I want is loving you and music, music, music*. Well, my grandmother and I were in the kitchen one morning … she was ironing or something … and this was playing on the radio. I must have sung along or said I liked it or something because she put the iron down, turned off the radio and marched through to the parlour.

"She opened her little walnut music cabinet that was stacked with sheet music and albums, and after a brief search removed a piece of music, put it on the piano, sat down, looked at me meaningfully … for I had followed her through as she had obviously intended I should, then played … "

"The Hungarian Rhapsody."

"Exactly. That's where the song had come from, I recognised it immediately and I suppose I learned something I have never forgotten. I suppose I play it because it reminds me both of the popular song and of grandmother playing the piano."

"I never saw you as a romantic, Bill."

He looked across at her feeling he had left his guard wide open, but her smile, he thought, was genuine. Then the back door opened announcing the arrival of Alistair, and Tom whom he had picked up from a friend's, and the conversation swung around to Alistair's day in the courts.

Later that evening, as he sat in front of his typewriter, Bill's conversation with Cat came back to him. He hoped what he had said might make things easier between them, particularly with Alistair. Then he remembered the latter part of their conversation, about music. Yes, he admitted to himself, it was as essential to him as the air he breathed or the food he ate and in some ways as he had got older, music had almost become more important than reading. From ever since he could remember, and that was really from his first days with his grandparents, music had been present in the foreground or the background. That, he supposed, was why so many of his childhood memories were associated with specific pieces of music. Take that Minuet.

I suppose I've heard it a hundred times, that Minuet. It was not a difficult piece for grandma but it was a favourite of grandfather's. I suspect he partly liked it for its simplicity, for though he loved to hear grandma play, even difficult pieces, he did not have a sophisticated taste in music. But there was another reason he liked it. His ship used to call regularly at Danzig, now Gdansk, in Poland. In fact, his ship might have just come from that port when they got stuck at Riga at the outbreak of the 1914-18 war. He liked the Polish people very much, knew quite a lot about the country and had several friends there who were very kind to him when his ship called. One, apparently, even turned up at their door in Newhaven, though I don't remember him of course, at the beginning of the 1939-45 war. I think he joined a Polish army unit of the allies.

After many decades of occupation by Russians and Prussians, Poland only became an independent country after the First World War and its first Prime Minister, albeit briefly, was Ignacy Jan Paderewski. Astonishingly, he was not only a politician, but also a composer and a very gifted concert pianist. Once, in Gdansk I suppose, grandfather was taken by a friend to hear Paderewski play. After that, knowing also his great patriotism, he revered him and even took some of his music back to grandma. One of the pieces was his Minuet which became very popular at the time.

Grandma played it many times for grandfather and it is the piece I most associate with them both. Every time I hear it I am back in that small cast-iron bed in their attic, late at night, listening to her playing behind the closed door of the parlour at the foot of the stairs. To be honest, I don't even know if she liked it: if she didn't, she never let on. However, the only specific time I recall hearing her play it was on the night of my 11th birthday, when a neighbour brought me home by the scruff of my neck. I remember I was standing in the hallway with the light from the vestibule shining through the coloured glass of the door, leaning against the hallstand with its walking sticks and umbrellas, trapped between Mr Hornsby and grandfather as the former relayed his anger and disgust over my head. I remember trying to concentrate on the music that filtered through from the parlour rather than hear his words, trying to will away their awful meaning.

As usual, I had a guilty conscience, though this time, somewhere deep inside me, I felt I should not. I also felt ashamed for grandfather having to listen to Mr Hornsby's tirade. Although the whole episode was painful at the time, it is quite funny in retrospect.

You see, I went to a boys' school and one of the few places I met girls was in the park opposite the house, and then I usually tried to avoid them because I never knew what to say: shades of my grandfather! There was one girl who was quite a torment to me who lived only a few doors down the hill. She was the same age as me, pretty, with short and straight black hair, and at least six inches taller than me. I was your age, so perhaps you will understand my confusion in her company better than most.

Faith, for that was her name, sometimes sat on the wall of her garden when I went past on my way to school. Sitting on the wall she would swing her long thin legs and say hello as I passed. I would mutter hello into my collar and hurry on. She had a kind of magnetic hold over me against which I had no defence. This went back a few months to a day when she and her friends came into the park to play when I was there already on the swings. She had hung upside down from a rail by the back of her legs and her short skirt had fallen over her waist revealing her green knickers. I must have been staring at these knickers, probably had never seen a pair before. She caught me staring,

"What are you looking at?"

I must have blushed crimson and said something like, "Me? Nothing."

I stopped the swing by dragging my feet, got off as casually as possible and walked off towards home. Something made me glance over my shoulder just before I left the park. She was still looking at me and I felt myself getting hot all over once again. It was an unsaid secret between us that this was unfinished business.

Faith's father, Mr Hornsby, was an elder in the local kirk. For me, that meant he carried out secret and imposing religious rituals, such as closing the massive church doors after the congregation was all in, taking in the collection plates and, at communion – which completely puzzled me – carrying round the tiny glasses of wine on the dimpled wooden trays that I could never see without thinking of a solitaire board. He had two suits. One was black and he wore that to church with a bowler hat. The other, which he wore to work every day, was dark blue and with it he wore a cloth cap and large, black, lace-up boots. He had a Ford Popular and he was a beanpole of a man, well over six feet tall, with long arms and legs to match. It was a wonder to watch him getting into his car for he closed himself up like a Swiss Army knife and then half-unfolded again once he was seated. He worked for one of the fish companies at Newhaven and he was often away for days at a time, travelling around the west and east coast fishing ports from Mallaig to Peterhead, buying fish. I remember his car because I was into cars at that age. Another neighbour, up the hill, had a Jowett Javelin. Now, that car was futuristic; it had a long sweeping rear without the usual bulging boot, and a sloping rear window. I wished we had one. It looked to me like the cockpit of an aeroplane. In comparison, Mr Hornsby's Ford Popular looked as exciting as an over-sized pram.

Mr Hornsby's face was as grey and unhealthy as a fish and I only once saw him smile, and that moment I will never forget. Not once do I remember him acknowledging me like our other neighbours usually did, and truth to tell, I was rather scared of him.

It must have been in connection with the church that I attended every Sunday with grandfather and grandma. I was sent with a message to Faith's house one day a few months after I had looked at her knickers. It was the last place I wanted to be, but my orders were firm and I couldn't get out of it. Can you imagine my feelings, having to enter that gate that I had passed so many times and walk up that gravel path to Faith's front door? I was almost shaking. I rang the bell and prayed that Mrs Hornsby, a wee mouse of a woman, would answer so that I could thrust the message in her hand and turn and run. Footsteps approached, I bit my lip and all but crushed the message in my hot little hand. The handle turned ... the door swung open ... I knew it. There was Faith, as surprised to see me as I was scared to see her. We stared at one another.

"Who's that, Faith?" Her father's voice called from the hidden depth of the house.

"It's wee William from up the road."

"What does he want?"

"What do you want?" she repeated.

I held out the letter in my hand.

"He's got a message ..." and more quietly, "I think."

"Tell him to come in."

Standing aside, she pulled the door open wide as if it was the gates of a castle. "Come in."

I stood in their hallway; everything was the same as ours but the opposite way round. Faith closed the door behind me and then walked past into what should have been the dining room, but was in fact their parlour. I followed her.

"Well, young man, what can we do for you?" Mr Hornsby said from one of the fireside chairs, as he put down a folded newspaper and pencil.

I thrust forward the message and he took it from my hands and opened it. I looked around the room as if I was interested, in order to avoid catching Faith's eye, and saw that the décor was very different from my grandparents' house. The furniture was much lighter in weight and colour, and instead of a heavy pelmet and long velvet curtains on the front windows there was a brightly chequered curtain that only stretched to the foot of the windowsill, halfway to the floor.

"Ah," he pushed his spectacles onto his forehead, "this will take a little time." He pulled out some paper from a shelf by the chair and picked up the pencil from the floor. "Can you wait?"

Before I could think of something pressing that demanded my immediate presence back home, Mrs Hornsby, whom I hadn't noticed, peered from around the wing of the other fireside chair in front of me and spoke.

"Of course he can. Would you like some lemonade?"

I nodded feebly.

"Faith?"

"I'll get it." She disappeared out of the door.

Mrs Hornsby started asking me questions about myself and I suppose I answered. It was almost a relief when Faith returned with two glasses, one of which she gave to me.

"Can I take William upstairs and show him my room?" She made me sound like a pet dog.

"Of course," said Mrs Hornsby, leaning across and tapping her husband on the knee with a knitting needle, "Henry will give you a shout when he is finished. Won't you dear?" He looked up briefly and gave an unintelligible "Hrrumph" in reply.

Faith turned on her heel. "C'mon," she said, without waiting and almost ran up the stairs ahead of me. I clutched my lemonade, trying not to spill it, and followed her.

Her room at the very top of the stairs, like the rest of the house, was identical to mine but the other way around. Whereas my bed was alongside the wall, hers stuck out halfway across the room. It had a large pink quilt and there was a row of soft toys, teddy bears and a moth-eaten dog with one ear and one eye, against the pillow. One wall and part of the sloping ceiling was covered in pictures of film stars cut from a film magazine. Faith opened a cupboard beside a small wardrobe to reveal boxes of games.

"What would you like to play? Ludo, snakes and ladders, snap?"

"I know knock-out whist."

"Okay."

She produced a pack of cards and we sat cross-legged on the floor and played a few hands. We must have talked about something for a little while as we played, but I was in no state to remember, and then she asked me if I liked the dress she was wearing. In my innocence I didn't see the way things were going. Maybe she didn't at that point. I think I answered noncommittally.

"This isn't my favourite dress you know. I've got a green taffeta one I like best. Would you like to see it?"

It was clear what my answer should be, but I could only swallow hard. She took that as a yes. I leaned back against the wall by the bedroom door and she opened the wardrobe and took out the dress. She held it in front of her and cocked her head questioningly.

"Yes … yup …" I managed.

"Is that all?" she retorted, with a hint of crossness that made me sit up.

Again I couldn't answer properly.

She threw the dress down on the bed between us and in the same movement began unbuttoning the yellow dress she wore from the neck to the hem. This, too, she threw on the bed and then I saw that she wore the same kind of knickers I had seen her wearing in the park, and a kind of vest with thin straps. Her body was elongated and thin and there were two small protrusions where her breasts were beginning to develop. Then she picked up the taffeta dress and put it on. There was a strange electricity in the room.

"There," she said, looking at me for a judgement.

My voice was husky in reply and I managed to say without thinking, "I prefer the yellow one."

"You … !" she said, and the word was so much meant for me, "prefer neither! Shall I take it off again?"

I could only nod. Faith stood once more in her underwear just across the room. Her hands were by her sides and she looked challengingly into my eyes. I looked at her long thin legs. My intense curiosity must have been engraved on my face. The next thing I knew she had taken off her vest and knickers. The effect of her standing there so rudely naked in front of me, in her own bedroom, was suddenly quite shocking.

To put it mildly, I was distracted as the door swung quietly open and from behind it, hidden from Faith, a smiling Mr Hornsby looked down on me. In a distant sort of way I was aware that the smile on his face was incredibly unnatural. Slowly, it contracted as he tried to read my expression of disbelief and impending disaster. He leaned his head forward quickly and caught Faith disappearing behind the wardrobe door pulling up her knickers. It was as if he had been electrocuted.

"What the blazes is going on here?" he bellowed, as he reached across to grab me. Why me, I thought, and ran around the bed towards Faith and the wardrobe. He lumbered after me and I scrambled back across the bed and out of the door. "Come here, you little bugger!" The stairs were steep and I ran down them as fast as I could, conscious of the reverberations of Mr Hornsby's great boots behind me. I might have got away but Mr Hornsby's shout of "Stop … you rapscallion!" brought Mrs Hornsby out of the door of the sitting room just as I was passing. We collided and before I had managed to get back to my feet I was collared.

Mr Hornsby brushed aside the faint squeakings of Mrs Hornsby and hauled me into the living room, slamming the door behind us.

We stood facing each other by the table in the centre of the room. He was breathing in great gulps and sat down on a chair to get his breath back. "What … just what do you think you were doing?"

I stared at the floor, "Nothing."

"Nothing! You call this nothing!" he shouted, his face swelling in anger. He made to get up from the chair. I really thought he was going to hit me or something.

Mrs Hornsby banged on the other side of the door. "Henry … Henry … now Henry …"

Mr Hornsby seemed to get a grip of himself, "It's alright, dear." His eyes searched around my feet and he took a deep breath. "Go and see to Faith, dear." Then he turned to me and almost in a whisper said, "You're a very wicked boy. You must learn to control yourself," and he rubbed his hands together as if he was nervous or they were cold.

I tried to relate what he was saying to what had happened. Somehow I knew it was not exactly wrong, but …

"It's a difficult age … I know … but we mustn't succumb to the temptations of the flesh." He was gathering pace but leaving me behind. "The body is a holy temple … we must keep it clean and pure for …" he searched for words, " … things you do not yet understand." I could see he was still searching for what he should do or say. His face softened a little. "We must pray for you."

I managed to get out in one hurried breath, "Mr Hornsby … can I go home now?"

I could see that unintentionally I had offered him another option. "Yes," and then more firmly, "yes … your father … grandfather … must deal with this." He got up. "Come along," and ushered me out, keeping one hand on my shoulder in case I bolted. But, of course, there was nowhere to go.

So there I was, a few moments later, in our own hallway, standing between Mr Hornsby and grandfather, listening to grandma playing Paderewski's Minuet as they discussed me in low tones way above my head.

That evening I was sent to bed early in sorrow and disgrace. Grandfather tried to ask me what had happened, but it was with some reluctance, as if he did not really want to know. I couldn't tell him, could I? I wondered what part I had played. Had I encouraged Faith, led her on? Was I guilty by association? I felt angry against Mr Hornsby but I also felt terrible. I had let grandfather and grandma down and on the very day they had given me a present for my birthday.

I have to admit that I cried myself to sleep that night as I lay watching the beam of the lighthouse – for that is what I had realised it must be. It was a clear, frosty night with a large moon. Must have been at the end of November; there were hundreds of stars through the window.

The incident with Faith certainly gave me a new perspective on life, but that night something else was to change it forever. I had woken up at some point, wide-awake, and suddenly remembered my present, still wrapped, lying on the table by the bed. I put the bedside light on, picked it up and unwrapped it. It was an illustrated copy of Treasure Island. *I opened the first page half-heartedly and began to read.*

'Squire Trelawney, Dr Livesey, and the rest of these gentlemen having asked me to write down the whole particulars about Treasure Island, from the beginning to the end, keeping nothing back but the bearings of the island, and that only because there is still treasure yet to lift, I take up my pen in the year of grace 17--, and go back to the time when my father kept the 'Admiral Benbow' inn, and the brown old seaman, with the sabre cut, first took up his lodging under our roof.'

I was hooked! I couldn't put it down. It was as if it was the first book I had ever read. I never knew until that night that this other world existed. Of course I had read comics and the set books for school, but Treasure Island *was something else. When I was reading it I was in another universe, safe from the one that seemed to bring me so much trouble.*

The night that I started reading Treasure Island, *inevitably, perhaps, I dreamed of Long John Silver. He appeared in my room as if that was where he naturally belonged, with his tricornered hat, a stained and worn blue jacket with wide lapels and two pockets as big as my schoolbag. He wore black breeches, one grey sock and a polished buckled shoe. His jacket hung open and jammed through the piece of cord that held up his breeches was a heavy looking pistol, the hammer uncocked. He was a large man and leaned his weight on his crutch as if it was the only thing that kept him upright. He had his back to me and was looking out the window.*

"Not a smuggler's moon, young William. I reckon I'll stay at me moorings tonight." It wanted an answer.

"Why?"

He turned and looked at me in surprise. His eyes were black, his face unshaven and his smile crooked. "Shiver me timbers, lad ... the customs men would see every reef point on a mainsail on a night like this, as clear as daylight, never mind a nervous man on the shore with a lantern and a boat on the breakers loaded with barrels of rum."

His right arm lay along the windowsill cradling a telescope. Balancing the crutch under his arm he rubbed his unshaven chin with his left hand and then, through his half-fastened shirt, scratched his chest. "So shipmate, they caught you with your hands in the stores again, eh?"

"What?"

"Up to no good."

"It wasn't my fault."

"That's no excuse, matey. The swabs'll still swing you from the yard arm."

He was right. I hung my head.

"Aw, c'mon, lad. If one of my crew hung his head like that I would say he was asking for it." He turned again to the window, shielding his eyes as the beam of light crossed his face. "That's a good light for spotting misdemeanours," and as he disappeared through the wall as if it wasn't there, he added over his shoulder, "fight your own corner, lad, fight your own corner ... we can outwit these lily-livered landlubbers ... you and me together."

Thus began a relationship that was to last for just about as long as Silver's with Jim Hawkins.

I slept deeply for the rest of the night, comforted that I had Silver on my side, but I wondered what grandfather would think of him.

Overnight, Starbank Park became a South Seas' island, the steep road a cobbled track to the shore, and the little harbour at Newhaven a nest of pirates. At night, the ship lights became those of smugglers and customs men and over it all shone the reassuring beam from the lighthouse. At last, I had a real companion.

CHAPTER 4

'There you go again!'

Edinburgh's ancient spine, a little twisted and a little worn by age is not a great deal changed from the time when it was the nerve centre of the old city. It is a narrow, descending ridge that runs from the castle at the top to Holyrood at the bottom. The steep sides of the ridge provided some sort of protection against marauders so that is where the old town germinated and grew. Naturally, everyone wanted to be safely on it, but because it is so narrow there is little room for building. The inhabitants, however, had an ingenious answer: they built their houses upwards, floor upon floor, so that the spine to the castle became encrusted with vertical growths like the back of a sleeping dragon. The citizens of Edinburgh warmed their flats by burning coal from the nearby coalfields, so this dragon did not breathe fire, but smoke, and became affectionately known as 'auld reekie'.

The road that runs roughly the mile length of the ridge from the castle to Holyrood is known as the High Street. Today it is still mostly composed of houses and small shops, but roughly a quarter of the way down the hill these buildings are dominated by both the temporal and spiritual centres of Scotland, in the forms of the Sheriff Courts and the crown-spired cathedral of St Giles. Here also was once the Scottish Parliament, and the prison, known as the Tolbooth.

A week or two after the episode with Faith and just after I had finished reading Treasure Island *for the first time, I was here at the Tolbooth on a school history outing that was tied in with a book we had to read for our English class … but we will come to that shortly.*

I didn't know what to do when I had finished Treasure Island. *There was just this great hole in my life and I had to find something else to fill it. For the first time I had a serious look at the books that were in a glass bookcase in my bedroom, which up until then I had dismissed as something of no interest. On the upper shelves I found that some of the books had belonged to my father when he had occupied this same room as a child. It was rather strange to see his name on the pages, written in childish writing very similar to my own. My grandparents hadn't initially told me that it had been his bedroom, apparently in case it upset me. By the time they did, thinking it might have a positive influence on me, my memory of him had already faded and the fact had little significance for me.*

The bottom shelf of the bookcase was occupied by large, worn and dull-looking, brown books that were propped up higgledy-piggledy. They smelled musty and old and I was loath, at first, to even touch them. When I took one out and laid it on the floor – it being too heavy to hold comfortably in my lap – I didn't know what to make of it. There seemed to be large amounts of text that normally would have instantly put me off, however, on most pages this was divided into columns, making it easier to read. Flipping through a volume I found that every so often there was a titled page with a large scrolled design and on almost every other page there were black and white drawings of dramatic moments from stories. One was of a white hunter in the act of discharging his gun at a large and ferocious leaping lion; another, a brave row of pith-helmeted British soldiers standing up against an overwhelming force of wild natives and yet another, a crew of whalers, one of them throwing a hand-held harpoon into an enormous leviathan that threatened to swamp their tiny open boat. It was those vivid illustrations that grabbed me and began to fill the space left after finishing Treasure Island *and I quickly cottoned-on that each titled page represented a new episode of a serialised tale.*

My appetite for adventure took me rapidly through all six volumes of those Boys Own Papers. *They took me to steaming jungles, arctic seas, snow-covered mountain tops, pirates' lairs, remote forts of the British Empire and set me down in the middle of titanic struggles between giant squids and iron-suited divers, British men-o-wars and Spanish galleons, lumberjacks and grizzly bears.*

But, quite propitiously for me, one of the volumes was missing. Several adventures therefore had gaps in them: the sailor who fell overboard in shark-infested seas was suddenly a captive of black and curly-headed natives on a palm-beached island; the half-clad, half-crazed gold miner who toiled in the arid wilderness metamorphosed into a dude with fancy clothes and a girl on each arm; the trapper who

had kissed his woman goodbye and set off into the snow, warmed by
black coffee and beans, lay with his back against a tree, his foot in his
own trap, his rifle out of reach and a large and wounded brown bear
eyeing him ominously.

It seemed quite natural to me that I should fill these gaps. I made
a cover out of cardboard that I decorated, very amateurishly, in
imitation of the six other volumes. Then I tore out the empty pages from
two old school jotters and started writing. For each of the adventures
I made up what I thought was a very plausible episode that linked the
existing ones together. Then I made holes in both the pages and the
cover and threaded through a couple of shoelaces I found in a kitchen
drawer. I was very pleased with my results and showed them to
grandma and grandfather, who, bless them, patted my head: they did
not know just what it was all going to lead to. For after that I began to
add adventures to the books I was reading, beginning with Treasure
Island. *At first these simply filled the empty spaces in my old jotters, but*
eventually I began to run out of them.

When I finished reading the volumes of the Boys Own Paper *I*
moved up to the next shelf and there found the novels that became my
evening reading on the chaise longue and my nightly bedtime reading
under the eye of the lighthouse, when I should have been asleep – King
Solomon's Mines *and* She, *by Rider Haggard,* Coral Island *by Captain*
Marryat, Tarzan *by Edgar Rice Burroughs and, my second favourite*
novel after Treasure Island, Kidnapped *also by Robert Louis Stevenson.*

It was the shortest day of the year and frequent snow showers had been
falling from the early hours. Between the showers appeared a pale blue sky,
otherwise it was a white blur, unpleasant to walk in. The centres of the streets
were clear of snow from traffic use, but the edges were beginning to build up
with soft furrows and ruts and the pavements were a wet mess of slush that
soaked through unsuitable footwear. Water dripped continuously from the
ledges and roofs of the buildings, spattering pedestrians. The crowd hugged the
middle of the pavement to avoid these and also left an empty space by the kerb
in order to avoid the occasional knee-high swathe of dirty brown snow thrown
from the wheels of buses and cars. People jostled and fought through and
around each other with increasing frustration as present-filled paper bags
caught and tore in the melee. Both Bill and Tom were wishing that they had
done their Christmas shopping earlier. But at least they were dry and warm, for
Cat had insisted that Tom put on his sensible shoes and winter coat while Bill
had opted for his standard Shetland wear; rubber boots, woolly hat, Fair Isle
sweaters and a heavy waterproof coat.

They had been shopping on the Bridges, where the deep valley on the south side of the spine of the High Street had long been bridged. Bill wanted to buy Tom a book for his Christmas, but did not trust his limited knowledge of modern teenage fiction. They shopped in one of Edinburgh's oldest bookshops on the North Bridge, in the main section of which he bought Tom his desired Terry Pratchett. Then he went downstairs to the children's department where he stood for a moment, paralysed by the packed shelves.

Eventually he found himself holding a modern edition of *Treasure Island* that he quickly bought while Tom was elsewhere. In the second-hand department he also bought an early edition of *The Heart of Midlothian* at a very reasonable price. He was not quite sure why he had bought the latter, none of his customers was looking for it. He rationalised that it was a good investment, but at the back of his mind an ulterior motive surfaced. Hence, when they left the bookshop, he led the way uptown to the High Street.

Unsurprisingly, he had to bribe Tom with the promise of some food to get him to continue trudging the streets, although secretly, he too was looking forward to something hot *and* a place to rest his weary legs. With only their books to clutch under their arms they made fairly rapid progress through the other shoppers. It was not unpleasant when the sun shone and they had turned up the High Street before a lowering shadow began pulling itself over the sky and the first flakes of a threatening snowstorm began lazily and innocently drifting onto their heads.

Bill grabbed Tom's sleeve. "In here."

They pushed their way into a small cafe and managed to squeeze into two empty chairs at a table by the window. Bill indulged Tom in a large piece of chocolate gateau and had his usual coffee himself. Tom wiped some steam off the window with the sleeve of his coat while Bill pulled a small box of pills from his trouser pocket. Hiding them on his lap, he knocked one pill into his hand and was swallowing it quickly as Tom turned round.

"What's that for?"

"Och ... the usual old man's ailment." He stuffed the box back in his pocket.

"What's that?"

"Something you'll not have to worry about for a long time." Then he changed the subject. "How's the cake?"

"Wicked!"

Bill laughed, and while Tom relished every forkful he sat with his hands wrapped around his cup warming his fingers and breathing in the aroma. By mutual agreement, when they had both finished, they had seconds: Tom of cake and Bill of coffee. When that was finished they sat back in satisfied silence.

Eventually Bill leaned forward and broke Tom's reverie. "What can you see out there?"

Tom wiped the window dry with his paper serviette, leaving little streaks of chocolate across the pane. "Not a lot, just people."

"What's across the street?" He nodded his head towards their right.

Tom peered through the snow in the direction indicated. "St Giles." Then looked around at his grandad conspiratorially, "Ahhhh …! So what are we doing here, I wonder?"

Bill lifted his shopping bag from the floor, extracted *The Heart of Midlothian* and put it on the table.

Tom picked it up and looked at the title. "Another old book."

"I was just thinking of this the other day. It was the first novel of Sir Walter Scott I had to read."

Tom opened the book and looked at the opening pages. "You had to read *this*?"

Bill smiled at him. "Not easy going is it? Do you know what the Heart of Midlothian was?"

"I've no idea."

"Neither had I until I was your age." He waved at the window. "Look out again. Can you see the square at the other end of St Giles?"

"Just."

"That's Parliament Square … where the Scottish Parliament used to be until we united with England. C'mon, let's go."

He put the book back in the shopping bag and got up. They left the cafe, crossed the cobbled street and made their way across Parliament Square. The snow had stopped falling and a pale pink was suffusing the western sky as it began to grow dark. A half moon stood in the southern sky. Bill stopped at the edge of Parliament Square and, looking down, waved his shopping bag at a large, heart-shaped pattern in the cobbles under their feet. "*This* … is the Heart of Midlothian."

A passer-by who overheard him stopped in his stride and looked down suspiciously. Tom stood back so that he was not actually standing on it.

"It's not a grave. I mean it does not actually contain a mummified heart or anything."

The passer-by shook his head and moved on.

"That's a relief."

"It is the site of the old Tolbooth."

"There you go again."

"Patience, Tom."

"I know … I know."

"The Tolbooth was the old city gaol."

"Ahhhh, right."

"Prisoners were held here, especially those who were going to be hanged."

"Here?"

"Yes. Right here, where we are standing."

"Brutal!"

"Sometimes you hit it square on the head, Tom … but c'mon, I'll show you something else." He checked the sky and guessed there wouldn't be any snow for a little while, then set off further up the High Street and crossed to a winding street that led down the south side of the ridge. While they walked he explained to Tom that Scott's novel was woven around the Porteous Riots in 1736, in which year a man named Wilson was sentenced to death for robbery.

"He wasn't innocent exactly, but he was attempting to redress what he thought was a wrong done to him by the Customs and Excise. He was also a rather strong man and he had helped, to his own cost, his accomplice make an audacious escape." They stopped at the bottom of the hill. "This is the Grassmarket and this is where hangings were carried out … in public."

Tom looked around him.

"Yes, there would be a great crowd around this spot on hanging days. It was a bit like a fair … public entertainment. Remember, there were no football games to go to on a Saturday then."

Tom's mouth hung open.

"In the case of Wilson, there was a great deal of sympathy for his plight from the ordinary man in the street. Poor Captain Porteous was the official whose job it was to escort Wilson from the Tolbooth … where we were … to here. Porteous had a detachment of soldiers to ensure everything went as it should and Wilson was duly hanged. It should have all ended there, but Wilson's body was left rather long on the gibbet, long after he was dead that is, and this affronted the crowd. Someone stepped forward and cut the rope, lowering him to the ground. Others pressed forward. Porteous, unfortunately, fearing public disorder, overstepped the mark, seized a gun and fired it at the crowd. His soldiers followed suit and several people were killed.

"Porteous was then put on trial himself and sentenced to death … to hang on the same spot as Wilson. Naturally, a large crowd gathered to watch his comeuppance and you can imagine the fever pitch of excitement as the hour drew near. Inexplicably for the crowd, the sentence was postponed and they were left very frustrated and angry. Porteous was being held in the Tolbooth and shortly afterwards the crowd, by now an organised mob, rioted. They took the Tolbooth by burning down the door, dragged out the unfortunate Porteous and lynched him."

"That was not very nice!"

"It certainly wasn't."

They walked slowly back up the hill to the High Street. Bill slapped his head, "Blimey ... I don't think we paid our bill at the cafe." He turned to a grinning Tom. "Maybe they'll lock us up in the Tolbooth?"

"Get a life, grandad!"

Bill rolled his eyes and shook his head. "C'mon, we must go and pay."

"But they won't miss it. They won't even remember us probably."

Bill made to grab Tom's ear. He ducked away. "We *must* pay. If we aren't honest with others, how can we expect that others are honest with us?"

"They're probably not," and he laughed.

Bill took Tom's shoulders in his hands and turned him towards himself. "Tom, when you are with me we do the honest thing. Okay?"

He nodded.

"And I hope you do the honest thing even when you are not with me."

Tom looked down at the cobbled street and shrugged his shoulders under Bill's hands.

Bill smiled at him. "Well ... in the future, eh?"

A relieved Tom looked up and smiled back. "Okay."

After they had returned to the cafe and paid their bill to a grateful waitress they looked around for a bus stop. Bill wondered which bus they should take. Tom said a 23.

"Could be," his grandad muttered.

"No. It is one we can take."

"Quite possibly then."

Tom planted himself in front of his grandad. "No, it *is* the right one grandad. Not 'possibly'!"

"Okay then."

Tom shook his head and pulled his grandfather over to the bus stop.

In the evening, before dinner, Bill sat down at his pianola and played the Minuet, which he did from memory. He could almost feel the presence of his grandparents as he played. Somewhere behind his back he knew his grandfather listened with closed eyes. Close beside him, hips touching, his grandmother watched his hands and turned the pages for him. He could smell the rose water in her hair, see the veins in her strong, small hands and on her wedding finger the silver ring set with the piece of jet. She had given him lessons until he could play that Minuet, but he could never play it, or anything else, as well as she did.

Then he took out the well-worn book of Beethoven and tried to play the Sonata in C sharp minor, the 'Moonlight'. The first movement he could manage with relative ease, as most beginners can. Even the second allegretto he could play with some confidence, but the presto agitato always defeated him. He never played in front of anyone since Alice had died, only for the ghost of his grandmother and he always apologised to her under his breath when he stumbled to a halt. Sometimes there was another ghost there, but the figure was indistinct. His grandmother had told him that his father had played quite well too.

His own playing always brought some comfort to him, but never satisfaction. Tonight, as usual after playing, he selected a record: this time of Richter hammering out Beethoven's 'Tempest' sonata. The sublime power of Richter's playing swept him up, carried him forward relentlessly, until finally, battered and exhausted, it dropped him onto a distant, silent shore.

When he had recovered from that exhilarating ride he wrapped up the presents he had bought and then turned to his mail. There were three requests for books, a negative reply from a supplier and a nice little cheque. There was also an envelope with a Shetland postmark in familiar shaky handwriting. He opened it to find a letter and another unopened envelope addressed to him at his cottage. He put both down for a moment. He had not thought of the place for some weeks. It seemed another world now and he wondered if he would ever go back to it? Turning his head, he looked at Alice's painting of the cottage and the shore. Beyond the latter were the skerries with two or three languid seals draped over the lower rocks and above them a snow of dancing, translucent, white flakes. He heard the joyful calls of the terns.

He got up and moved to the window that looked out on the snow-covered garden. The terns would not be there right now of course, but far away. The skerries would be deserted apart from visiting shags and on the sea would be small flocks of long-tailed ducks from Iceland and his regular guest from Canada, a solitary great northern diver that patrolled in aristocratic splendour just to seaward of the skerries from late autumn until spring. On Cat's bird table in the centre of the lawn he watched two robins scrap for seed. Was he getting used to being here? Perhaps he was, but he still missed the background breathing of the sea, the roar of the wind, the sweep of the horizon and the immensity of the Shetland sky.

He picked up the letter and smiled at Magnus' brief covering letter. All was well, the cottage dry, nothing damaged in the gales. His son Peter had given Bill's bike a run and an oil change. The enclosed was the only mail that seemed to have slipped the redirect net. Would he be home in the spring? Bill looked at the small brown envelope that was also enclosed and saw that the date stamp was over a month old. Opening it, he found a printed official-looking note from the local GP. It confirmed the diagnosis and required him to take the note to his new GP in Edinburgh. Nothing had really changed he thought, so there was no rush.

At dinner, Alistair informed his father that they were planning to go abroad for Christmas. It was going to be a skiing holiday. He had booked a self-catering chalet and there was plenty room for Bill if he would like to come. Bill sensed an apology in his tone and was a little more reassuring than he needed in his response. He would be quite happy to stay and look after the house. He even asked to see the brochures and the maps and managed to sound enthusiastic in his queries and questions regarding the resort and its facilities. After that they all relaxed. Bill then excused himself early from the meal pleading tiredness, which was genuine, and thus confirmed for Cat and Alistair that he would be better off staying at home rather than coming with them.

After he had left the table and returned upstairs to his flat the conversation, quite naturally, turned to him. Alistair wondered if he needed to ask someone to keep an eye on Bill and Cat thought it would be nice if she could freeze some meals for him. They agreed that he would want the minimum of fuss. Tom thought they might get some videos for him, his mum and dad were dubious, but agreed that someone should ask him. Tom then realised that 'not having a particular interest in films or videos' was only one of many things that he did not know about his grandpa.

"Did grandpa always work as a journalist, dad?"

"I think he did a few adventurous things in his youth, but latterly, yes … a free-lance journalist."

"What's that when it's at home?"

His mother cut in as she cleared the table. "Thomas, I wish you wouldn't use that expression."

"Sorry, mum."

Alistair continued. "It means that he didn't work for anyone … any paper or journal … in particular."

"Does it make a lot of money?"

He picked up a golf magazine and began flicking through it. "Only if you are very good I would think."

Tom persisted. "Was he good?"

His father scratched his head. "I honestly don't know."

"Oh, come on, Alistair … " Cat interrupted again, "you know his pieces appeared regularly in the national papers. He must have been good … but I don't think he earned a lot of money."

"I suppose you're right," Alistair conceded, "but of course my mother also sold her paintings quite well … so between the two of them they made a reasonable living. I can't remember ever being denied anything."

Tom sat up from slouching in a fireside chair. "Are those her paintings in grandpa's room?"

Alistair thought for a brief second. "Yes, those are my mother's." He got up, walked over to the wall opposite the fireplace and tapped a large framed gouache. It was of a terraced house on a steep road by a park, with two figures on a summer swing seat in the garden. There was a man lounging against the front door and a woman with yellow hair at the gate. "This is one of hers. Did you not know?"

Tom stared at it, opened his mouth to speak and then bit his lip quickly.

"It's the house where your grandpa was brought up. She painted it for him. When my mother died he insisted we take it."

This time Tom spoke. "It's at Newhaven, isn't it?"

"Yes, it is."

"Grandpa told me."

CHAPTER

*'Shiver me timbers, William. Treasure is not worth
your life ... somebody else's maybe ... '*

The phone was ringing. It took Bill a few moments to recollect where he was. He put down a scrapbook of fifty-year-old newspaper cuttings, pushed his feet into his slippers, pulled his dressing gown around him and struggled to his feet.

"Hello ... hello." He could not quite catch who was speaking and what they were saying.

"Happy Christmas, grandad."

It was Tom of course. "Thanks, Tom ... and a happy Christmas to you too. Plenty of food there I hope?"

"Buckets. Thanks for the Terry Pratchett. I promise I will start reading it tonight."

"Oh, you don't have to promise."

"Mum and dad send their love too. Oh, I nearly forgot. I got a new iPod for Christmas."

"A what?"

"The thing with the headphones that you said wasn't good for me ... remember?"

"Yes, I know."

"Well, I'm going to record some of your things when I get home ... you can choose the ones you want. It will be for your birthday. You can have my old Walkman and then you can listen to your music when you go for your walks."

"Ah ... " he hesitated doubtfully.

"What, grandpa?"

"Nothing. That would be very nice, Tom. Thank you."

He saw himself reflected in the window, rumpled, untidy and grey and was painfully reminded of his bladder problems.

"Grandad?"

"Sorry."

"You okay?"

"Absolutely."

"I'm sorry you're not here."

"I'm not … sorry that is … but don't repeat that."

"It's great here. There's lots of snow and lots of people. I've met some other boys … and girls too. You should have come."

"Dream on!"

"Hey, cool, grandad."

"I'm just fine. Can't ski, can't eat all that food, can't drink all that booze. I'm writing about a Christmas fifty years ago for you."

"Can't wait to read it. By the way, mum says … is the house alright?"

"No, it's burned to the ground."

"Wicked!"

"But of course. Tell her everything is fine."

"Dad wants to speak to you."

"Okay, Tom, enjoy the New Year too, but don't ring me too early."

"Bye, grandad."

"Hello, dad."

Bill closed his eyes for a moment. Alistair's voice had penetrated his usual paternal reserve. He put it down to the glass of Drambuie that he had indulged in when he had got up. "Happy Christmas, son."

"And to you. Everything okay with you?"

"Just fine. I'm not entirely on my own you know."

"Pardon?"

"I've got a drinks invite in the afternoon."

"You're a dark horse. Who with?"

"Give you one guess."

"Emmm … not with … Mrs … what's-her-name down the road?"

"Merryweather … yes, but don't worry, she has assured me there will be others. Safety in numbers you know!"

"Well well. Oh … on the mantelpiece in the sitting room you'll find a wee present. But please consume it in the flat. You'll understand."

"Thanks, Alistair. Happy Christmas to Cat. Have a good time yourselves. See you all in a week or so."

Bill put down the phone and found he was still holding one of the newspaper cuttings in his other hand. He looked at the aerial photograph of the cargo ship. It was slightly out of focus, having been taken through perspex on a grey and windy winter afternoon. He laid it on the desk and went down the stairs and through the kitchen to the sitting room. Right enough, on the mantelpiece was a slim wrapped object. The card attached said 'I shouldn't encourage you, but enjoy!' He smiled to himself and returned to his own room with the present.

Before he opened it he decided to have some breakfast, a walk and a bath. In fact, it was not to be until after he had returned from Mrs Merryweather's little drinks party, sat at the pianola and played a few old favourites, that he finally sat down once more with the cuttings by the typewriter, opened the package and took out and lit up a King Edward cigar.

> *Grandfather had several habits and routines that grandma and I breached with extreme caution. It was not that he had a bad temper. It was just that, if crossed, he could be very grumpy and uncooperative for the remainder of the day. Grandma could do all the apologising she liked but he would be very stubborn – wonder where I got that trait from! There was one sure way she could obtain forgiveness – for my minor transgressions too, thank goodness – and that was to sit down at the piano and play some of his favourites; only it had to appear that her desire to play had no connection with his grumpiness. It was a fine line.*
>
> *One of the little idiosyncrasies that he demanded of everyone was that tea should be poured into milk and not the other way around. He swore it had to do with colloidal solutions and would not be persuaded that it made no difference. Maybe he was right; I for one never tried any empirical experiments with his tea. Another was complete quietness while he listened to the early evening news, which he enjoyed with his cup of tea – milk poured first of course. This was high tea, when we had scones and jam and usually something cooked, like poached fish, fresh from Newhaven. Until they died they had high tea and then supper at about nine, before I went to bed. Supper was always a chatty meal. As long as I could keep it going I didn't have to go to bed. High tea, on the other hand, at least until the news, sports results and shipping forecast, were over, was a silent meal, broken only by the radio, subdued sounds of eating and the occasional muttered and rhetorical remark from grandfather. My chair at the table was nearest the radio where it sat on the sideboard and I was given the responsibility by grandfather of turning it off and on and of raising or lowering the volume, but rarely tuning as he considered that a skill I did not yet possess. I enjoyed turning it on and off because the bakelite knob gave a very satisfying and solid click.*

I cannot remember if that particular Christmas was snowy for us or not. I do remember though that there were continuous gales in England right through into the New Year. I was probably concentrating on eating my tea, a day or two after Christmas, when grandfather told me to turn up the sound on the radio.

' *… all the passengers have been taken off … 30 degrees list … only Captain Carlsen left on board … And now to sport …'*

"What is it?" I asked grandfather.

"An American freighter."

"What's that?"

"A cargo ship … she's just left the Channel on her way home."

"What's the Channel?"

He made to open his mouth and say something but I saw grandma catch his eye. He started again, "… It's that narrow piece of sea between England and France."

"But what has happened?" *I wanted to know.*

He repeated, "An American freighter in the Channel has developed a list …" *This time he anticipated my question and leaned sideways in his chair to illustrate a list. Grandma, on the other side, grabbed the arm of his chair.* "The weather can't be good and some of the cargo may have shifted. But they do seem to have gotten everybody off."

"But not the captain," *grandma broke in.*

"Why hasn't he left, then?"

He looked at us both. "As long as he or some of the crew remain on board, the ship and its cargo belong to the owners. If they all were to leave and others were to board her or secure a line … and manage to get her to safety … they can claim salvage … the value of the ship and her cargo." *He wiped his moustache with his napkin and put it down on the table.* "A captain also gets attached to his ship. Abandoning a ship is like abandoning … not just a responsibility but an old friend."

"So the captain is going to stay?"

Grandfather nodded.

"What'll they do now?"

Grandfather looked at the table. "They will probably try and get a tug to her, get a line on board and then tow her into the nearest port."

I tried to imagine the scene and then I wondered, "Did you ever abandon ship, grandad?"

He laughed. "Only in Riga! But joking apart, I've often been in bad weather but never in a situation quite like this."

"How far is it to the nearest port?"

He pointed to the small bookcase that was usually hidden behind the open kitchen door behind me. "Fetch the atlas."

Grandma took the dishes off the table and made room for grandad to open the atlas. He searched the pages before spreading it open on the table. I leaned on my elbows beside him.

He poked his stubby finger at the English Channel. "Here we are," then moved it hesitatingly across the page south-westward beyond Ireland and out into the Atlantic. He drew an imaginary circle around a small area of sea in the middle of nowhere. "Somewhere about here I would guess." His finger moved again a short distance north-eastwards. "Maybe 300 miles south-west of Fastnet." He tapped the spot and shook his head.

I looked at all the unfamiliar names that hung like name-tags from the coastline of Ireland. "Where would the tug tow the ship to?"

His eyes shifted their focus on the map and his bushy moustache twisted as he compressed his lips. "You ask a gey lot of questions, William. Depends on the weather ... the size of the ship ... and when, and if ... a tug can get to her." He turned the map and scanned the southern coast of Ireland. "Maybe Cork," and then the English south coast, "or maybe Falmouth."

The questions were cramming into my head and I couldn't stop asking them. "How long would that take?"

He turned and looked at me from under eyebrows that were miniature and untamed versions of his moustache. I smiled hopelessly. He put a finger in his ear to placate an itch and I noticed for the first time that the same white hairs also sprouted there. "If the weather holds and *there is a tug not too far away ... maybe a few days."*

Later, just before I went to bed, I asked him the name of the ship and learned that it was the Flying Enterprise. *That night I dreamed of Silver and I struggling with the heavy wheel as the sea swept over our ship. Mr Hornsby rowed away from the* Hispaniola's *side with grandma and a crew of pirates.*

"We've got to save your grandfather and the treasure," Silver said.

In front of us on the lower deck grandfather tied ropes around boxes and barrels that were all wrapped in Christmas paper. Loosed sails cracked and snapped in the wind and then, as with dreams, the end became a little hazy. In the morning I hastily began another story in an old notebook that I had managed to wheedle out of grandma.

Grandfather and grandma didn't really celebrate Christmas, though they went through the motions for me. I always had one of grandfather's thick stockings over the end of my bed, bulging with fruit and lots of wee presents individually wrapped. They always tried to get me something special: a sledge one year and a bicycle when I was fourteen. Each year they gave each other the same thing … she gave him a bottle of his favourite malt and he gave her bath salts and rose water. There was something very special about their exchange of presents, the way they thanked each other. Christmas was only one of the two or three occasions when they kissed each other in my presence. They would hold their presents in one hand and look at each other like a couple of children, and I knew, in their embrace, that they still regarded each other and their bond with a kind of wonder. I could have felt left out of it, but they always turned to include me in their arms, even though I had given nothing.

Hogmanay, however, was the really special time of year for them and they looked forward to it excitedly. Grandma baked shortbread and a heavy, dry, black cake in a pastry crust, called black bun. Grandfather laid out his bottles on the sideboard. He polished the glasses to a sparkle with a kitchen towel and then fussed around the coal fire to ensure the room was warm and welcoming. It was the one night of the year when I was allowed to stay up very late. In fact I was allowed to see in the New Year and was given the very special privilege of being their first-foot. Grandma would insist I put on my coat then she would put a piece of black bun in one of my hands and a lump of coal in the other and send me out the front door. I had to wait a few minutes after they had closed it on me and then knock. After a few moments they would open it as if surprised to see me and I would give them the black bun and the coal and we all would wish each other a Happy New Year. After that there were always several visitors, usually old sea-going pals of grandfather. They would knock back grandfather's malt and yarn away into the wee smaa hours and at some point Grandma would see me up to bed.

It was a couple of days after New Year, and before the holidays were over, that grandfather showed me the picture in his paper. It was taken from the air, was black and white and a little out of focus. It was obviously blowing a gale of wind and rain, and the ship was partly obscured by spray. The photograph was of the Flying Enterprise wallowing in a heavy sea with one rail almost under water. In one corner of the photograph was an enlarged inset of the ship's bridge. It was very grainy and a black circle had been drawn around a white dot

that might have been a face. The caption said 'CAPTAIN CARLSEN
STAYS WITH HIS SHIP'. *Grandfather stared at it with admiration.*

"Is there nobody else with him?"

*"No, he's been four nights and days on his own out there. Only
emergency lighting and probably no heating." He spoke with
reverence.*

*I tried to imagine the cold and the wet, the floor sloping steeply,
the walls and stairs at strange angles, the silence of a dead ship broken
only by the occasional crash of loose objects. Had he been able to get
a hot drink, never mind a hot meal in those four days? He seemed to
me to be a hero like Gary Cooper the film star. I could see his clenched
jaw and steely look as I read the text under the photograph.*

"What's a list of 60 degrees, grandad?"

*Grandfather put down the paper, looked around and then went
over to the kitchen door. He took a firm hold of the doorknob then
slowly leaned away outwards until it seemed he could lean no more. He
gasped, "That's only 45 degrees," and then the door moved, his fingers
slipped and he crashed heavily onto the floor.*

*"Ouch! That was sore." He looked across at me gawping at him.
"Quick, help me up."*

*We were halfway back to his chair when grandma came rushing
down the stairs, her stick rattling against the balustrade. She looked at
us both suspiciously. "What was that?"*

*Grandfather looked at me and then pulled me towards his chair.
"William was just showing me a trick of his when he fell over." His
hand tightened painfully on my elbow. "Are you alright now, boy?"*

*I looked at him and then managed to redirect my gaze to grandma.
"I'm fine now ... really."*

*"Well, just the pair of you sit down and behave yourselves." She
gave us each a peremptory stare and went on through to the kitchen.*

*Grandfather staggered to his chair, sat down, winked at me rather
painfully and put a finger to his lips. "Mum's the word, boy."*

I nodded in reply.

*This time, to illustrate the 60 degree list, he took the couple of
books and his ashtray off the wee table by his chair and instructed me
to tilt it. I kept on increasing the tilt and even before he told me to stop
I knew that had I been standing on the table I, and anything else not
attached to it, would have slid off.*

"That's about 60 degrees!"

It dawned on me that everything on the Flying Enterprise – *cargo,
ropes and wires, chairs and tables, crockery, books, clothing, food and*

anything else loose – had to be lying in a tangled heap on one side of the ship.

Silver came to me again that night. The storms in the south had now reached us, the wind was blattering around the walls of the house, the trees in the garden thrashed themselves into a wild frenzy and the rain was lashing on the windowpanes, dimming the lighthouse beam. He stood in his usual place with his collar turned up around his neck, gazing into the darkness outside as if watching the Flying Enterprise.

"Shiver me timbers, William. Not even treasure is worth your life … somebody else's maybe … but not yours nor mine. Do'in his duty is one thing. But he needs to get his carcass off there, matey."

I wanted to argue but he frightened me a little.

Over the following week the papers and the radio were full of the story of the Flying Enterprise *and its brave captain. At school we talked of nothing else, even football took second place and I couldn't wait to get back home to hear the news from grandfather. He was following the drama, day by day, hour by hour and minute by minute with a sort of enthusiastic trepidation. Grandma said that it was just as if he was back at sea. He dug out his old nautical books and showed me diagrams and pictures to illustrate Captain Carlsen's predicament. I learned a whole new language of 'heaving lines', 'bollards', 'focstles' and 'weather rail under'. I learned the names for the different members of the crew and the various officers; of all the parts of a ship; which was port and which was starboard; which showed a green light and which a red. I learned the names of the sea areas used in the shipping forecast and those for all the wind speeds. They were magic names to me, bursting with new meanings, each with its own weight and texture. They were so real I could almost hold them in my hands. Not comfortable names to cuddle but names that burned my fingers. I absorbed them hungrily like someone who had been starved of language. But they were not words I could use in conversation, except with grandfather and even then I felt self-conscious saying them. So I wrote them into my stories. Using these wonderful new words was a whole new adventure in itself and I even asked grandma for a dictionary for my next birthday.*

The real story, however, went on. The Turmoil, *a deep-sea tug, set off from Falmouth to try and tow the* Flying Enterprise, *but Captain Carlsen was unable to secure the towrope on his own. Grandfather took me down to the harbour at Newhaven to show me how thick and heavy a towrope might be. A rope that would have to be dragged from the tug once a thin heaving line had been thrown across to the* Flying

Enterprise. *He described the slippery, sloping deck, the freezing wind, old hands, the ship and the tug heaving and plunging dangerously close. Somehow, the first mate from the tug, a Mr Dancy, managed to get aboard the* Flying Enterprise *and after several attempts he and Captain Carlsen got the towrope on and made it fast. They set off for Falmouth.*

Another few days of more reasonable weather went by and the Turmoil *steadily towed the* Flying Enterprise *half-way to Falmouth. In another couple of days they were due off The Lizard, the extreme south-western tip of England. Agonisingly slowly they were making their way to safety and as long as the weather held maybe they would make it. The two men were now able to take turns on watch, grabbing what sleep they could, always with the thought in their heads that another roll of the ship and she might go under. Eleven days after all but Captain Carlsen had left the ship, and only 57 miles from Falmouth, the towrope broke. The two men, though near exhaustion, somehow managed to secure another. Then the weather deteriorated once again and they were forced to cease towing and to heave-to.*

The next day the Flying Enterprise *was wallowing in heavy seas and rolling to an incredible 80 degrees: she was almost on her side. I asked grandfather how dangerous it was now for Captain Carlsen and Mr Dancy.*

"Very, very dangerous," he said. "What happens now is entirely unpredictable … in the short term that is … in the long term, if they don't make port soon … she's going to turn over." He looked at me squarely so he was sure I would understand … and I did. "These are very brave men."

I thought of Silver. "What would you have done, grandad … if it had been your ship?"

I was sitting on the chaise-longue cutting out the articles and pictures from the paper, for by now I too had become rather obsessed by the drama of the Flying Enterprise *and I was making up a scrapbook. Grandma was knitting in her chair on one side of the fire and grandfather was sitting in his on the other. She put down her knitting to listen to what grandfather might say. He got up and filled his pipe from a jar on the mantelpiece by the clock. He took an inordinately long time to reply and I nearly broke into the silence. Finally, he spoke.*

"Things are rarely as straightforward as you might think."

I wondered if he was looking for an excuse.

"If, for some reason, the master … Captain Carlsen … felt that he was responsible for the situation his ship was in, he might stay aboard

longer than if he felt … there was nothing he could have done in the first place."

I put down the scissors I was working with. "D'you mean he's to blame?"

"No. I mean I don't know … that's what I am saying. I can't tell … probably no one can at this particular moment. He can be the only judge." He drew on his pipe. "But to answer your question … I would not have wanted to be on that ship for the last … what has it been … almost two weeks." He looked across at grandma and then at me. "I think I would maybe have been off before now." He rubbed his face and smiled in a curious way. "Mind you, it's not my ship."

I decided, rightly or wrongly, that grandfather would have stayed.

Before I went to bed that night we listened to the late news, almost in silence, 'Captain Carlsen and Mr Dancy were picked up safely. They left the Flying Enterprise *just 50 minutes before it sank. Well that, sadly, is the end of an epic struggle …'*

Grandfather switched the wireless off and poured himself a glass of malt.

"It's sad to lose something isn't it, especially after you have struggled so long and hard to save it? At least these two brave men are safe," but he shook his head slowly at the loss of the ship.

"Maybe I'll be a sailor when I grow up." I suddenly blurted out, but as I said it I wondered if I could ever be as brave as Captain Carlsen.

"I'll drink to that," grandfather said, raising his glass, "but I don't think your mum and dad would have wanted that."

"Your grandmother neither," said grandma, launching into her knitting with a frown.

"Did you like being a sailor?"

A wistful look came into his eyes. "Ah well, some of the time. Things were pretty rough in my day though." He sipped his dram.

"Tell me something that happened to you?" I leaned forward to encourage him. Grandma tugged violently at the ball of wool that had slipped onto the floor.

He laughed gently. "Another time … another time." But he never did.

That night, however, he did leave me a legacy of his knowledge of the sea, tucking in another loose strand of my world in the process. He came up to my room to say good night, something grandma usually did but he, rarely. I expect it was to do with the Flying Enterprise. *As he switched off the bedroom light my lighthouse beam swept the room. I asked him where it was from.*

He went to the window and, standing almost in the footprints of Silver, looked out. "It's the Isle of May lighthouse." And he explained to me that each lighthouse has a different sequence of flashes and if you count them and the intervals between, you can tell exactly which one it is. He then tried to explain something about bearings and finding one's position, but that was beyond me. He added, as an afterthought, that the May was one of the oldest lighthouses in Scotland.

Knowing the source of the light and the fact that it was a kind of constant was very comforting. I cried a little that night thinking of my mum and dad, but they were not tears of grief. I had a strange feeling that I can't put into words ... somehow the light held their presence and in a sense they were still here. That night Silver stayed away.

CHAPTER *6*

'I never thought I would ever be as scared again.'

"*Y*our dad was out for quite a long time this morning."

There was no reaction. Alistair was completely absorbed. Hypnotised, is how Cat would have described it.

"Hello … hello … Cat calling Alistair."

He shifted in the chair, put the lager can on the floor and belched surreptitiously, "Uh hu."

"Language problems, dear?"

"Mmmmm?"

She walked in front of the screen as somewhere in Florida, on grass as short and green as a billiard table, flanked by bushes with flowers worthy of a botanic park, around a couple of hundred adults in oversize shorts and undersize ankle socks held their collective breath. A small, white and dimpled ball rolled to a stop on the very lip of a neat round hole in the ground. "Oooohhhhs" filled the room.

"Chicken shit," said Alistair, leaning over the arm of the chair to see around Cat's legs.

"Alistair! Dearest."

"Sorry, love." He pulled himself up, "What was that?"

"Your father."

"What about him?"

She moved away from the screen so that his eyes would follow her and sat down on a low antique nursing chair. She pulled up her legs and wrapped her arms around them, putting her chin on her knees. "Your father didn't wear his usual ragbag when he went for his morning constitutional today."

He took a sip from his can. "Maybe he went downtown," his eyes wandering back to the screen.

"He wasn't gone that long."

"Maybe he went to the post office to send off some books, or to the bank?"

"Hhmm," she murmured doubtfully.

"Did you ask him?"

"I couldn't think what to ask."

Alistair groped for the remote with his free hand, pointed it at the screen and switched it off. "What are you worrying about? Surely he can get dressed up and go out without any ulterior motive? Hey … maybe he went to call on our merry widow?"

Cat frowned at him. "Who?"

"Mrs Merryweather, at number 62."

"Oh Alistair, grow up."

"Well, I really think you are worrying about nothing." He crushed the empty can in his hands. "He hasn't done anything strange … has he?"

She unwrapped her arms from her legs, stretched them out and leaned back. "Perhaps you're right."

"I think he has settled in very well, considering."

She nodded in agreement.

"He and Thomas seem to get on very well."

She smiled at him. "Does that please you?"

"Yes … I suppose it does … makes it easier for him and me too." They looked at each other. "How are you getting on with him?"

"He's a bit crusty on top and a bit stuck in his ways, but I suspect he's really a bit of an old dear underneath. Do you think he is a good role model for Thomas?"

"Just a minute. *I'm* his role model!"

"Of course dear, but … you and he don't share many views."

"Hang on there, Thomas and I … "

"Not Thomas you fool … I mean Bill."

"Oh! D'you think he might influence Thomas."

"Of course, he will." She rose, went over to him and sat on the arm of his chair, putting her arm around his shoulder. "But then, so will everybody." She stroked his cheek with her free hand. "I think your dad is just a wee bit of a vagabond, so we ought to keep an eye on him and Thomas."

He looked up at her with a hint of wickedness in his eye. "Just remember, I'm his son … and just look at me."

Later, at dinner, Alistair commented that he would have to work on Saturday, apologising to Tom that he would not be able to come and watch him playing rugby. Before he had thought about it, Bill found himself volunteering to go in Alistair's place. He brushed off Cat's protestations. The following day he wished he had not, but it was too late to renege. The weather had turned mild and with it had come wind and rain. It teemed down and even Tom, a keen rugby player, was no longer looking forward to his game. Cat ordered a taxi and insisted they took it. She also stuffed some notes into Bill's hand to pay for it. When he heard the name of the destination Bill recognised it as a place where *he* had once played rugby, though he had never liked sports. He wrapped himself up in his Fair Isle sweaters and beret and green boots, though he did wear his better raincoat over the top of it all. He also took a large coloured golf umbrella from the stand in the hall. Tom wore his school uniform and carried his gear on his back in a kind of rucksack.

When they got to the grounds, however, they found that the game had been cancelled. There was nothing for it but to find the bus stop, stand in the shelter and wait for it to take them home. The only other occupants were three other schoolboys who had been dropped off for the game and who also had to find their own way home. Two chased each other around the shelter, stamping through a puddle from the overflowing gutter and punching and pulling each other playfully while their sports bags soaked up the rain. The third was in a different uniform and looked pretty miserable. Bill recognised his cap badge as that of his old school. They seemed to wait a very long time until a bus came. It was not the right one for them, but the two pals and the single lad took it. As the latter boarded in front of them Bill nudged Tom and nodded his head towards the disappearing boy.

"I went to that school."

"Well, it's just as well the game was cancelled because that's who we were going to play against! Who would you have supported?"

"You, of course."

"Would you really?"

"Ych. I didn't like my school very much."

"Why not?"

"Oh, for a lot of reasons … some my own fault."

Miraculously, the wind and rain eased off and a pale watery glow began to brighten in the west as the weather front moved away to the east. They decided maybe they had missed the bus they wanted so they began to walk towards town where they might pick up another. This took them along the length of the playing fields that were surrounded by high, blue-painted, metal palings and lined with trees that were bare and wet black poles. Beyond them were acres of pitches, mud and puddle covered. Tom scuffed with his feet among the leaves littering the pavement.

"In my day, when it was too wet to practise we were supposed to run around the grounds instead."

"Supposed to … ?" Tom left the question trailing.

"I was a thrawn wee lad. I didn't see the point of getting soaking wet when it was too wet to play rugby. Mind you, I didn't see the point of getting wet even when we could play."

Tom laughed and kicked boisterously at a large pile of wet leaves blown together at a corner of the road. He began to turn it and found that Bill had stopped behind him.

"Right here ... " he banged the ferrule of the umbrella on the spot. "One day, over fifty years ago, the prefects, probably under instructions, checked the names of all those dutifully running past. Of course ... "

"Your name wasn't taken," Tom shouted triumphantly. Bill just grimaced at him.

"My name wasn't there right enough." He walked on and Tom followed at his side, looking up at him.

"What happened?"

"On the following morning I was given a written order from the prefects to appear at their court after school." He looked down at Tom with a wry smile on his face. "The school was a little old fashioned, to my mind barbaric, and the older boys were allowed to punish younger one. They found me guilty of failing to participate in the run and I was sentenced to six hits on my bottom with the traditional implement ... basically a piece of wood."

"Yoww! Was it sore?"

Bill turned to Tom as they walked along, "Yes ... it was."

But it was not exactly as he had told Tom

> *It was just as Mr Thomson, the games master, was telling us that there would be no rugby but that we should change into our kit, nevertheless, and run around the playing fields, that I became aware of Silver lurking at the end of the veranda of the changing rooms. As Mr Thomson led the others in to change and, as I was hesitating in the doorway, Silver beckoned me. I made the decision in a second and regretted it ever after. Of course, I got caught.*
>
> *I never thought I would ever be as scared again. I was wrong as it happened. There were two of us on trial that afternoon, both of us for the same offence. The prefects' court took place in a little building next to the gym. It had once been a squash court. The ceiling was very high and the walls were as smooth as the floor. It was always bare and cold in there. We were called in turn to stand at attention in front of the table at the far end of the room, behind which the prefects sat in judgement. It's not that I hadn't been reprimanded before, but then it had been by adults and, although I could not have articulated it, I was instinctively aware of some reluctance, or control, when punished by an adult. What*

I was well aware of – what child is not? – was that the rules of engagement between children or youths are not usually respected by the stronger side. The four prefects I faced showed no reluctance, no doubts. They heard my case, sentenced me to six hits and sent me outside into the corridor to await punishment. I was scared. I stood there with the other boy and tried to control my shaking body. I was close to tears, close to wetting myself, close to grovelling at their feet if it would get me off.

The door opened and I was led in. Only three prefects now sat behind the table, the fourth stood by the door with his hands behind his back. I was told to bend over and put my head below the top of the table. Through sobs, I stared down at three pairs of dirty shoes. I was like the condemned man in his awful fear and clumsiness breaking all the little formal routines of retribution and, in so doing, upsetting the dignity of the occasion and angering the officials. Years later I remembered this moment when a dog I had to shoot sensed its impending doom and struggled terribly against my grip, causing me to lose my temper and abuse its trust.

My legs buckled and I was physically forced into the right posture with whispered oaths of annoyance. The prefect administering the punishment then hit my presented bottom through the thin material of my trousers with the flat piece of wood. Oh how it stung and yet it was a relief at last to know exactly what the pain would be. There were five more hits but I don't think I felt the last as by then my backside was numb. The real pain came afterwards as I walked with difficulty down the corridor, across the playground and onto the bus. I could hardly sit down for the stiffness and burning.

My grandparents knew that something was wrong but I couldn't tell them what had happened. They had a long debate after I had gone to bed that night. I heard grandma's determination to visit the school and find out and my grandfather's equal determination that they must respect my silence. They learned the truth of the event a couple of years later and I wonder now if it would have changed things had grandma had her way. In retrospect, I think that up to this point I was holding my own without the love of my parents, but it was about then that I began to lose it.

That night I lay on my side in bed for my backside and the tops of my thighs were red and tender. I watched that familiar beam of light from the May way out on the edge of the Forth and I cried myself to sleep, just as hard as I had the very first night I had lain there.

He came again of course, that night.

"Aye, take it like an honest man and keep your own counsel. That's what I would say." He turned towards me from his usual position by the window. "They're an ill-gotten crew, shipmate."

He stroked his chin with his broad, brown hand and gave me a sly look. "We'll think of sumit, you and me lad, sumit that will sink 'em. And if not, we'll just steer a course around 'em as if they weren't there."

Silver swung his crutch as naturally as if it was part of his own flesh and bones and loped across the floor to my bedside. So close did he stand looking down on me that I could see that his clothes were stained and dirty. He gave me a conspiratorial smile revealing several large black teeth dispersed among the white.

"We don't need 'em, William. You and me, we'll find our own passage." He fingered the cord that held up his breeches. "Just like the strands that make up a hawser ... that's how we are," and he gave me a leering wink before slipping through the wall.

A bell rang. Bill looked at the figure of Tom slumped against the glass beside him utterly absorbed in a book. He gently tilted it up in Tom's hands to see the cover. It was Tolkein's *The Lord of the Rings*.

 "Are you enjoying it?"

"F...aaannntastic!" Tom replied, his eyes glued to the page, "but it's a bit complicated."

He recalled the feeling. "Have you seen the film?"

Tom glanced up. "No, not yet."

"Would you like to?"

He put the book down. "How d'you mean?"

"Well ... I know the story and I would like to see it, but I would feel a little ... embarrassed to go on my own. I mean ... can you see me queuing with mums and children ... and sitting on my own trying to eat my ice cream without drawing attention to myself?"

Tom grinned at him. "Maybe I could take you?"

"Would you? Seriously?"

"Play your cards right."

"You're teasing your old grandad."

"Sorry."

"Tell you what, I'll suggest it as soon as we get home."

"Great!"

So they went to the film the following weekend. It was showing in an enormous cinema complex that quite horrified Bill. He followed Tom closely, lest he lost him, through snakes of people criss-crossing a vast indoor concourse, hideously coloured and lit only by narrow beams of light. He bought tickets from an over-familiar young man then they descended the shallow slope of a long, dark corridor past numbered doors, Bill stumbling as he shuffled forward blindly. Finally, they entered a kind of private lounge that was the anteroom to their screen. It was decorated in plush crimson and lit by crimson lights, appearing to Bill, for all the world, like a bordello. As they approached the swing doors he would not have been surprised if they had met an exiting Toulouse Lautrec in the company of painted ladies. He kept his thoughts to himself as Tom led him up steep narrow steps to wide and well-padded seats. Just as his eyes had become accustomed to the startling décor and his body had gratefully accepted the comfortable seat, his ears were assailed by an ill-judged level of decibels that penetrated the very bones of his head and ricocheted endlessly around his skull.

He closed his eyes and was on the point of fleeing, his arms gripping the armrests like a drowning man clutching onto driftwood. He tried to relax as Tom chattered about the various trailers and gave him a very brief, inaudible and unintelligible, rundown on the story of the main film, which he knew better than Tom anyway. However, once it began he forgot where he was and found himself utterly absorbed. He even forgot his aches and pains and it was only when the film was finished and he tried to stand up that he realised how long he had been sitting and how stiff and sore he was.

The next day when Tom came to see him in his flat his grandad admitted that he had not enjoyed himself so much for a long time. Tom tentatively offered his copy of the book to his grandad to read. Bill was touched.

"Actually, Tom, I've read it."

"Did you like it?"

"Did I like it! *The Lord of the Rings* is probably my third most favourite book."

He put it down on his desk next to another which he picked up. It was slim and small by modern standards, the cover tooled with the outline of a ship, its pages almost as fine as tissue, the edges tinted with gold and the print tiny. He handed it to Tom who opened the pages with difficulty. The first was blank but had an inscription in a childish scrawl that read, *'This book belongs to William Manson'*. The next page held the title, *Treasure Island*.

"You'll have read this?" Bill said to him.

"No, though I've heard of it," he reassured him.

"You haven't! I don't believe it!" They looked at each other and Bill saw that Tom felt he had disappointed him. "Maybe you've read *Kidnapped*?"

"Oh yes, we read that last year. That's great."

"Well, the author of *Kidnapped*, Robert Louis Stevenson, also wrote *Treasure Island*. You must read it." He picked up *The Lord of the Rings*, "I think I'd like to read this again … you can read mine. What d'you say we swap?"

"Okay," but he handled the thin-leaved book nervously.

Bill glanced at it and at the Tolkein book in his hand. "Tell you what," he said, as he put it down and gently took *Treasure Island* out of Tom's hand, "I just happen to have another copy for you." Tom's eyes opened in anticipation as Bill picked the copy he had bought from the shop before Christmas and handed it to him. Tom began flicking through the pages, stopping briefly at the illustrations as his grandad went on talking. "This copy got me the belt anyhow. Don't want it to be catching."

Tom put his new book down and looked at him eagerly. "Tell me about it."

Bill settled himself on the couch. "Make some coffee then. There's some orange juice in the fridge and some chocolate biscuits in the tin if you want any."

"You don't have any Irnbru?"

"There you've got me, but I'll get some if you like."

"Yes please … but don't tell dad."

He looked up from the couch at Tom in the doorway. "Are you addicted or something?"

"Get a life, grandpa."

"Pardon?"

"It's just a soft drink, but dad doesn't approve."

Bill puckered his mouth. "I could get into trouble."

"Just say it's yours," suggested Tom.

"Hmmm."

"Please."

"Okay then, but be it on your head."

Tom poured the hot water into the cafetière.

Bill picked up his copy of *Treasure Island* and waved it in the air. "My grandparents gave me this for my birthday when I was eleven. I took it to bed that night and even after my lights were out I remember reading it in the beams from the lighthouse that crossed my bedroom." He laughed out loud and half-shouted through to Tom in his kitchenette. "Daft! I could only get a phrase at a time." He waited until Tom came through with his mug. "Nice and strong I hope." He sipped it and winked at Tom in approval.

"Lighthouse?"

"My bed in my grandparents' house looked out towards the sea where there was a lighthouse. It shone in on me all night." He looked at Tom casually. "Cool, eh?"

"Right on, grandad!"

"Where were we? Ah yes … I took this to school the next day … I just couldn't put it down." He flipped idly through the pages, stopping at one and tapping it with a forefinger. "I was just finishing chapter seven and starting chapter eight, now I remember." He shifted his weight on the couch and looked at Tom. "I was early for class and must have sat down and opened the book while I was waiting. My seat was in the front row."

Tom nibbled at the edges of his biscuit and listened.

"It was at the point in the story where Jim Hawkins, a young lad like yourself, meets the ship's cook, Long John Silver, for the first time … only he doesn't know at that point that Silver is actually a pirate." Bill began to read, "*'His left leg was cut off close by the hip, and under the left shoulder he carried a crutch, which he managed with a great dexterity, hopping about upon it like a bird. He was very tall and strong, with a face as big as a ham – plain and pale, but intelligent and smiling'*. I was hooked. I suppose I had been reading for about five or ten minutes and I was utterly unaware that the class had settled and that the teacher, Mr Bartholomew, had begun the lesson. I had got to the line," Bill turned the pages, "where Long John Silver, *'took my hand in his large firm grip'*. It was so real I felt it. He lifted my hand … from off the book and then lifted up the book itself. I looked up at his face and it was Mr Bartholomew!

"There was utter silence in the classroom as he took me and my book to his desk. He glanced at the cover and then muttered that I would be better sticking to the set readers rather than wasting my time, and his, on adventure stories. He put the book in a drawer from which he took his belt and then gave me six of the best! I didn't get the book back for a couple of weeks and I think I was more upset at the loss of the book than getting the belt." He anticipated Tom's question.

"Yes, it was sore, but it was over so quick. A pal told me afterwards that Mr Bartholomew had spotted I was not paying attention when he was sitting behind his desk. His eye had alighted on me like a hawk and the class had followed his gaze and watched the promising scenario with bated breath, as he stalked me, slowly and silently."

"I've never had the belt," said Tom. "Corpr … copra … "

"Corporal," Bill interrupted, "from the Latin *corpus*, the body."

"Well, corporal," he enunciated carefully, "punishment isn't allowed anymore."

"Good thing too." He sighed and closed the book. "Unfortunately our set readers at school were Scott … Sir Walter … rather than Stevenson."

"Don't know him."

"Yes, you must … *Ivanhoe*?"

Tom's face lit up, "Saw the film."

"Well, there you go … but you never saw a film of *Treasure Island*?"

"No, I don't think so."

"Then we must try and get one of those tape things out. There must be one of *Treasure Island*."

"You mean video?"

"That's it."

"Actually, they are DVDs now grandad."

"Well, whatever the damned things are called, we'll get one and you can see what a great story it is."

After Tom left with his new copy of *Treasure Island*, Bill put *his* copy back on the shelf beside the other Stevenson novels. He ran his hand along the shelf until he came to another old book. He pulled it out and was returning to the couch when he remembered something else and went to his desk instead. There he picked up Scott's three-volume edition of *The Pirate*, published in 1822. It was due to be sent off to a client – an expatriate Shetlander in New Zealand. The book he had taken off the shelf was *The Heart of Midlothian*. Both had been required reading at school. He set them down on the couch and began idly leafing through *The Pirate*.

> *Mr Bartholomew was a tall, bulky man and because of that or his name or his strength with the belt, no one knew which, it was so long ago, he had been nicknamed Atlas. There, any resemblance to the bronzed, muscle-bound man in the magazines we were not supposed to read, ended. For Mr Bartholomew was fat, had thinning hair and wore a mustard coloured suit with a matching waistcoat that I could not imagine on Charles Atlas. He was said to have a second identical suit but only the cognoscenti could tell one from the other, I certainly couldn't.*
>
> *"Now, Sir Walter Scott was an antiquarian, an historian who actually turned to writing to pay off his bills." He gathered his gown, chalky and glazed with age, around him and perched his overflowing bulk on the edge of his desk. "But Scott was also a romantic." He smiled benignly as he shared this little anomaly with us. "He used historical fact as the background to his romances." Lifting himself off the desk Mr Bartholomew picked up a piece of chalk, turned to the blackboard and wrote up two words – HISTORY and ROMANCE.*
>
> *"Now, when I use the word romance," he said, turning surprisingly swiftly for his size, "I do not mean the kind of thing that goes on between Mr Stewart Granger and Miss Deborah Kerr." There was an approving and measured snigger from the class. "We shall find in* The Heart of Midlothian, *as in all Scott's novels, that the historical*

setting, which is the frame on which Scott weaves his romances, is a time not long before Scott's own.

"We will find in The Heart of Midlothian, *the macabre and the gothic … goodness, or at least nobility, challenging evil: the age old struggle between the forces of darkness and light."*

In the corner of my jotter I noted down the words gothic and macabre for future use.

Mr Bartholomew looked around the class and I hastily concentrated on the well-thumbed book on my desk: to no avail.

"Manson?"

Reluctantly I looked up.

"Would you do us the honour of beginning the first chapter of a real piece of literature?"

Of course it was a rhetorical question. He was just rubbing salt into the wounds he had inflicted a few days previously over the episode of Treasure Island. *The class grabbed the chance of a cheap laugh at my expense.*

"Yes sir." I stood up, found the first page and balancing the book in my hands began:

" 'The times have changed in nothing more (we follow as we were wont the manuscript of Peter Pattieson) than in the rapid conveyance of intelligence and communication betwixt one part of Scotland and another. It is not above twenty or thirty years, according to the evidence of many credible witnesses now alive, since a little miserable horse-cart, performing with difficulty a journey of thirty miles per diem, carried our mails from the capital of Scotland to its extremity. Nor was Scotland much more deficient in these accommodations, than our richer sister had been about eighty years before. Fielding, in his Tom Jones, *and Farquhar, in a little farce called the* Stage-Coach, *have ridiculed the slowness of these vehicles of public accommodation. According to the latter authority, the highest bribe could only induce the coachman to promise to anticipate by half an hour the usual time of his arrival at the Bull and Mouth'."*

Thus began my introduction to Sir Walter Scott.

I struggled on through many more such tortuous sentences, the beginnings of which I had long forgotten before I had reached the end, until at last the bell brought the torture to an end.

Luckily this introduction to Scott happened after I had discovered my own adventure stories, or I might never have picked up a book again. How could the opening of the Heart of Midlothian *compare with the opening of* Treasure Island!

CHAPTER 7

'By the sea wall, I hesitated.'

"*G*randpa!"

Bill heard him burst through the landing door into his sitting room.

"Grandpa. Where are you?" He clattered into the kitchen.

"I'm in the bath. What is it … an earthquake or something?"

Tom put his forehead against the bathroom door and shouted through, "Lennox Lewis has just won the world heavyweight championship!"

"Quite possibly."

"Grandpa. He *has* won it!"

He heard his grandpa moving around inside and the bath emptying. "Just coming, just coming. Tell you what, you … "

"I know, make some coffee." He shook his head and went into the kitchen where, to his delight, he spied a couple of bottles of Irnbru on the worktop.

"He's Canadian, isn't he?" Bill said over his shoulder as he came into the sitting room from the bathroom in his dressing gown, rubbing his hair vigorously with a bright green towel.

Tom came through with the coffee and a glass of Irnbru for himself. "No, he's British, but he was brought up in Canada."

"Ah." He sat down on the couch. "Was it a good fight?"

"I didn't see it. Dad did though and he said it was great."

"He must be the first British heavyweight champion for years."

Tom sat down beside him. "I guess so." He turned to Bill. "Who was world champion when you were young?"

"Well … there were a number of champions of course, but I think they were mostly American." He put down the towel on the arm of the couch and took up the mug of coffee. "The one I remember best, apart from Muhammad Ali, of course, was Rocky Marciano. He was a real bruiser, looked as if he had just come off the Rock … Alcatraz. You know what that is, or rather, was?"

"No ...o ... o ... " said Tom shaking his head slowly.

Bill smiled. "Well, it was a famous island prison in San Francisco Bay ... in America."

"I know where San Francisco is, grandad," Tom muttered under his breath. "Did any British boxers fight him for the championship?"

Bill sat down on the couch, cupping his mug in both hands. He sighed heavily. "Yeh, one did and it was a very sad, not to say humiliating, fight." He looked over the mug at Tom. "D'you want to hear?"

He answered with a grin.

"Well ... here's where I illustrate that a story needs a beginning ... because this is all beginning." He settled back against the cushions.

"We had no great heavyweight when I was a kid, but we had two wonderful light-heavyweights, Don Cockell and Randolph Turpin. Turpin was a handsome, dark-skinned, upright and elegant boxer. He moved up to light heavyweight and then beat the French champion at that weight. Cockell, on the other hand, was a modest and gentle guy, smaller and stockier with a slick of black hair. He wasn't such an all-round boxer as Turpin but he was a tenacious fighter. He was the British light-heavyweight champion and in the same year Turpin beat the French champion, Cockell beat the Italian champion. Inevitably, everyone wanted to see a match between the two, before one might possibly challenge Marciano."

Tom listened avidly.

"You know," Bill stroked his chin, "physically, Cockell always reminded me of Lou Costello ... of the comedy duo, Bud Abbot and Lou Costello ... but you wouldn't remember them?"

"Dream on, grandad."

"Right, sorry. Anyway ... both men were the epitome of sportsmanship and although each had his own followers and lots of bets were placed on each, there were few people who would openly support one to the detriment of the other."

"What do you mean, grandpa?"

"They were such nice guys and good boxers that I think we all hoped for an honourable draw. Anyway, I was allowed to get up very early in the morning and listen to the fight with my grandfather, much against grandma's wishes. She stayed in bed. Come to think of it ... " he looked down at his apparel, "I was probably dressed just like this, except, of course, the dressing gown and pyjamas were a little smaller!" He laughed and put the empty mug down, then turned more seriously to Tom. "Imagine it. Your two heroes are to fight each other ... a gladiatorial combat."

He stood up, wrapped the towel around his neck like a boxer, tucked in his dressing gown and reached up for an imaginary microphone. In a loud voice he began, "Ladies and Gentlemen. This is a challenge contest for the British light-heavyweight championship." With his free hand he grandly introduced the boxers in each corner. Tom sat transfixed. He imagined the great cheers that went up for both men. Bill then introduced the referee, judges and timekeeper. He let go the microphone and called Turpin and Cockell into the centre of the ring. He put his arms around their shoulders and huddled there with them. " ... Clean fight ... no fouls ... break on my command ... back to your corners and come out fighting." Tom clapped.

Bill sat back down on the couch, a little breathless, and described the fight to Tom as if it was happening just in front of them.

"In the opening round they circled each other tentatively, jabbing and parrying. Turpin, with his longer reach, immediately began to pick up points – but Cockell was never put off by being on the receiving end of punches. He took them, ducked others and landed a few of his own. To begin with they were even, but it was ominous for Cockell that Turpin was able to keep him at a distance and pick him off." Unconsciously, Bill rubbed one hand over the fist of the other.

"In the third round Turpin landed a good punch on Cockell and put him on the floor. There was a groan from Cockell's supporters and a cheer from Turpin's, but Cockell got up easily within the count. As the fight progressed Turpin landed more and more telling punches."

Bill turned to Tom briefly. "Grandfather and I were supporting Turpin, I'm not quite sure why ... maybe because he was the better boxer. But our hearts sank for the plucky Cockell. Through all the punches, head down, he kept coming forward to try and find a way through Turpin's defence."

"Suddenly, at this point in the fight the referee stopped it and drew both boxers together in the centre of the ring. Grandfather and I listened to the commentator as he expressed his puzzlement, 'I'm trying to hear what the referee is saying to the two men. It's been such a clean fight I can't imagine what it is. Well, well, my goodness ... he has asked them to stop apologising to each other'." Bill looked at Tom. "Can you believe it? Have you ever heard of that in *any* competition, never mind the rough sport of boxing?"

Tom shook his head in disbelief.

Bill continued. "As the fight went into the later rounds it was obvious that Turpin was well in front and that Cockell was taking a terrible beating. He never gave up though ... just kept coming forward. We winced every time we heard the commentator exclaim ' ... and there's another beautiful right cross to Cockell's head'. In the ninth and tenth rounds Cockell took more and more punishment. Everyone was wishing it was all over. Finally, in the eleventh, Turpin hit Cockell with a tremendous punch and put him flat on the canvas."

They stared at the floor, wishing he would stay there.

"Before the count was out Cockell struggled to his feet, but it was clear that he had nothing left. The referee counted him out on his feet and Turpin won by a knock-out."

They were both silent. Eventually Bill spoke, "I remember being very confused as to how I felt. There was no winner really, both men were heroes."

"So Turpin went on to fight Rocky Marciano?"

Bill shook his head. "No, but he did go on to beat another American, Sugar Ray Robinson, and win the world middleweight title. It was Cockell who went to America to challenge Marciano for the heavyweight title." He shook his head. "He was beaten into a pulp. Marciano retired undefeated."

"I don't think I would want to be a boxer."

"What would you want to be?"

"Dad would like me to go into Law, like him."

Bill twisted round on the couch to face him. "But what would *you* like?"

Tom hesitated, started to say something, stopped, reached into his back pocket and pulled out a piece of paper. Shyly, he gave it to Bill who slowly unfolded it, then, putting it flat on his knees, smoothed out the creases with the back of his hand. He looked at it for a moment.

"Lennox Lewis?"

"Yes," then tentatively, "I drew it from the newspaper."

"Its good," he looked up briefly, "I mean it."

"That's what I like doing best, but dad says I shouldn't waste my time scribbling. You know, I saw grandmother's picture in the sitting room for the first time the other day. I had never really looked at it before." Then he remembered, got up off the couch and looked around the walls of his grandpa's room. He walked over to the painting of the cottage, Bill watched him. "That's her picture, isn't it?"

"Yes, it is."

He stood in front of it. "I didn't know grandma painted until dad told me."

Bill looked at him over the back of the couch. "Well, there you go."

"I would like to be able to do that."

"And why not?"

He turned. "D'you think I could?"

Bill glanced down at the drawing of Lennox Lewis. "Well, you seem to have a little talent. I'll say that." He held it up. "But you need to learn to draw from life."

Tom took the drawing from Bill and looked at it as if to try and discern what was wrong with it. "What d'you mean?"

"I don't know an awful lot about it ... if you had known Alice ... your grandmother ... she would have explained. I just know that copying is not the way to learn to draw." He caught Tom's eye. "Nothing wrong with it mind, but if you really want to learn, to get better at it, then you need to draw *things* ... " he waved his hand vaguely round the room and then tapped himself on the chest, " ... and *people*."

Tom clutched the drawing in his hand. "D'you know," he hesitated, as if unsure to tell his grandad, "I've dreamed about it but I've never really thought about it seriously before ... I mean as something I really could do. I don't know how to say it ... that it was important to me ... until dad told me about the picture in the living room." He turned to look at his grandmother's picture, "Somehow, knowing grandma had done it and then recognising it was where you lived ... then just knowing that the people were your grandparents ... " he looked at Bill, who nodded, " ... and you," Bill nodded again, " ... and grandma ... all made a kind of sense and something just ... I knew somehow for certain that that was what I wanted to do."

Bill got up and ambled over to Alice's painting. Tom followed. With one hand he shared the piece of paper and with the other tousled Tom's hair. "I'm happy for you, Tom. A talent is a very special gift ... sometimes a burden ... but if you pursue it, it will give you something nothing else can ever match."

Tom looked down at his drawing proudly and then his face fell. "But I don't think dad will let me."

"Can I give you a bit of advice?"

He looked up at his grandfather.

"You can't change the world all at once. Be patient ... with your dad I mean. Work at your drawing. Do the other things you have to do. There's plenty of time." He stood in front of Tom with both hands on his shoulders. "Right?"

Tom looked at the floor, clamped his lips doubtfully then shrugged. "Okay." He looked up and smiled shyly. "Thanks, grandad." Then, in a more confident tone, said, "Can I come and draw you sometime?"

Bill laughed. "Of course."

After Tom had gone, Bill got dressed. He picked up the three packages and the several letters he had to post and then went out for his walk. In the garden he noticed that Cat had de-headed the daffodils that had peopled the grass for the past couple of weeks like a yellow fanfare for spring. The exotic lips of the tulips were opening to the warming sun and the leaves on the trees were stretching speculatively out of their buds like the tender wings of emerging insects. He had an appointment and he was a little concerned about it.

As he walked slowly down the road dressed in one less Fair Isle sweater than usual, he wondered if he should have said the things he had to Tom or if there was anything else he should have said. It gave him a warm feeling to think that Alice's talent may just have been passed on and then he felt so sad for her that she was not there to see and nourish it. How proud she would have been. He glanced around, put down his packages on top of a low garden wall, took out his handkerchief and furtively wiped a tear from his eye and blew his nose. "Jesus!" he muttered under his breath.

Halfway down the hill towards the shops there was a bench on the pavement under some trees. He sat down and closed his eyes. Even from behind his closed lids he could feel the warm sunlight. Right this moment he didn't know quite what to do about the next part of his story for Tom. Since the day it happened he had never thought to put it down on paper and he did not know if he could face a re-examination of it.

He sat up straight, put the packets down beside him and took out his pipe. He filled it, took out the matches, struck one and held it over the tobacco. He watched the flare of the flame inches in front of his face. Watched it grow smaller, slowly fade, die and the match end turn black, without making any attempt to draw the pipe and light the tobacco. His hands, clutching the pipe and box of matches, fell to his lap.

Breathless voices broke into his reverie. He looked up and a party of chattering and anorexic cyclists in baseball caps and skin-tight lycra vests and tights, of all the colours of the rainbow, swept past him up the hill like a zany flock of budgies. As they disappeared over the rise the synchronised weaving of their wee bums brought a smile to his lips. He stuffed his pipe and matches back in his pocket, got up and continued his way downhill towards the shops and post office. He still had not decided what exactly he would do. Half-an-hour later, the result of his appointment, however, had made the decision for him. That afternoon he settled himself in front of the typewriter beneath Alice's painting and began the most difficult part of the story.

> *To my great relief we at last come to the end of* The Heart of Midlothian *and I now waited apprehensively to see what Mr Bartholomew would come up with next. In the time that we had read that book in class I had read* Treasure Island *for the second time,* The Adventures of Huckleberry Finn, *whose exploits on the Mississippi, as unlikely and yet believable as Jim Hawkins, I could only envy, and was now reading* Kidnapped.
>
> *In my head was a melange of heroes and villains. The Forth on our doorstep became the Mississippi and somewhere in its upper reaches, among heather-covered hills, redcoats and broadswords,*

there was a little paddleboat with a one-legged captain, smuggling whisky and black cattle. My scribbled stories in the night owed a lot to Robert Louis Stevenson, Mark Twain and to Coral Island *and* Mr Midshipman Easy, *but very little to Sir Walter Scott.*

"*In* The Pirate *we will meet Mordaunt Merton, the young man of good family, grappling, metaphysically, with Clement Cleveland, the worldly and mysterious stranger he rescues from drowning. We will also meet Norna, a sort of witch, cum seer, who seems to be in touch with the supernatural.*"

With a title like The Pirate *and new words such as 'metaphysical' and 'supernatural', I had high hopes for our new class reader. As usual, most of Mr Bartholomew's introduction went over our heads. Nevertheless, it hinted at excitement and danger. It was a promising beginning.*

Mr Bartholomew perched, as usual, on the edge of his desk in front of us, his thighs stretching his trousers to bursting point. He made to cross his legs and then, finding that impossible, spread them apart; they settled like sacks of flour overflowing the lip of his desk. For those of us in the front row this posture revealed two, short, unmatching socks of green and blue held up by suspenders that disappeared up the trouser legs around two fat and black-haired calves. He opened the book and began to read aloud to the class.

"The Pirate, *chapter one, 'That long, narrow and irregular island, usually called the Main-Land of Zetland, because it is by far the largest of that Archipelago, terminates, as is well known to the mariners who navigate the stormy seas which surround the Thule of the ancients, in a cliff of tremendous height, entitled Sumburgh Head, which presents its bare scalp and naked sides to the weight of a tremendous surge, and forms the extreme point of the isle to the south-east. This ...'*"

I wondered if Zetland might be Shetland, as his voice droned on soporifically over my head. That could be exciting ... a story was beginning to form in my mind. I wished I had some paper, but having run out of it at home I wondered if I could get some extra pocket money to spend on another lined notebook. After twenty minutes of Mr Bartholomew's recitation and a further twenty minutes of silent reading I realised that this Scott novel was going to be another dud, maybe worse than the first!

It was a coincidence that I should not have noticed. At the end of the class Mr Bartholomew opened a wall cupboard and handed out new jotters to everyone. I found myself looking at the shelves neatly stacked with little brown paper packets of lined jotters. There were so many nobody would miss one or two. I knew the thought was wrong, immediately felt guilty and turned my face away. I was sure someone, even Mr Bartholomew, had seen my acquisitive gaze. I glanced around but no one was paying any attention to me. That night, after I had put down Kidnapped and switched off the light, I heard Silver's voice.

"Cast your deadlights over them writing books, did you, eh, shipmate?"

I did not answer but lay with my eyes open watching the May light sweep the wall, momentarily etching and erasing a black shadow of the branches of the tree just outside the window.

"Makes you go cold inside, eh?" He swung his crutch and his leg over to my bed. He leaned against the wall, propped up his crutch and scratched his head. "Ah, I do recall my own first taste o' piracy. Piece of cake, matey. I'll wager you'll pull it off easy as reefin' the mainsail."

In my head I wondered if I could do it. Maybe if I went in early …

"Afore the captain and the crew arrive, eh?" He looked down on me and gave an exaggerated wink. "Conspiracy, eh!"

What's in a word! I saw it like a flag in front of me, as potent and frightening as a skull and crossbones and yet, curiously, it gave me courage … CONS … PIRACY. Silver touched me on the shoulder, "See you on the early watch," and tucking his crutch back under his arm he swung off through the window.

I was in the classroom early the next day and had long since opened and closed the cupboard and tucked a nearly full packet of new jotters securely – I thought – in my bag, before anyone else arrived. After that I thought excitedly and briefly of all the paper I had for my stories and then, when the class began, never gave the jotters another thought.

As these things happen, Mr Bartholomew decided on that day that he would have one of his 'resettlements'. It was his custom every so often to move the reformed to the back and the recalcitrant to the front. I was to be moved to the back, a rare error of judgement that Mr Bartholomew was soon to discover. He stirred us around like peppercorns in soup until he was satisfied with our new distribution. Then he instructed us to pass on our schoolbags to their new desks. He should have instructed us to take our bags with us as we moved, but he never did it the sensible way. Not that that had ever bothered me before, but this time in boisterous enthusiasm someone slung my bag from the front to my new desk at the back of the classroom. It hit another desk in front, burst open and the contents, including the new jotters, spilled out at Mr Bartholomew's feet!

I died in that moment before he understood what he was looking at and before the whole class picked up the electricity in the air and slowly and silently regarded me with a new kind of awe. I was numb and frozen, not feeling anything, but in a kind of limbo. I don't remember the rest of that lesson, nor the next. I came back to the present, or to a version of it, when someone brought a note summoning me to the headmaster's office; a place to which I had never been.

It was the first time he had even spoken to me, or me to him. I stood in front of his desk and was questioned. It was as if I was acting a part in a play. I knew my lines … I knew the plot … I knew the ending … and there was nothing I could do about it. I couldn't explain why I had taken the jotters. It was not something that an adult would understand and it was so important to me. I felt I would lose that secret fulfilment I found in writing my stories if anyone else appropriated it. I therefore answered every question with "I don't know."

Eventually he seemed satisfied that no one else was involved and he informed me that he had no choice but to punish me. I did not know what that might be, but I felt it could not be worse than having to face my grandparents. In retrospect I was right and it was the least of the many hurts that followed. He meted out the punishment immediately: six of the cane on my bottom. It was sore but no worse than the beating I had had from the prefects.

It was not until I got back to my class that I began to understand just how seriously everyone was taking my crime and what a seismic shift had occurred to my world. There was no kudos this time for what I had done nor for the punishment I had received. I had broken some fundamental rule and I was ostracised. No one would even look at me, never mind speak to me and that seemed to include the teachers. The headmaster had told me that he would give me a letter to take home at the end of the day. And just in case I might lose it he had let it be known to me that he would also post a copy direct to my grandfather if he didn't receive a reply.

I don't think I can express how I felt giving that letter to grandfather. I never saw its contents and I could not watch his face as he read it. Grandma was in tears that evening. I sensed she wanted to be sympathetic, but I knew that grandfather would not let her. Poor *woman, she must have felt some responsibility, some failure in herself and I couldn't tell her how innocent she and grandfather were, no more than I could explain anything to the headmaster. Grandfather struggled to understand. I know he did not want to believe that I was just a petty thief – which is what I was I supposed. He ended up giving me a very incoherent morality lesson and sent me to my room. I broke something in him that night.*

Later, he *was there of course … Silver … in my room.*

"We caught it broadside there matey, eh?"

He waited for me to reply, but I didn't.

"Maybe time to lie doggo … or … maybe time to pull up the anchor, eh?"

Still I didn't answer and after a moment he shrugged his shoulders and loped off.

I never needed that comforting sweep of light from the May as much as I did that night. I lay awake for hours under its repetitive gaze. All the adventure stories, read and written, seemed like nothing. All the loving times with my grandparents seemed to be destroyed. The past had no connection with now, or the future. What was the future anyway? I did not so much feel unloved as unlovable, undeserving of love.

I thought of Jim Hawkins, Huckleberry Finn and David Balfour and I decided to run away.

The day after Tom had shown his grandfather his drawing, he came across him in the garden, sitting on a cushion under the branches of a large elm tree with a loose-leaf folder on his lap, listening to some music on a small transistor radio. Bill was editing his manuscript, as he now referred to it, although at that precise moment he was leaning against the trunk with his eyes closed.

"That's nice."

Bill opened his eyes and put his finger to his lips.

The piece ended, Bill switched off the radio and patted the ground beside him.

"What was that … was it a violin?"

Bill shook his head in mock sorrow. "It was the prelude of Bach's Cello Suite … in G Major."

Tom stuck his tongue in his cheek. "Still, it was nice."

Bill reached out for his arm and pulled the laughing Tom down on the grass beside him.

"One day … " Bill threatened, then said more seriously, "I want to tell you about something I did … that I'm not very proud of … rather a long time ago."

Tom rolled onto his stomach and propped up his head with his hands, his elbows spread apart on the grass, and looked at his grandfather.

"I've written it down in the story," Bill said, indicating the folder, "but I would rather first tell you about it verbally." Then he explained to Tom at length about his early ambitions to write and the disastrous decision to steal the jotters.

"If you ever need paper or materials, Tom, ask me first will you? Don't do anything silly like I did."

Tom sat cross-legged pulling up lumps of grass as he listened to Bill. "That must have been awful for you. I can't imagine my pals not speaking to me." Then he stopped plucking the grass and looked round at his grandfather. "But they must have started speaking to you again at some point?"

Bill shook his head slowly in reply. "They never had the opportunity. I left that school."

Tom laughed. "Wicked!" Then saw that his grandfather was staring into the distance, perhaps into the past, and seemed shaken. He had upset him somehow. "Sorry grandpa … I didn't mean to … "

Bill interrupted him. "Its okay … its nothing … " He changed the subject. "Have you got a map of the Edinburgh area anywhere?"

"I think dad keeps a few maps in his car. I'll go and see."

"If you look in my kitchen you might just find some refreshment too," Bill winked.

Tom returned with a couple of tins of Irnbru and some maps. He put down one can and the maps beside Bill. Bill ignored the can and after looking at the maps selected one and opened it up on the grass in front of them. He put a finger on Newhaven and drew an imaginary line along the south side of the Firth of Forth towards Stirling.

"I decided to run away."

"But weren't you … I mean … what about your grandparents?"

Bill stared at the map. "It's difficult to explain and I don't know, of course, that my memory is one hundred per cent. I suppose I thought that I was taking trouble out of their lives. I mean … in my state of mind and at the age I was, I didn't doubt that on my travels I would find a new life. I never thought that I would be back." He turned to Tom. "A little naïve, eh?"

Tom leaned forward under his grandfather's gaze to get his attention. "Naïve?"

He looked at Tom's face so close. "Innocent … simple-minded, I mean … what's that expression of your's … get a life!"

"Well done, grandad."

"Thank you."

"But why did you go that way?" And he pointed vaguely towards the inner end of the Firth of Forth on the map.

"Ahh," Bill thought for a moment, "perhaps three reasons. The first is that I suppose I knew what lay the other way … mostly houses and the coast road to Dunbar and Berwick. I didn't know what lay to the west beyond South Queensferry. Not even beyond Granton that was only a mile or so away."

Tom squirmed.

"Yes, I know that sounds illogical, but *not* knowing allowed me to fantasise freely as to what *might* be there." He stretched his back against the base of the elm. "I don't know if you can understand that?" He carried on without waiting for Tom's response. "The second reason was that I could see part of the Forth Railway Bridge from the bottom of our street and that glimpse always fascinated me. How big was it really? I had always wanted to see it close-up. The third and fourth reasons … "

"You said."

"I know, I know … were Twain and Stevenson."

"They sound like a band?"

"Mark Twain and *Huckleberry Finn*, and Robert Louis Stevenson and *Kidnapped*."

"Of course," Tom said, "Queensferry … Hawes Inn, that's where David Balfour was kidnapped!"

"Well done. But I had my sights set further west, somewhere vaguely in the Highlands, where I would disappear into the country of Alan Breck. I would retrace their path, when they fled from the Campbells and the Government Troops, but in the opposite direction. Shall I read a bit?"

Tom nodded from his prone position then waited patiently while his grandfather searched in his pockets for his pipe and tobacco, lit up and then manoeuvred himself against the tree so that the sunlight did not fall directly on the pages. Tom turned over on his back and lay with his arms behind his head, looking up into the sky.

> "*It was a Saturday, a beautiful day at the beginning of June, or thereabouts, a week or so after the theft of the jotters.*"

He looked up. "A bit like today, but maybe not quite so warm." He picked up the tin of Irnbru that Tom had brought him, opened it and took a swig. Tom raised his eyebrows quizzically. His grandfather shrugged noncommittally, took another swig and then continued:

"'One of those days when you wake early and it is misty, still and cold, and you know that by not long after breakfast the mist will dissipate; that it'll warm up and stay that way all through the long day ahead until late into the evening. The promise is there and you believe it without further thought. I made some excuse to my grandparents about a school event and meeting up with some of the boys from my class. They were reassured that I would be home after lunch. I pinched some money from a little box of change grandma kept in the kitchen, and some food from the pantry. As for clothes, I didn't think that I might need anything warm or waterproof. I probably wore sandals, short trousers, a shirt and a jacket of some sort. I carried my food in the canvas shoulder bag in which grandfather had kept his gas mask during the war. I shortened the strap and put it round my neck and it hung rather snugly against my side.

At the bottom of the road by the sea wall I hesitated. To the right were Newhaven harbour, the tram stop and the shops; the direction I took nearly every time I stood on this spot. Turning left would be irrevocable. I heard the thud of wood on the stone of the pavement, the shuffle of a shoe, and felt the pressure of a hand on my shoulder. I turned and caught sight of the tops of the Forth Railway Bridge a little more than ten miles away. We set off!

From Newhaven I made my way along the shore road towards the adjacent suburb of Granton. In those days there was a railway embankment between the cobbled road and the sea and on the landward side, behind tenements and terraced houses, rose a steep hill. The stone of both the tenement buildings and of the retaining wall of the embankment was black, the former facing north and the latter shaded for most of the day by the buildings opposite. Perhaps because of the lack of sunlight and because the road was at the bottom of the hill, it was nearly always wet and dirty. I was depressed walking along it; trapped in a dark and miserable canyon. For those who lived on the ground floor of the tenements it must have been like living in a cellar. I knew the first part of the road, for about halfway along was a gateway to another world: a short pedestrian tunnel under the railway line onto Granton beach.

You have probably gathered that I was a rather solitary child. Living with grandparents did not encourage me or other children to make friendships. I used to wander quite a bit on my own. Usually it was down to the busy harbour at Newhaven, but, unbeknown to my grandparents, I occasionally used to go to this beach at Granton that was the only accessible sandy beach along this part of the shore.

Along this road I could also get a close look at the railway engines and the coal wagons that otherwise I only heard from a distance in bed at night. I used to love to run down the dark, dripping, echoing tunnel onto the beach, especially when a train went overhead and the whole structure rumbled and vibrated. The beach was filthy and probably a very unhealthy place to be, but that never bothered me. From the beach I could scramble up the huge stone blocks onto the breakwater of Granton harbour that ran a crooked half-mile out into the sea. I loved the end of that breakwater. It came to an end at a railed, wooden platform with open boards beneath which you could see the water. There was something just a little disquieting about it. It seemed to me to be a springboard on the edge of the world. Looking back eastward towards the mouth of the Forth I could see the horizon, a straight line beyond which there was nothing.

Granton was very much grander than Newhaven with its little wooden fishing boats. There were always big, rusty steam trawlers coming and going. At least they seemed big to me, and there were often one or two of the ships that brought esparto grass from Spain for the paper mills outside Edinburgh. Incoming trawlers throbbed past within feet of the end of the breakwater, low in the water, exuding the rich, raw aroma of fish and escorted by mobs of raucous gulls. The esparto grass ships, on the other hand, were almost spotless. They not only had holds filled with bales of grass but deck cargoes of the stuff, stacked right up to the bridge, like toy boats packed by a child, so that I imagined the captain on tip-toes trying to see where he was going.

But there was one boat … ship … I don't know what you would properly call it, that I most looked forward to seeing when I went to Granton, particularly after grandfather had explained lighthouses to me, and that was the Pole Star. *She was the lighthouse supply ship and she was a royal yacht compared to all the others. Immaculately painted and maintained, she had scrubbed wooden decks and a crew smartly dressed in blue. From my bedroom window I often saw her steaming in or out of the Forth. If I had gone to sea like my grandfather it would have had to have been on the* Pole Star.

But I digress. That June day I went on past Granton without going onto the breakwater; past a ruckle of sheds and yards, workshops, and derelict and abandoned boatyards and marine engineering businesses. Then I went on past the gasworks with its twin inflating towers and strong, unpleasant gaseous smell, until, about two hours after leaving home, I came to the golf course and an unbroken vista of the Forth estuary. This was the very limit of my

*territory. I knew that Queensferry and the railway bridge lay further
west, but I did not know what lay between me and my goal.*

*But then, there was Silver, swinging along beside me on the
fairway. "Rum country this matey, but easy walking ... if walking you
can call it!" and he laughed coarsely as he swung his good leg along.
"How far d'you reckon it is then, William lad?"*

I shook my head. "I don't know."

"Well, we'll just hold this course for a bit yet."

*A golf ball landed quite close behind me and ran on past. I turned
and saw a group of men waving and shouting, telling me to get off the
fairway.*

*"Swabs!" roared Silver, leaning heavily on my shoulder and
waving his crutch.*

I hurried him on.

*At the end of the golf course was a rough path that led off along
the shore. I had come only a few miles and thought I was nearly there.
So when, after another half a mile or so, I came upon a tall grey stone
tower house, I imagined it was the House of Shaws and that South
Queensferry lay just beyond. I hurried on, keeping an eye on the
building as I passed. I could almost hear the creak of the great door
and Ebenezer Balfour's wheedling voice as it opened. Actually, I was
just halfway, almost at the village of Cramond and very shortly I came
to the unexpected barrier of the River Almond. The river is not very
big, but too wide and deep to wade. In despair I sat down where the
mouth of the river meets the sea. How was I going to get across to
Queensferry?'"*

Bill put down the folder and sipped his Irnbru tentatively. "Have you
been to Cramond, Tom?"

"No, I don't think so, but grandad ... "

"It's a pretty little village. Before the bridge was built further upstream it
must have been one of the main routes between Edinburgh and South
Queensferry."

"Was it the House of Shaws you saw ... and ... ?"

"I thought it was at the time, but no ... that doesn't really exist, does it
... but it might have been the inspiration for it."

"So, how did you get across the river?"

"The way you still can today."

"There's a bridge?"

"Hang on." He put down the can, "Bit sweet for my taste," and picked up
the folder. A large cloud floated over the sun.

"Grandad," he said urgently, "Before you go on … who is Silver?" Then quietly, "Was it Long John Silver?"

Bill put down the folder. "Ah … can we come back to that when I have finished?" And before Tom could disagree he picked up the folder once again and resumed reading.

> "'The river mouth is just below Cramond and I turned and walked disconsolately up towards the neatly painted cottages of the village. And then I saw a man standing in the middle of the river, sculling a little wooden boat. I ran onto the road between the village and the river and saw that he was ferrying people across from Cramond to the far bank. I joined a small queue at the head of some steps to the river and nervously waited my turn. There was a notice board with the tariff. I had more than enough money to get across and nobody was paying any attention to me.
>
> Once on the boat I sat in the bow as if it were mine, and the extended family of parents, children and a grandparent that occupied the two thwarts, were my crew. I watched the ferryman and tried to work out how he sculled the single oar. Swans and ducks followed us looking for bread. Silver sat next to the ferryman in the stern. He smiled broadly and winked at me as he trailed his fingers in the water.
>
> Landing on the western bank of the Almond was like stepping onto a foreign shore. We had left the village on the eastern bank and now only the ferryman's cottage lay between me and Queensferry, or so I thought. It was lunchtime and I was hungry so I sat down just off the path above the bank to eat some of grandma's cakes and scones. I looked back across the river to the village that I had left behind. I watched couples and families pass me without a glance, some returning to Cramond and others setting off along the path to South Queensferry, and revelled in my secret. Beside me, Silver lay on his back, his tri-cornered hat over his face, snoring loudly.
>
> The second half of the journey to South Queensferry was a lot longer than I expected. The afternoon was wearing on and I was beginning to get a little tired. But at last I saw again the frame of the Forth Railway Bridge, its latticework of huge, rusty red tubes describing a series of gigantic leaping diamonds across the Forth, through the middle of which – in slow-motion such was the size of it – a tiny train trailed white smoke and crimson carriages en route from Fife to the Lothians. My heart lifted at the sight and I hurried on to where the path meets the main Edinburgh road right beneath the great stone pillars that support the railway line before it joins the vaulting bridge structure proper.'"

A small raindrop pattered onto the page in front of him. Tom was on his feet folding up the map. "Mustn't get it wet or I'll get into trouble."

Bill struggled more slowly to his feet.

"I've never been to South Queensferry." He gathered up the other maps and his empty Irnbru. The raindrops became heavier. "I have been over the bridges though. Could we go sometime?"

Bill tucked the folder under his arm and stuck a battered panama on his head. They hurried across the lawn to the back door as the rain began to wet their shoulders. Bill was feeling particularly good. He reckoned he was midway through his story.

"I've just thought of a better idea, matey," Bill said, laughing, "leave it with me."

"But you were going to tell me about ... "

"Patience, Tom, patience.

CHAPTER 8

*'In trying to escape my crime I had become responsible
for another. This time, someone was dead.'*

*I*t was a pleasant surprise and Alistair could not work out what had come over his dad. Nothing had come up in the conversation that suggested he was looking for a favour. He had come to the conclusion, therefore, that this was purely a social occasion and that they were being entertained out of the goodness of his heart. Maybe, on the other hand, it was a kind of thank you. He looked around the table at the relaxed and smiling faces of Cat, Thomas and Bill. It was so good to see his family so happy and to see young Thomas behaving quite the young man. He sipped his coffee and the small port he had allowed himself. It was a beautiful mild and clear night after the rain. He looked out of the restaurant windows at the magnificent spectacle of the illuminated Forth Railway Bridge that filled the view above South Queensferry below them and at the car lights on the Road Bridge less than a mile to the west. Maybe it was a good moment to ask his dad a favour?

He caught Cat's eye and, as if she had read his thoughts, she smiled tenderly, stretched across the table and squeezed his hand. Tom's slightly flushed face grimaced. He had managed to get just a little more wine than had been intended. Bill, a little warm and distinctly uncomfortable in one of Alistair's plainer shirts and matching tie, leaned back in his seat to find if the base of the landward pillar of the bridge was visible, but it was not. His old blue corduroy jacket with the patched elbows hung on the back of the chair behind him. He took out his wallet and gesticulated to a waiter nearby for the bill.

"Dad."

Bill sighed inwardly. He wished he would call him Bill. He smiled.

Alistair looked at Cat then switched his gaze back to his father. "We've got a favour to ask you."

"Go on."

"Well, I have been asked to give advice at a trial in the West Indies. In St Kitts to be precise."

Bill and Tom responded in unison, "Wonderful / Wicked."

Cat frowned at Tom.

"I would like to take Cat and Thomas." He looked at Tom beside him and put his hand on his shoulder. "Unfortunately, it's all happening just before the end of term and you have your exams. I don't think you can come. I wish you could but … "

Cat broke in. "We wondered, Bill, if you would stay with Thomas until we get back." She looked for confirmation from Alistair.

The waiter came over and took Bill's proffered credit card.

"It will only be for a couple of weeks before and after his holidays begin."

"But of course," Bill answered. "I shall sit with a whip over Tom and make sure he passes his exams and in the holidays I will set him essays to keep him busy."

"Oh, you won't have to do that … "

"Only joking, son."

And Tom got in his too. "No way, grandad."

"Thomas!" said Cat sharply.

"Oh mum … "

Bill, stirring some more cream into his coffee, jabbed the spoon towards Tom. "Don't worry, I will teach him some lessons."

"Anyway, where is St Kit-e-Kat exactly?" Tom joked.

Bill put down his spoon and reached to punch Tom in the midriff. He doubled up in laughter.

"If you behave," said Alistair, "I will show you when we get home. Actually, it is a tiny island, part of what is called the Leeward Islands."

"Still British then?"

"Yes, exactly."

They sat back and sipped their coffee.

"Is it a big case?" asked Bill.

"Well, it's more of a complex case and a peculiar point of law. Bit of a precedent really."

"Hmm. I should feel quite proud."

"Don't you?"

Bill saw that that question was far from flippant and so did Cat. He looked at his son, nodded, grinned and said, "Yes. Yes, I am. I'm *very* proud."

The waiter returned with Bill's card. He signed the slip and thanked him, tucking a folded banknote behind it. The waiter acknowledged his thanks with an imperceptible nod of his head and said he hoped they had had a good meal.

Cat picked up her napkin and fanned her face. "It's quite warm in here. I could do with some fresh air."

"Where'll we go?" asked Alistair.

"Why don't we go to the old ferry slip down there?" suggested Bill, gesturing out of the window towards the bridge, while at the same time surreptitiously digging Tom with his elbow.

"Yes, we'd get a nice view of the bridge down there," Cat replied. "C'mon all of you." She got up and Alistair slipped her stole over her shoulders.

Where the road swings around a corner by the base of one of the bridge piers, just before the old ferry point at South Queensferry, they passed the beginning of the path to Cramond. In the back of the car Bill drew Tom's attention to it. Immediately after, they pulled up in front of a large pub. Bill pointed to the sign, "The Hawse Inn, Tom. Where David Balfour was kidnapped."

"Cool!"

"Cruel, you mean."

"Where now?" said Alistair.

"Just here will do fine."

Alistair swung the car around and they parked by the kerb and a low stone wall, beyond which lay the sea. They got out and strolled along the pavement towards the broad slip that shelved out and down into the water right opposite the Inn. Alistair and Cat stopped and admired the spectacle of the bridge and its huge frame picked out by lights. Bill put a hand on Tom's arm and guided him down the slip a little way.

"This is the Queen's Ferry, or the South Queen's Ferry to be exact. The North Queen's Ferry is over there." He pointed in the darkness across the Forth to the shore of Fife over a mile away. "Do you know how it came to be called the Queensferry?"

"No, but you're going to tell me."

Bill pretended to cuff him. "I bet you can't guess how long it has been the Queen's Ferry."

"A couple of hundred years?"

"More."

"Five hundred years?"

"More."

"I don't know."

"Nearly 1000 years!"

"Wow!"

"And it was probably a crossing point for thousands of years before that.

If you look at a map you will see that you would have to go another 15 miles to the west to find the next place where the Firth of Forth gets narrower than this. Anyway, it was named after Margaret, who became Queen of Scotland when she married Malcolm Canmore in the 11th century. After that the ferry service lasted right up until 1964! Until that was built," and he pointed to the slender suspension road bridge that ran parallel to the rail bridge.

Bill's tone changed. "When I ran away from Newhaven there was no road bridge of course and I came here to catch the car-ferry across to Fife."

"Right here?"

"Right here, where we are standing, more than 50 years ago."

"Where did you go when you got to the other side?"

"Nowhere." He gripped the wall beside them. "I came back on the same ferry."

"How come, grandad?"

"When I have written it you will find out for yourself." He looked around the scene, one more time, at the far shore that he never arrived at and at the cold dark waters under the bridges, took a deep breath and exhaled it slowly. Then he took Tom's arm again. "Let's go back to the car."

> *I emerged onto the main road at South Queensferry about teatime or early evening. I was astonished to see the Hawes Inn: I never knew it actually existed. I could feel Silver's hand on my shoulder guiding me in, but I shook him off and walked across the road to the ferry. The north side of the Forth looked quite close from here, much closer than at Newhaven. I think there were three ferries that operated at the same time, one on either side, and one in the middle, so to speak. They were broad, squat, blunt ended boats with names like* Mary Queen of Scots *and* Robert the Bruce. *Cars were queuing in a line down the slip and one by one slowly driving onto it. I checked the fares again on the board and still had just enough money to get across.*
>
> *I hesitated.*
>
> *"Get aboard, matey," Silver said in my ear. "We've had a fair passage so far. No time for second thoughts. I'll wager Alan Brett is pacing the shore over yonder."*
>
> *I followed others walking down the slip past the cars as if I was part of a family. I had been full of confidence walking along the shore track from home and the sight of the Hawes Inn had given me a lift, but now that I had to get on the ferry and there were lots of people around I began to get a little nervous. There was a ramp onto the ferry and a turntable on the deck that revolved the cars and pointed them in the direction in which they were to park. I walked up the ramp and dodged through the cars.*

Once safely on the ferry the excitement of the adventure came back to me, but did not outweigh a growing apprehension. The ramp was pulled up, the ropes cast off and the ferry began its journey across the Forth. Some people stayed in their cars but most milled around enjoying the view and the feel of the sea under their feet. Crossing the Almond in a wee boat was one thing, but pushing off from South Queensferry into the Forth, with the wind in my face and the waves slapping and bursting against the hull of the ferry, was a bit more like running away to sea and into the completely unknown. I found a sheltered corner where I would not be too obvious, but from where I could watch the sea. There, I sat down on some ropes and opened grandfather's bag. Most of the food was gone but I still had a slab of cooking chocolate. I broke off a chunk and ate it as I looked up at the enormous railway bridge towering above the ferry. I felt very small and for the first time began to wonder what I was going to do when it got dark. A chill of foreboding ran through me.

Silver sat on a bollard beside me. He closed his eyes and lifted his head up as if into sunlight. "Ah … salt wind on the old canvas." He heard something, opened his eyes and spotted one of the other ferries coming towards us. He took up his telescope from under his free arm and held it to his eye. It was comforting to have him beside me.

"What shall I do if Alan is not there?"

Balancing the crutch under his arm he pushed home the telescope and slipped it into one of his coat pockets.

"You won't go away?"

He screwed up his unshaven face in mock surprise as he sat facing me. Our knees almost touched.

"I gives you my affidavit, lad."

I gazed past him under the railway bridge towards the sea where the Forth opens out, but I couldn't see Newhaven. Home now seemed many miles away. Far overhead, a train rumbled across the bridge.

"William?"

It was not Silver speaking. It was another man's questioning voice, somehow familiar, unsure if he recognised me or not. I froze and looked down at the bag on my lap, hoping the voice would go away.

"It is William, isn't it?" The voice persisted as it came closer.

I bent my head down more.

"What are you doing here? Are you with your grandfather?" He was standing right beside me now and by the sound of his voice he was looking around. "Where is he?"

A large white and bony hand gripped my shoulder. I followed the long arm up and there was Mr Hornsby's long and enquiring face looking down at me.

"Run lad, run!" said Silver, propelling himself like a pole-vaulter onto his foot and with surprising swiftness disappearing between the cars. I hardly needed his advice as the memory of my last intimate acquaintanceship with Mr Hornsby came back to me.

I clutched my bag, squirmed out of Mr Hornsby's grip that had tightened on my shoulder and scampered after Silver. "Wait Silver, wait!"

"Hey! Hey, come back," Mr Hornsby shouted, as he ran after me.

I hadn't taken half-a-dozen steps after Silver when I heard Mr Hornsby behind me cry out in a strange, somewhat surprised, voice, "Whoops!"

It all happened in slow motion and in another world. His cry made me turn my head. I tripped, and as I flew through the air I saw his upside-down face, bearing a puzzled expression, above the side of the ferry. His head hit the broad metal gunwale with a sickening thud and the hand, that moments before had been on my shoulder, slid across it. Then he was gone. Coincidentally, I heard another voice shout, "Man overboard!" Then I hit something that knocked the breath right out of me so that I lay semi-conscious on the deck with my eyes open and yet unable to move or speak. The enormity of what had happened seeped through me like an icy fluid, clutching my chest like a clamp. In trying to escape one crime I had become responsible for another. This time, someone was dead. How could I ever be forgiven? It seemed that Silver had betrayed me.

Bill gently pulled the last sheet of paper out of the typewriter with a shaking hand, punched holes in it and added it to the folder. It was two o'clock in the morning. Re-living the events of that day almost 60 years ago had sapped his energy. Several times he had questioned his uncertain memory and discarded some of the answers he had found there, torn out a sheet of paper and rolled in another. The one memory that never left him was the only one of which he was entirely certain and whose image, he knew, would haunt him to the end of his life.

It was a warm night and it was not until he staggered to his feet, almost knocking over the chair, that he realised he was sweating profusely. He had a shower and made a cup of coffee. Then he pulled a chair over to one of the speakers and put on a record, carefully lowering the volume. He wanted to put on a Bach organ concerto, full blast, but of course he couldn't at such an hour. Instead he put on a Busoni transcription for piano. The recording was by John

Ogden and despite his exhaustion Bill smiled to himself as he recalled the apocryphal story of Ogden, so pampered by his mother that he could not even tie his shoelaces when he got married!

Many of the pieces that his grandmother had used in teaching him to play the piano were Bach's. They were always a source of great comfort to him. He listened as Ogden rippled down through the chords and the music rolled over an enormous landscape with a sharpness that the intended instrument, the organ, could not have achieved. Bach's line was so pure, momentous, logical and, inevitable. Absorbing himself in such music was like being relocated to his proper place on earth: putting everything else in perspective.

Poor Mr Hornsby. He must have made an instant decision that day that he needed to collar me again, if only for my own good. Today, Bill knew it had been an accident, but still *his* fault. Poor Faith, and her mother, he still felt badly for them both. They had moved house shortly afterwards and he had never seen Faith again.

It was now a little more than a week since he had taken them all to the restaurant. Alistair and Cat were due to fly out to the West Indies the next day and Tom's exams began a couple of days later, finishing with the end of term in a week's time. Bill went to bed after three o'clock, completely drained and a little ill. The pain seemed to be becoming more persistent. He would have to go back to the surgery. He resolved to give Tom the instalment he had just written, so that he could read it himself.

In the event, it was not until Alistair and Cat had left that he passed over some sheets of paper to Tom. He had been afraid that in Tom's carelessness his parents might find them. Somehow, he did not want them to read anything, not yet at least. He had never shared real intimacies with Alistair and he couldn't start now. Besides, they might question his influence on Tom just when he was really getting to know him and enjoy his company.

Now that there were just the two of them they ate in the kitchen. Between them they managed to heat up the meals Cat had prepared in advance. Bill insisted on doing most of the preparation and washing up, but he also insisted that Tom used his time to study. The only time off he sanctioned was to allow Tom to read what he had written.

He was full of questions after Bill had called a halt to revision just before supper and allowed Tom time to read the pages. Tom was at the kitchen table and Bill was mashing the potatoes by the sink. Around his waist he had tied one of Cat's pinafores.

"Were you arrested, grandad … and what about your grandparents? And … tell me about Silver this time … it *was* Long John Silver?"

"I'll come to Silver in a moment, Tom. Firstly, I have little direct memory of exactly what happened. What I know now I pieced together from the

fragments of my memory of the event, because that is all I have, just fragments
– Mr Hornsby's face, the grip of his hand, the sound of his head hitting the
gunwale, Silver's flying coat tails as he fled, thumping the deck with his crutch
and a sea of solicitous adult faces – *and* from what I can recall of the questions
that were asked of me later at home, both by the police and by grandfather." He
turned off the gas under a pot on the stove.

"But Long John Silver!"

"Hang on. I'll get there in a moment." Taking two plates from the rack he
proceeded to ladle mince from the pot. Then from the Pyrex dish he added the
mashed potatoes.

"Apparently, a combination of bouncing off the boot of a car and the shock
of what I had seen had left me speechless. They turned the ferry around and
searched for Mr Hornsby, but there was no sign of him. No one had seen or
heard anything other than the seaman who saw him, as I did, poised upside
down over the gunwale, prior to disappearing. The seaman had not seen me
immediately."

Bill handed one plate with a fork to Tom. "Is that enough?" Tom nodded
eagerly. Then he fetched a beer and an Irnbru from the fridge, took the other
plate and sat down opposite Tom.

"No one was allowed off the ferry until statements had been taken and all
the names and address had been recorded. The authorities had a mystery on
their hands. In Mr Hornsby's car – he had been on his way to a fishmarket in
the north – there were papers that gave his name and address, so they knew who
he was. But how had he fallen overboard and what, if any, was the relationship
between this unfortunate event and the shocked boy who seemed to be on his
own?"

Tom stopped mixing the mince and mashed potatoes together for a
moment. "You?"

"Yes ... the mystery deepened when grandfather's address was found
written in ink on the inside of the shoulder bag I was carrying. The boy and the
man lived on the same street! A doctor examined me and decided that I might
be suffering from more than shock.

"By the time I was taken home by police car it must have been very late.
Our local doctor, a friend of grandfather's, was waiting to check me over. I was
sedated and put to bed and grandma sat by me until I eventually fell asleep. The
police concluded that Mr Hornsby and I had met by sheer coincidence, but not
until after some potentially embarrassing, not to say unspeakable, theories were
discounted through the delicate questioning of quite a number of people,
including neighbours and members of the local church. The police could not be
sure exactly what had happened. There was oil on the deck where he went over
and it was decided that he must have slipped on that. Being a tall man, the top

of the gunwale would have been level with his waist. Under certain circumstances he could have fallen over, but he would have to have been leaning over the side or had some momentum, perhaps he had been running. There was no suggestion of foul play or suicide. Nobody could explain what had happened to me, unless it was that I had seen the accident, run away in shock, not looking where I was going, and tripped. Physically, I could not have been responsible for the accident, of that they were sure. It was decided therefore to leave me out of any press report and record Mr Hornsby's drowning as death by misadventure. He never knew the irony of that and they never found his body."

Bill pushed the plate aside.

"Did it sink to the bottom?"

"I expect it got washed out the Forth into the North Sea."

"Maybe he got swallowed by a whale, like Jonah?"

"Hmm. I expect his disappearance was much more prosaic than that."

"Grandad!"

"I mean … without describing the gory details … his body probably broke up and he ended up eaten by the crabs."

"And Long John Silver?"

Bill repeated with a sigh, "Long John Silver. D'you know that Stevenson took the name Silver from a man's surname in Braemar?"

"Grandad!"

"You don't believe me?"

"No, grandad, I mean how *would* I know where the name came from!"

"Well, I'm telling you."

"Is there any ice-cream?"

"Yes, I'm sure there is. You go and get it. None for me."

While Tom scooped out as much ice-cream as he thought he might get away with, and more, Bill ruminated on where to begin with Long John Silver. "It's one of these things that I cannot ever be precise about – the point at which Silver left my dreams, so to speak, and sort of became a companion. It seemed to happen so naturally I never questioned it. Of course, the last thing I would have done would have been to have mentioned it to an adult." He turned to Tom as he sat down with a large bowl of ice-cream. "You would understand that?"

"Right on, grandad."

"You see, I had come to rely on all these adventure stories I read and those I created myself, to take me away from … the things that made me unhappy, and in the process I must have become rather obsessed by Long John Silver. In all the stories I read he was the only one who befriended a boy, He was my friend too."

"Not a very reliable friend."

"You put your finger on it, Tom."

"Did your grandparents know about Silver?"

"Ah well … I was just coming to that." He picked up Tom's bowl and the plates and took them to the sink. "Years afterwards, not long before grandfather died, I asked for his forgiveness for the shame and hurt I had caused him and grandma, particularly in running away from them. He told me that they had been hurt, that he could not deny, but that they had forgiven me long ago. In fact, it was that very night when I was brought back from Queensferry that they realised they had to do something more radical to help me. The doctor's diagnosis also gave them the excuse. It seems that I was close to, if not already suffering from, a nervous breakdown, and that as I tossed and turned in my bed grandma had heard me raving about my intended adventures and my terrible guilt and she distinctly heard me talking fearfully about a man named Silver. It was grandfather who put two and two together when he picked up the well-thumbed copy of *Treasure Island* from the pile of books by my bed. He also read, for the first time, all my childish adventure stories scribbled in the spaces of my old notebooks … in which Silver featured rather prominently … and then he guessed the motive for my previous crime."

Bill turned briefly from the sink. "Incidentally, they never told *me* at that time that they knew of Silver's occupation of my head … so to speak … and I don't think he told the doctor or the police." He returned to the washing up. "The doctor suggested that the best thing for my grandparents to do would be to distract me from the events that had brought on the breakdown. If possible, they should take me away somewhere for a while, from all the associations." He stacked the plates back in the rack

"Shetland?"

Bill turned and leaned against the worktop. "Yes, they decided they would take me for a long holiday. Grandma still had a sister living there. She had been down once or twice to visit us, but I hardly knew her. She arranged for us all to go and stay with her, and her man, on their croft."

He found himself looking at the calendar on the wall as he spoke. "Oh, by the way, Tom, if I am not here when you get back tomorrow, I won't be long. I just have an appointment at four-thirty, that's all."

"I've got a half-day tomorrow because of the exams, so actually I'll be home at lunchtime."

"That's okay then, I'll be here. How many more exams do you have?"

Tom counted with his fingers on the table. "I had six altogether and I have had four. So I just have two left … English tomorrow morning and maths on Thursday, then I am finished."

"Did you see the card from your mum and dad?"

"Yep. They're having a cool time. Especially mum in all that sun, and diving too … lucky her. I wish I was there."

"Did you see that they will not be home now for another ten days or so?"

"Yeh, that's really rough. Dad promised he would take me somewhere special."

"Well, maybe we'll think of something."

Tom got up and shyly extracted a piece of paper that Bill had inadvertently covered by the pages of the manuscript.

"That's for you."

"Oh." Bill took it in his hand. "It's Long John Silver!" He turned to hold it under the light. "I like him … he's got a real wicked, yet friendly grin. You didn't copy *him*!"

Tom shook his head proudly.

CHAPTER *9*

'I fell asleep under the moonlight, rocked
gently by the roll of the ship, soothed by the soft
susurration of the sea against its iron hull and
by the deep heartbeat of the engine pulsing through me.'

*B*ill fiddled with the blank piece of paper in the typewriter. He wanted to introduce Tom to Shetland in the same way he had wanted to make him think about Edinburgh, history and culture, at the opening of his story. These things were important to him. It is a pity, he thought, that there are probably no famous Shetlanders that Tom would know. Ah, well. His eyes wandered over the room looking for inspiration and alighted on the books lying on the settee.

What was the opening to The Pirate? *'That long, narrow, and irregular island … stormy seas … furious tide …' I am holding the three-volume edition in my hands and I cannot believe that it is nearly 200 years old! Well, if the wind is a reminder to the Edinburgh citizen of the proximity of the sea, in Shetland reminders are not needed, for there is nowhere that is more than five miles from any shore. Nevertheless, that does not inhibit the wind from ensuring that no one forgets this: indeed, it just seems to redouble the wind's determination. In Edinburgh, one notices the wind, in Shetland one notices the days the wind is absent.*

If one stands on the top of Ronas Hill on such a day, when eyes are not stung to tears in the blast, the northern and southern extremities of the islands – Muckle Flugga some 30 miles to the north and Fitful Head some 50 miles to the south – can both just be discerned. Between those points lies the archipelago, a fragmented jigsaw of islands. The sea is rich and the land is poor. There are probably more seabirds on its coasts than people in Edinburgh! In Edinburgh, people make their living in well insulated offices; in Shetland, the living is made predominantly from the sea.

There is a saying in the North Isles that, 'Orcadians are farmers with boats and Shetlanders are fishermen with crofts'. It could equally well have been said that Shetlanders were seamen with crofts. For they have served in disproportionately large numbers in Britain's Navy from the 18th century, in the Greenland and Antarctic whaling and in the British Merchant Navy until its demise in the late 20th century.

But this is not Scotland, make no mistake, the islanders' blood is more Norse than Scots. Shetlanders have been longer under the rule of Scandinavia than under Scotland. The dialect and the culture is therefore a blend with a strong and independent Norse element.

Bill had cut this passage down, but still he wondered if Tom would find it as irrelevant as he had the very first page? Perhaps initially, he thought, but maybe the story will grow on him and take him back to seek his roots. He wondered what impression Shetland would make on him. The blood attachment was growing thinner with every generation. Either you fell for the islands or you disliked them. Either the overwhelming domination of the sea and the bare landscape were seen as freeing the eye to the enormous impression of space, or the exposure was cruel and unremitting. It was not Alistair's scene, but Alice had loved it, caught the expanse and the light, maybe Tom would too.

I remember, quite clearly, that time between the conclusion of my abortive attempt at escaping my mismanaged and unhappy life and the preparations for going to Shetland. I was treated like an invalid. I have recollections of spending a great deal of the day in bed, lying on the chaise longue in the parlour or walking slowly with grandfather or grandma to Newhaven. Adventure stories were not allowed and I remember I was given colouring books and crayons and models to make that I never completed, picture books and comics, books about aircraft and ships, and only lighter modern fiction including one of morally uplifting stories entitled Uncle Arthur's Bedtime Stories. *I found all that dreadfully boring and my interest in reading only revived when grandma gave me a handbook on birds, which she said might help me identify those I would see in Shetland. That was when I learned that I might soon make my first visit to these islands.*

Unexpectedly, I found myself fascinated, first by the Latin names for all the birds and then by the system of classification of the families and species, of which the names were an intricate part. I had never before thought that there might be a pattern into which all living things fit. Only then did I begin to look at the illustrations carefully. Although I had been aware of all the gulls around Newhaven and on the shore road, I had not been aware that there were actually several different kinds, nor that in some the young were very different to the adults. Grandma was actually quite pleased when I insisted on dragging her down to the harbour so that we could look at them and she pretended a great interest, even though it was tiring for her to walk far. I even persuaded grandfather to allow me to borrow his old binoculars that bowed my head with their weight and whose strap left a red weal around my neck.

Grandfather continued my marine education in preparation for the sea journey we were to make from Leith via Aberdeen to Shetland. He gave me his seamanship book that contained a mass of information on such topics as the structure and parts of a ship and how to make knots for every purpose. There were three coloured pages in the book. One had all the different flags, such as the yellow one for quarantine and the red and white one that meant a ship had a pilot on board. The second coloured page illustrated the special lights that a ship carried, such as red for port and green for starboard. The third was of matchstick men with sailor's hats who held little flags in their hands in all sorts of different positions. This was semaphore, used for sending messages before the wireless was invented.

When I was not arguing with grandma as to the proper identity of a seagull, grandfather was teaching me how to tie knots and to signal in semaphore. He made a pair of makeshift signal flags out of one of grandma's old, and one not so old, dishtowels, and stood at one end of the back garden, with me at the other, moving the flags from one position to another with such speed that they cracked sharply in the air. Eventually he would start coughing and grandma would come out and take them away from him. I was never more aware of just how exceptionally kind and loving they were than during that time, just as I had taken their love for granted beforehand.

When I was sedated I slept so soundly that I do not remember any visits from Silver. Thereafter, grandma made me drink one of her herbal concoctions before I went to bed, but once again, as I watched the Isle of May light, I became conscious of his shadow in the corner by the window. Then I had nightmares of Mr Hornsby's face as he disappeared over the side of the ferry. The worst were those when the face seemed to become grandfather's. I would awake desperately *trying not to think of him. It became a diabolical game; if I did recognise him he would suffer the same fate and I would again be responsible.*

It was just before mid-summer when we left for Shetland. The steamer was called the St Magnus *and we sailed from Leith. It was actually the first time I had been into Leith docks even though they were quite close to the house. We went by taxi to the docks, past the policeman and through the great wooden gates. I had thought that Newhaven or Granton were busy places, but they were nothing to the size and bustle of Leith. The place was alive with steam engines and lorries, shunting and reversing, loading and unloading, whining and straining, empty and full. Ropes swung, wires tautened and spinning winches banged and screeched. There were smells of fresh cut timber, steam and oil, tar and coir, fish and livestock and many others I could not place and, permeating them all, the smell of the salt sea.*

In the narrow spaces between the ships and the great open sheds, gangs of rough looking men pushing heavily loaded barrows, or holding wicked-looking cargo hooks, laughed and bantered; swung rope slings around burlap-wrapped bales and boxes and even cattle, then looped them over hooks that hoisted them up into the air and over the sides of the ships. The cattle bellowed in terror. I was swept up by the smells, the noise and bustle, in the rawness and coarse language of the stevedores. It was the most exciting place I had ever seen.

The taxi stopped by one of the sheds and we took our luggage through its cavernous interior to the narrow gangway that slanted almost vertically up the black painted side of the St Magnus*. At the first sight of the gangway grandma shook her head, but with encouragement from grandfather she eventually managed to struggle up, with a great deal of muttering under her breath. Grandfather and I followed, holding on with one hand to balance against its swaying motion against the steamer's hull. I watched some cargo on the end of a wire keep pace with our ascent. At the top, where grandma and I had to wait until grandfather had been back down the gangway twice to collect all our things, I watched the pistons of the crane pumping and clanking laboriously as a load was swung over the ship's side, then they reversed rapidly as the load dropped down into the hold. Inside the accommodation we were met by a steward neatly dressed in black trousers and a tight fitting white jacket. He took the tickets from grandfather and snapped his fingers over his shoulder. Another, younger steward appeared and took our cases.*

"If you'll just follow me sir, madam," he said and he led us off in single file through a narrow doorway, down a staircase, or properly a 'companionway' according to grandfather's book of 'Seamanship', and down a corridor or 'alleyway'. The alleyway was so narrow that we had to squeeze past people going the other way. It was panelled in dark polished wood, as was the whole interior of the accommodation. The cabin doors were like those of a row of cupboards along the alleyway, each separately identified by brass numerals.

"Numbers 21 and 22 ... ?" The older steward looked enquiringly at grandfather.

"William's with me ... we'll take 21 and Mrs Manson will take 22."

The steward looked again at grandfather. "Captain Manson?" he asked tentatively.

"Retired," grandfather answered briefly.

"Good to have you on board sir. Going home for long?"

Grandfather was taken aback, but pleased to be recognised. "A month or two, perhaps."

"Well sir, anything you or Mrs Manson want, just ring the bell."

Grandfather smiled and acknowledged the offer with a nod of thanks.

The stewards then opened the doors and put in the luggage. Grandfather fumbled in his pocket and handed something to the older steward whose fingers quickly enclosed it. "Sir," he said, nodding his head and disappearing back up the alleyway, pushing the younger one in front of him.

The cabin was tiny and panelled with the same dark wood as the alleyway. On one side was a padded bench seat, on the other, a rectangular wooden box hinged down from the wall to reveal a mirror behind it and a small hand-basin within it. On the side opposite the door were two bunks, each with little curtains drawn back at both ends and on the bulkhead above the upper bunk was a brass-rimmed porthole.

"Can I have the top one?" I blurted out.

"With pleasure, William. I doubt my limbs could get me up there anyhow."

At the foot of the bunks was a small ladder. I scrambled up. In other circumstances I might have thrown myself flat on the bunk, but the sheet and blanket were folded so faultlessly and the pillows so immaculately plumped-up, without a sign of a crease, that I felt totally inhibited. In the exact centre of the folded blanket was the emblem of the shipping line, a circle enclosing two crossed flags, around which were written the exotic words 'The North of Scotland, Orkney & Shetland Steam Navigation Co'.

Grandfather and I went up on deck just as a steward appeared, ringing a hand bell vigorously and shouting "All ashore who's going ashore". Grandfather pointed out the Blue Peter flag that was being pulled down and replaced by the pilot flag and I stood proudly by his side as we steamed out of Leith and into the Firth of Forth. Grandma had gone straight to her bunk and we did not see her again until we were tied up at Aberdeen many hours later. Most of that time I sat well wrapped up in a blanket with grandfather in a shelter at the after end of the accommodation. In the excitement of the voyage, for I had experienced nothing like this before – the restrictions of the war had prevented anyone travelling far from Edinburgh for a number of years – I almost forgot about recent events.

Not long after leaving Leith and as we passed out of the mouth of the Firth of Forth, grandfather pointed out the Isle of May and the lighthouse. It was a very strange feeling to be so close to the source of that familiar and comforting light. The lighthouse was not particularly large or imposing, just a white building with a little tower. It perched above the cliff on the south side of the island and below it wheeled tight flocks of little black and white seabirds. No seaman could ever have wished to have seen that light with a greater depth of desire than I did.

We steamed out of the Forth and on past the North Carr lightship and later the Bell Rock when grandfather retrieved his telescope from the cabin and I had my first look at a real lighthouse. Its perfect cylindrical shape seemed to rise straight out of the sea.

"Completed by Robert Stevenson in 1810," grandfather said, "after three years work. The reef that it is built on is under water at high tide. What must it have been like … 150 years ago … landing the great blocks of stone and fixing them together as if they were just bricks on a building site?"

I shook my head. It looked as if it had always been there.

After calling in at Aberdeen we left again in the evening for the overnight sail to Lerwick and once more grandma disappeared into her cabin. Grandfather took me on a conducted tour of the ship to show me what many of the names I had learned from his book actually referred to. One of the crew, in a white boiler-suit, even took us down via oil-slicked metal steps and gratings into the engine-room, where in a cacophony of hammering sounds and steam, men in grimy clothes *with filthy handkerchiefs knotted around their necks, flung shovels of coal into a boiler, and shining pistons as big as lampposts cranked around the propeller shaft. I didn't realise just how hot it was until we re-emerged into the freezing wind on deck. There, a row of passengers in anoraks and woolly hats, with their trousers tucked into thick socks above leather boots, leaned against the rails and stared over the sea. Around their necks hung binoculars and every so often one of them would shout and simultaneously they would all raise their binoculars and follow a seabird skimming over the waves. Before I could ask him a question, grandfather reminded me that grandma, not he, was the one who could answer any questions about 'ornithology'. Then we heard the steward circling the deck, ringing his bell and shouting that high tea was being served and grandfather insisted we "repair to the cabin" and wash our hands.*

There must have been a swell, for as grandfather and I walked along the alleyway to the saloon the whole ship creaked and groaned like an arthritic old animal and I found that I was keeping myself upright with a hand on each bulkhead. In the saloon the round tables were fastened permanently in position and even the heavy round-backed chairs were chained to the deck. I had never eaten out and at first I wondered how grandfather could be so at home and relaxed. We sat with other passengers and he chatted while I tucked into breaded haddock and chips. Then, of course, I remembered that this had been his life. Until he had retired, not long before I had come to live with them, he had probably spent more time at sea than he had at home.

Everything on the table seemed to have been made for a small giant. The plates, cups and saucers were so thick and heavy that I needed two hands to lift them up while the cutlery seemed as solid as grandfather's tools. After the fish there were scones and biscuits. The biscuits were round and dry and almost an inch thick and they splintered into handfuls of hard flakes that I shovelled off my lap and under the table. I wondered if this was the hardtack on which seamen and polar explorers had subsisted?

Later, lying in the top bunk, after I had slid myself, like a letter into an envelope, under the folded bedclothes, I was aware of Silver trying to make himself comfortable on the bench. I wanted to tell him to go away, but when I opened my mouth to speak he put a finger to his mouth and nodded in the direction of grandfather below me. So I turned over and looked out of the porthole.

The waves of the sea were dark and only inches away. I pressed my forehead against the glass and could feel their coldness. The movement of the surface of the sea at first appeared chaotic and then I gradually discerned a pattern. First there was an underlying swell of large slow waves coming obliquely towards us that was causing the steamer to roll with a regular and gentle motion. This was the memory of yesterday's weather, for superimposed on the swell were today's short, steep and wind-driven waves. These were cutting across the swell, seemingly intent on erasing it, and when the wave and swell tops coincided they clashed like gladiators sending up plumes of spray.

For a moment in that dark coldness I saw Mr Hornsby's face and drew back from the porthole and then something happened that changed the whole scene. The thick, dark clouds broke and the full moon that had been hidden shone through and lit up the sea with an unearthly, silvery light. The broken surface glimmered like a living skin. The sea became an ever-changing pattern of shape and light that completely entranced me and, for the first time in weeks, I resolved to start a new story to be set on a tramp steamer. I fell asleep under the moonlight, rocked gently by the roll of the ship, soothed by the soft susurration of the sea against its iron hull and by the deep heartbeat of the engine pulsing through me.

Bill was looking at Tom's picture of Silver that he had pinned on the wall beside Alice's painting of the cottage. It was lunchtime and he had just hauled himself through from the bathroom where he had been sick. It was not the first time this had happened lately but on this occasion the combination of nausea and pain rather depressed him. He forced himself upright in the chair, took a couple of tablets from a bottle on the desk in front of him, washed them down with a glass of water and waited. Gradually he regained his composure. He was glad Tom was next door with a pal.

If he was going to do it, he must do it now, very soon ... but what about Tom? There was one possible course he could take and he knew that neither Alistair nor Cat would be happy with it. First though, there were a few things to be taken care of, such as completing his second-hand book orders.

Later, sitting in the kitchen, he wondered just how much he should tell Tom.

"Don't you like my pie, grandad?" Tom looked across the table as Bill raised an eyebrow. "Well, okay, it is mum's, but I did heat it in the microwave all on my own."

"I'm just not very hungry, Tom."

"Can I have your potatoes?"

Bill picked up his plate and handed it to Tom who scraped off the potatoes onto his own.

"Do old people not eat a lot of food?"

"Careful with the 'old'! By the way, did you put your clothes in the wash?"

"Yes. Do you know how it works?"

"How do you think you have had clean clothes since your mum left? Anyhow, now you're on holiday you can hang them out tomorrow morning." He watched Tom packing away his supper like only growing children can.

"Tom."

"Yep."

"Get me a cup of coffee will you?"

"Sure."

"And a glass of water."

As Tom made the coffee Bill took the bottle of pills from his pocket, popped one in his mouth and washed it down with a mouthful of water.

Tom watched him as the kettle came to the boil. "Got a headache, grandad?"

"No, it's not that, Tom," he answered, as Tom poured the water into the small caffitiere, "I'm just not very well at the moment." He saw Tom turn and look at him. "Nothing to worry about though."

Tom put a cup and the coffee down in front of him and fetched an ice-cream carton from the fridge. Bill shook his head at the proffered chocolate chip. Tom gave himself a generous helping then returned the carton.

"Tom."

"Hmm?"

"How would you like to come and stay in my cottage?"

"In the holidays d'you mean?"

"I mean ... now ... now that your exams are finished."

"But ... "

"Don't worry about your mum and dad. I'll tell them." The bitter taste of the coffee gradually erased that of the pill.

Tom reflected for just a moment. Then, with the emphasis on the second syllable he replied, "Wicked!" unaware that his grandad intended to delay sending Alistair and Cat a postcard about his plans so that they would not know for another week.

"Okay." He poured himself some more coffee. "I sort of thought you might say yes ... so I booked our seats on a flight from Edinburgh tomorrow."

Tom's eyes widened and he looked at his grandfather with a new respect.

"Now, you clear up and then we must pack some clothes for you."

When Tom was in bed, and after some hesitation, Bill wrote the card to Alistair. Then, after more hesitation, he left a new message on the phone's answering machine. Later, he packed a few things, poured himself a glass of whisky and sat down and played the pianola for what he intended would be the last time. In memory of his grandparents he played the Minuet and several of their favourite Schubert pieces. Later, he fell asleep on the couch while listening to one of Beethoven's late quartets, crying through the second molto adagio movement, not in grief or self-pity, but in a kind of joy: he always imagined it as a kind of 'movement of the spheres'.

CHAPTER *10*

' "So," said Magnus, easing his bulk onto the resting
chair that creaked and gave visibly under his weight.
"Foo lang is du hame for?" '

"*G*randad. It's morning."

The light was bright on his face. Bill screwed up his eyes. His back and his neck ached. The couch was not the place to sleep.

"Morning, Tom." He swung his legs onto the floor and struggled to get upright.

"You must have slept well."

Bill put the palms of his hands on his lower back, straightened and muttered doubtfully, "Mmmmm."

"I'll make breakfast, shall I?"

"That's a good idea, Tom. Just coffee and toast will be great. I'll be with you in a moment." He rubbed his unshaven chin.

Tom spun on his heels and clattered back down the stairs two at a time to the kitchen.

After breakfast they gathered their things together at the front door, Bill having dragged his two bags down the night before. He checked that Tom had packed lots of clothes and some books to read. "There's no TV at the cottage." Next, he double-checked that all the doors and windows were locked. Finally, he looked at the burglar alarms in the hall-cupboard and the piece of paper that Cat had left him. He stared at the dials and buttons. Tom watched, shook his head, pushed past Bill and keyed in a set of numbers. Bill shook his head in turn and left him to it.

The doorbell rang to signal the arrival of the taxi.

"Now, have we got everything?" He looked around at his bags, Tom's bag and his wee rucksack. There was something missing. "Take these out, Tom. I'll just be a moment." Then he went back up to his flat. There he checked the bathroom to see that he had all his pills, but it was not those that he had forgotten. He looked around the sitting room and saw it on his desk. His typewriter, he had almost forgotten his typewriter! He snapped the lid on it and made for the door, stopped, turned back, put the typewriter back down on the desk and walked over to the wall where he ran his fingers over Alice's painting. He stared at it for a moment and whispered something before picking up the typewriter once more and making for the door. He took one last look at all the old familiar objects, closed the door, and hurried after Tom.

As the plane left Edinburgh airport and crossed the Firth of Forth on its way north, Bill looked over Tom's shoulder through the window. For a brief moment there it all was before him: South Queensferry and the bridge just below; in the middle distance, Granton, Newhaven and Leith; immediately to the south, Edinburgh and the castle; and in the far distance, he thought he could make out the Isle of May. Then they were over Fife and climbing into the clouds.

The flight took nearly two hours and Bill was feeling extremely uncomfortable by the time the pilot announced their descent to Sumburgh airport at the southern tip of Shetland. Tom craned his neck and stretched his seat belt to try and see ahead as they swept past the cliffs of Fitful Head as if they were going to land on the surface of the sea. At the last moment the shore and the runway appeared and the engines roared as they braked rapidly on the short runway.

Their impressions and feelings could not have been more different as they left the airport in Magnus-the-boat's old car. For Tom, although he had been briefly to Shetland once before, with his mum and dad, everything was so different to home, from the strange dialect to the all-dominating presence of the sea. The road from the airport skirted dunes and beaches where long waves boomed on the sand and little birds raced back and forward just out of reach of the lapping water. It circled cliffs and deep bays in which sat little boats, then climbed over a hill to reveal a panorama of small fields and scattered houses and yet more cliffs, beaches and an endless number of small islands, stretching into the far distance. Away from the fields everything seemed to be covered in peat. For Bill, after five minutes, it was as if he had never been away, as if the last nine months had not existed. He devoured the familiar scenery while Magnus brought him up to date with the local gossip.

Tom liked Magnus instantly. He was enormous and cheerful with it, filling the driver's seat to the roof and spilling onto the adjacent passenger seat. Once, when he had still been lobstering, he had been a powerful man and the bulk of his girth had been muscle, but now in old age he had gone to fat. When he laughed, which was often, his huge face folded into a mass of creases. When he lifted his cap to scratch his head, which was as much a habit of his as laughing, Tom saw that abruptly above the line where he settled his cap, his head was completely bald and as creamy white as a baby's bottom. Below that his face and the rolls of his neck were weathered brown. What fascinated Tom most though were his hands that spanned the steering wheel like a couple of hams.

Magnus drove as he had used to steer his boat. Initially this was very disconcerting for his passengers. He seemed to anticipate the need to turn the wheel and then waited for a moment for the car to respond before he corrected it. He also tended to forget to use the gears. The car wandered continuously and consistently on long trajectories, especially on corners, from the centre line to the verge and back again. Once Tom saw that there was a pattern to Magnus' driving, idiosyncratic as it was, he relaxed.

"Boy, I'm blyde to see dee hame," said Magnus, after a lull in the conversation, patting Bill's knee and swinging the car across a corner.

"It's good to be here, Magnus. I wasn't sure I would be back."

"I put the water and your fire on this morning. The cottage is fine and dry."

"Thanks."

Magnus glanced across at Bill's drawn face. "Du's lookit better."

Bill stared straight ahead. "Just something I've picked up."

"I trust du's something for it?"

Bill nodded, glanced across at Magnus and smiled briefly. Magnus nodded too, but doubtfully. Then he swivelled his head.

"And tell me, boy, aboot dis young man du his wi' dee?"

Bill half turned in his seat to look at Tom. "Tom is my grandson … my only grandson … my best grandson." He looked at him proudly. "Alistair's boy."

Magnus exchanged glances with Tom in the rear-view mirror. "Ah, is du yon peerie boy dat was here just a couple of years ago?"

Tom nodded.

"Weel, weel! Maybe de an me 'ill get de auld graandfaider oot fishing while you're hame. Du looks laek a strong young man and, by God, we baith need a bit o strent nooadays." His body shook with quiet merriment. "Eh, Bill?"

"Too right, Magnus."

Tom felt wrapped in the warmth of the two old mens' conversation. They included him in their banter and yet he knew he did not have to respond.

The drive took just about as long as the flight had. They drove up and down the sides of long inlets that Bill informed him were called 'voes', past innumerable lochs and lochans and across peat-covered hills. Tom saw a scruffy mountain hare loping across the ground towards the road, stop, sit up on its hind legs and watch them nervously for a moment, before it dropped onto all four legs and took off at speed, zig-zagging away from them. Occasionally, they passed scattered groups of houses, some old but many modern and large. It all looked rather bare to Tom. Eventually, descending a long hill, they crossed a cattle-grid, passed a sign and came into Sandness.

"A beautiful flat of corn, grass and meadow," said Bill of the landscape ahead of them. "The Reverend George Low, 1774."

Tom groaned theatrically.

Magnus surveyed the scene ahead of them. "No quite dat noo, boy," he sighed. "But I suppose we sood be tankfil at it's no aa doon ta silage."

Despite Magnus' comment Tom liked Sandness: everything was in miniature. The fields were full of yellow flowers and small sheep with tiny lambs of various shades of black and from dark chocolate to light coffee. It seemed a lot gentler than the barren hills they had just passed through. Gradually, the road grew narrower, winding through stony outcrops surrounded by green grass and clear, shallow lochans, until it finally ended above a perfect little bay surrounded by rocks, in which sat several small boats.

"Weel, here we are," said Magnus, swinging the old car up to a gate behind which a track led down to a cottage. Tom immediately recognised it from his grandmother's painting.

Despite, or maybe because of his familiarity with the place, Bill's heart pounded. He got out, opened the gate and waved Magnus through, gesturing to him just to keep on going down to the cottage. A few hundred yards further down the track Magnus stopped and slowly extricated himself from the right hand side of the car with much grunting, while Tom literally flew out of the left hand door. Bill closed the gate and stood with his back against it. He sighed deeply at the scene that lay before him.

Below the cottage, sheep regarded them with a passing interest and continued to graze a green sward that dipped sharply to the sea. Beyond that there lay a small group of rocky skerries on which seals lazed and above which a white cloud of terns bickered and squabbled. Beyond that was a broad reach of sea, partly enclosed by the land that swung from the south on their right in a great arc, ending on the horizon some 10 miles in front of them.

The cottage itself was built to the plan used by crofters throughout the Highlands and Islands of Scotland for generations. The low walls were of stone, three feet thick, pointed with a lime mortar and painted white. On each gable were two chimneys and in the middle of each of the long walls, front and back, between the small sash windows, was a small porch. Bill's cottage faced south and in the front porch that had additional light from two side windows he had kept geraniums. The back porch, however, had no windows and here Bill stored his coats and boots, a wooden box for peat and several shelves with tools. The roof that had once been thatched, then felted and tarred, now consisted of aluminium sheets.

In the downstairs of the cottage there were two rooms, each twelve-foot square, with a little box-room in between and a short passageway connecting them. Upstairs, or more accurately, up the ladder, were two low-ceilinged attic rooms lit only by narrow skylights. The inside had hardly changed in 150 years. The downstairs ceilings were unlined, exposing lightweight beams, while the walls were lined in broad panels of tongue-and-grooved wood that Bill had painted in greens and blues. Some of the panelling in the kitchen had been hand-cut from sea-driven timber and was riddled with the holes of shipworm through which draughts had poured, like water through a colander, before Bill had plugged them. Both the front and rear porches were flagged, but otherwise the floors were boarded.

In the kitchen Bill had put a stove. Apart from that the only heating consisted of an electric radiator in each room. The middle box-room was now the bathroom and the far room his office and bedroom. Over the inside doors and the windows Bill had hung heavy curtains and, with the exception of the worst winter gales, the cottage was quite snug.

As Bill reached it, Tom rushed off down to the shore scattering sheep and their well-grown lambs.

"Don't go too far now and mind the cliff edge," he shouted after him.

Tom waved over his shoulder in reply.

Magnus gave Bill a hand to carry the bags and the typewriter into the kitchen. The stove was lit, the cottage was warm and draped over the chairs and hanging on the pulley were sheets and blankets. Bill looked in the fridge; there was milk, a lump of cheese, bacon and eggs. On the dresser was a loaf of bread. Bill looked questioningly at Magnus. "Maisie," he responded.

Bill smiled gratefully.

"So," said Magnus, easing his bulk onto the resting chair that creaked and gave visibly under his weight. "Foo lang is du hame for?"

Bill stared out of the window and watched Tom throwing stones into the sea. "For good."

"But I towt … "

Bill interrupted him without turning and said simply. "I'm ill, Magnus."

"Oh!" Magnus uttered slowly with understanding. "Can I ask … ?"

Bill turned from the window and looked at his old friend and neighbour. "Month … maybe months." He shrugged his shoulders. "I want to be here," he looked around the room and once more out of the window, "in this place."

Magnus pulled himself up, raised an arm to put it on Bill's shoulder and then dropped it again uselessly. "I understand, boy … and Tom?"

Bill turned again. "He doesn't know … at least how serious it is, at present."

"Aw shite," Magnus groaned in frustration.

It was Bill's turn to raise his arm. He clapped Magnus' huge shoulder, looked into his eyes and smiled. "I somehow knew it was coming and I'm prepared. Only one or two things left I want to do. So … " he punched Magnus playfully on his chest, "I don't want to hear any grief … especially from you!"

Magnus forced out a smile in reply. "Onything du wants. Onything we can do. Just ask … will du?"

"Of course."

Bill saw Magnus back to his car and returned to the kitchen. Through the window he watched Tom picking his way among the rocky pools. He felt tired and his limbs, heavy.

> *There was only stillness and silence. It was very early in the morning. I awoke slowly and stared at the ceiling only a couple of feet above my head. Then I sat up and looked out of the porthole. A row of neatly painted, slim, double-ended, wooden boats lay in the middle of the little harbour between the steamer and the far harbour wall opposite, against which several black-hulled and untidy fishing boats were tied up. Along their low bulwarks, on top of their wheelhouses and on the adjacent harbour edge, were lines of still and silent gulls. They seemed to be waiting for something. I recognised that they were mostly herring gulls, but indiscriminately placed among them, head and shoulders taller, were a few greater black-back gulls with wicked yellow eyes and beaks like clasp knives.*
>
> *Grandfather was snoring and I managed to get down from the bunk, dressed and out of the door without waking him. No one seemed to be up, the alleyways and saloon were deserted. Outside it was fresh and cool and I could see that the* St Magnus *was alongside one arm of Lerwick harbour which seemed to be just an extension of the street. The shore was composed of grey stone houses that rose straight out of the water and beyond them, up the hill from the sea, the roofs of others jostled above each other as if for the view.*
>
> *The gulls seemed to be the only living inhabitants of the place. They shuffled uneasily and meowelled softly. Occasionally one would stretch its neck and break the stillness with a harsh and raucous call, unsettling all its neighbours. I hesitated for a moment at the top of the gangway, but, apart from the gulls, there was nothing to intimidate me. I felt like an actor entering a scene that was waiting for me.*
>
> *The main street lay just behind the first row of buildings that, on my right, were fronted by an esplanade. The street was surfaced with*

worn flagstones and so narrow and winding that a bus could not have passed through it and even a car would have had to go carefully. My first impression of a stage-set was reinforced by the intimacy of the shops and houses that seemed to lean over the street. Between them, every so often, even narrower lanes and steps led both up the hill and back down to the esplanade.

I walked along the flagged street for several hundred yards, listening to the echo of my own footfalls, before I decided to turn back. But then a wonderful aroma filled my nostrils. I followed it down a steep lane until I came to the open back door of a bakery. From the threshold I saw a skinny man in a crumpled white hat, white overalls and a dirty white apron held up by a piece of string, draw out a wide tray of rolls from an oven and replace it with another unbaked tray-full. He turned and saw me.

"Weel boy, du's up an' aboot airly dis morning." I nodded my head, though I was unsure what he said. He took off a large protective glove and scratched his ear. "Wid du laek a roll, eh?" And he tore one off and tossed it to me.

Until then I had forgotten that I had had no food since high tea last night. I sank my mouth into the hot and spongy interior. The baker looked at me a little more closely then turned back to his work, addressing me over his shoulder.

"Is du on holiday, den?"

I pulled another mouthful from the roll, chewed and nodded my head in the general direction of the harbour

"Whar's du gyaain ta bide?"

I stopped chewing and looked at his back blankly.

He pulled another tray out of the oven, set it down and, turning around, spoke to me slowly. "Whar is du biding in Shetland?"

I shrugged. "Don't know."

He laughed. "Weel, wherever du bides, geng an catch dee twartree troots. Du'll enjoy dat."

Seeing that I had finished the roll he threw me another. "Noo, du's keepin me fae me wark."

It was time to go and I managed to mutter, "Thanks for the rolls," before turning down the lane to the esplanade and back to the steamer. There, grandfather was standing in his vest with his braces hanging down, shaving, and grandma was sitting on the bench, fully dressed.

After what seemed like an interminable time since we had finished breakfast we were at last standing on the pier waiting for grandma's sister and her husband to pick us up. Silver was lying against the wall *of the harbour shed picking his teeth. He grinned and waved his arm to catch my attention but I looked the other way.*

Shortly afterwards, an old Morris 10 drew up beside us. The lower bodywork and the wheel hubs were bottle green and the upper half and mudguards were black. It was a beautifully cared for, box-shaped little car, with a broad running board, four doors with large chrome handles and square windows that were turning brown in the corners. The seats were of brown leather. An old lady, whom I recognised, flew out the passenger door and flung her arms around grandma. It was Aunt Ina, her sister: my grand-aunt. She was much taller than grandma and elegant with it. Grandfather went round to the driver's door where Uncle Bertie, I assumed, emerged to shake hands with him and me.

Uncle Bertie had been a crofter nearly all his life, apart from a spell at the Antarctic whaling as a young man. He was the only son in his family and had had little choice but to return and take up the croft as his parents aged. Even in his seventies he was tanned, wiry and strong, and quiet with it. Most of the time, he deferred to Aunt Ina, except when he was asked about the croft. Aunt Ina's and grandma's parents, on the other hand, had pushed the girls out and on to seek better things. Ina had been a bright child like grandma and had gone to college to train as a secondary teacher in English. Perhaps because they had no children of their own, Aunt Ina had carried on teaching. Aunt Ina, grandma used to tell me, was a poet and I was immediately somewhat in awe of her.

Grandfather sat in the front of the car with Uncle Bertie and I sat in the back, squashed between Aunt Ina and grandma. The seat was very deep and slippery and my feet couldn't reach the floor if I leaned against the back. If I had not been jammed between the pair of them I would have slid all over the place like a piece of jelly on a plate. They chatted over my head all the way back to their croft and I saw little until we arrived there after about an hour.

It was a low, cosy-looking building with a black, tarred roof surrounded by a dry-stane dyke. Poking just over the top of the dyke, sheltered against it and crowded within the small garden, were roses and fuchsias. There was a bright green gate in the wall behind which two very excited black and white collies whined and wagged their tails. Before he opened the gate Uncle Bertie spoke to them firmly and they flattened themselves on the concrete path. There they continued their welcome with such vigour that their whole bodies squirmed and shook from their noses to their tails. As soon as the gate was opened they were all over us, or rather me, when they found that I was the only one to respond in like manner. I rolled in the grass with them before being called inside. The dogs, however, remained outside and no amount of cajoling from me could entice them in.

The first thing that struck me about the inside of the cottage was that the sitting room was the only room with a carpet. Everywhere else, apart from the kitchen which was flagged, was covered in a shiny, dark brown linoleum. From the kitchen, adjacent to the front door and the sitting room, a narrow corridor ran to an extension at the back where there were three bedrooms. I was put in the smallest, between the other two: which reassuring position I was to appreciate later in the semi-dark, when I lay and listened to snores and other strange noises from either side. It was not until Uncle Bertie took me outside after breakfast and across the track to the far end of the byre, where he opened the door of a tiny wooden hut and showed me the toilet, that I realised there was no bathroom in the cottage and that the only running water was at the kitchen sink. There was no light in the toilet, just as there was no electric light in the house, but the door was ill fitting and there were many small holes in it through which streamed little beams of daylight alive with dancing motes. From the seat, if the door was open, there was a wonderful view of the fields and, in the distance, sand dunes and the sea.

I was a little frightened about going to bed that night; it seemed such a long way away down the narrow corridor from the kitchen and all the adults, but at nine o'clock it was still light. In fact it never really got dark at all at night for the couple of months or so that we were there. Aunt Ina took me into the living room on the way to bed to let me choose a book to read. Against one wall of the room there was a little upright piano and against another a large glass-fronted bookcase, packed with books. She opened the doors to let me choose. I ran my eyes across the spines. One, with a loose cover and the picture of a man standing in a boat with a spear in his hand caught my eye. The title was equally intriguing, so I picked it: its title was Moby Dick.

Most of these memories are like rather poor, out-of-focus snapshots – the door of the outside toilet, the cold linoleum floor of the corridor, the small wooden bed I slept in, the dogs, even the faces of Aunt Ina and Uncle Bertie. My clearest memories are from my senses: the sweet aroma of the peat fire and the smell of the oil lights; the barking of the dogs; the hissing of the Tilley lamp; the drumming of a stream of water hitting tin as one of the grown-ups peed into a chamber pot in the middle of the night; and the mechanical notes of the little piano.

Actually, it wasn't exactly a piano and instead of the usual small foot pedals it had two very large ones. A couple of days after we arrived I was sitting at it doing the lessons that grandma had set me. She must have decided that, despite, or maybe because of, my breakdown and this 'retreat' to Shetland, there needed to be some continuity and discipline and had brought my exercise books with her. My attempts at my lessons drew Aunt Ina into the room and she sat and listened for a while.

"Aunt Ina."

"Yes, William."

I indicated the large pedals with my feet. "What are these for?"

"Don't you know?"

"No."

She stood behind me and leaned over my shoulder. She smelled of lavender.

"It's a pianola."

"What's that?"

"I'll show you."

She lifted my lesson book from off its support. Then she opened the top of the piano, swung up the music support, slipped it under the lid and then closed it again. Then with her long thin hand she grasped a little knob on the centre panel of the pianola and slid it open. I had never looked inside a piano before and I didn't know what to expect, certainly not the curious brass mechanism of rollers that was revealed.

She looked at me and smiled at my surprised expression.

"D'you like Chopin?"

"I think so." I said doubtfully.

She turned to a matching, and elegant, two-doored cabinet that sat beside the pianola. Opening it, she searched through slim, long, cardboard boxes that were neatly packed on its shelves. They were all slightly battered and worn with handling and on the end of each was a printed label. She examined them in turn and selected one.

"This is a little mazurka."

"A what?"

There was a hint of playfulness in her voice that I liked. "It's a little fast, but I think you'll manage it," and she winked at me mysteriously.

I watched as she opened the end of the box and slid out a roller wound with stiff brown paper. She unrolled about a foot of the paper and I could see that it was perforated with tiny rectangular holes. At first glance the perforations looked random, but then I thought that maybe there was a pattern to them. I still had no idea what it was all about and Aunt Ina was enjoying herself knowing just that.

She leaned over me again and inserted the roll into the mechanism in the pianola, fastening the free end of the paper onto a fixed empty roll.

"Right. Now you must pump the pedals, firmly, but rhythmically."

I adjusted myself on the seat because my legs only just reached the pedals. Then I began to pump. The first thing that happened was that the rollers began to turn and the paper began to run from the full one to the empty one.

"Keep going now," Aunt Ina urged me. "That's just about the right speed."

Then to my astonishment the piano …pianola …began to play the Chopin mazurka all by itself.

I was speechless. This was wonderful. Here I was playing Chopin. Aunt Ina clapped her hands as if in delight at my playing. I pumped away totally delighted and absorbed in the music. I heard the floor creak and when I looked over my shoulder Aunt Ina was dancing lightly around the room!

After I was finished she showed me how to load and unload the rolls myself, but only on the condition that I still diligently practised my lessons. I remember how firmly she emphasised how much care I must take. She held a roll in her hand and explained that it was irreplaceable. It was several evenings later, when I was playing the pianola on my own, that I found the box containing Paderewski's Minuet. On the cover it said that the recording was carried out by the maestro himself!

It was most satisfying, pumping the pedals and hearing that so-familiar minuet come to life without the sight of grandma's fingers on the keyboard. It was a surprise for grandfather and grandma too. I was not conscious of them tiptoeing into the room and standing behind me, but towards the end of the piece I felt her hand on my shoulder and it was one of the weirdest and most pleasurable feelings of my life.

Bill struggled to pull open the door of the front porch that had swollen with the winter's damp. He managed to move it just sufficiently to get the catch out of the lock in the jamb then he went through the house, out the back door and around the gable to the front so that he could attack it from the outside. Grasping the handle, he threw his shoulder against the door. After a couple of thumps it reluctantly swung open, scraping and screeching on the stone floor. The effort tired him and he dragged out a kitchen chair onto the grass in front of the cottage and collapsed onto it.

For a few moments he sat there, leaning back in the chair against the wall of the cottage. The flat wooden seat caused pain to shoot from the base of his spine and he shifted uncomfortably to ease it. Perspiration dampened his brow and he felt the nausea rising from his stomach. He closed his eyes and took several deep, slow breaths. For a few moments in his self-enforced darkness all he was aware of was his sick body. He willed his control over it and gradually the pain and nausea subsided. He became aware of the air lightly caressing his face. Without opening his eyes he tried to identify the various sounds he could hear.

First there was the long swell surging over the skerries, dissipating itself on the shore, rinsing and combing the pebbles and extracting a deep growl from the throat of the beach. Then there was the lazy meowl of a black-back gull, the loud song of a wren from the roof above him and he thought he heard a seal bark. Above those sounds were two repeated high notes. The first he recognised instantly as the arctic terns on the skerries, but it took him several moments to recognise the second as the distant sound of Tom's voice. He opened his eyes and saw Tom perched on a black rock on the very limit of the land, idly throwing stones into the sea from a small heap on his lap. He was holding a one-sided conversation with the birds and the waves.

Bill cupped his hands around his mouth. "Tom … Tom … c'mon and let's get unpacked and see what we have for supper."

Tom waved back, gathered up the remaining stones in his lap, threw them in a handful into the sea and scrambled back to the beach over the rocks.

In the kitchen Bill got Tom to carry out an inventory of the basic supplies that Maisie had purchased for them. Then they made out an additional list of things they needed, including Irnbru and tobacco. While Tom wrote it down, Bill laced up a pair of heavy boots.

"But how will we get them, grandad?" Tom said. "We haven't any transport."

"Oh yes we have," said Bill, as he searched in the back porch through a collection of oilskins, anoraks and overcoats that hung on the wall above a collection of leather and rubber boots on the floor. He turned to Tom with a cut-down yellow oilskin in one hand and a faded and sea-worn, red hard-hat in the other. "Now, you better wear these."

Tom clutched the hard-hat and pulled a face at Bill. "We're cycling?"

Bill shook his head and pulled on a large and thick black overcoat with an obviously unmatching broad green belt and buckle, borrowed or stolen from its original owner. From a high shelf he brought down, what looked to Tom, like the black helmet of a miner or pot-holer. Wrapped around the outside of the helmet was a pair of goggles and inside, and spilling out, was a pair of large leather gauntlets.

Holding up the hard-hat to his grandad, he said, "I'm not wearing this."

Bill shrugged. "Then you're not coming to the shop with me." He turned, went out the back door and tramped off towards a large double door into the old byre. Tom followed, dangling the hat by its plastic strap. "If you are coming," said Bill over his shoulder, "please shut the door behind you."

By the time Tom had pulled the door to and rejoined his grandad the latter had propped open the double doors with a couple of stones and was gazing fondly into the gloom of the unlit byre. Tom stopped beside him and followed his gaze. Facing them on the worn black cobbles of the byre floor was a large and rather old, to Tom's eyes, motorbike and sidecar. The bike had no windscreen and even the sidecar only had a tiny one. Its frame and mudguards were painted black and from the cylinder head twin chrome exhausts, polished and shining, curved backwards on either side. The exposed engine, with all its ribs and tubes and pipes, its nuts and bolts and wires and levers, looked to Tom like an untamed animal, like raw power awaiting its trainer.

He gawped at the sight. "Wicked!" was all he could say at first sight.

Silently, Bill approved his statement.

"What is it?" Tom asked him.

"It's a Panther ... with sidecar, as you can see."

"You're joking."

"No, I'm not. That's the name of the make and this is one of the last they made." Bill walked into the byre and crouched down by the side of the bike as he inspected it closely. "Peter's done a lovely job on it. It's even better than when I left it."

"How old is it?"

"Forty years old, believe it or not, built in the early 1960s ... though I didn't buy it until 1985 I think. You might find it a wee bit noisy. It's a big engine ... 645cc."

Tom peered into the sidecar.

"Sorry ... that's a bit of a mess. I have only used it for carrying things ... not people."

"I've never seen a sidecar before."

"Well, no one uses them now. They went out of fashion after the war when cars became cheaper and the working man could afford them."

Bill fastened the chinstrap of his helmet. "Got the list?"

Tom nodded.

"Okay. In you get then."

There had once been a seat in the sidecar, but Bill had long since removed it to make room for carrying shopping, peats, driftwood, or anything else he required to transport. He hunted around the byre until he found a couple of pieces of foam that had originally been the stuffing of a chair.

"Here, put this underneath and behind you."

Tom crouched in the sidecar feeling as if he was sitting inside a second-hand torpedo. It was surprisingly comfortable. He felt Bill's hand on his shoulder.

"Oh … by the way, Tom," and he gestured at the bike, "don't mention this to your father ... at least not at the moment, eh?"

Tom grinned at him. "You bet!"

Bill slung his leg over the bike and sat down. He checked various levers, primed the petrol, swung out the metal starter pedal on the right then stood up on the left pedal. He said a silent prayer for both himself and the bike and then came down hard and firm with his right foot. The machine coughed loudly. Tom looked up at him. Bill winced, took a breath and kicked again. The bike literally roared into life, deafening them in the confines of the byre. He looked down at Tom, smiled in pleasure and pulled the goggles over his eyes.

"Hold on now!" he shouted above the noise as they began to choke on the exhaust fumes.

Tom felt the clunk as the gear engaged and watched as Bill twisted the throttle on the handlebars. He jammed the hard-hat firmly down on his head and grabbed the bar that traversed the sidecar in front of him. The large bulk of his grandad and his clothing loomed above him like a pioneering aviator. He did not know quite what to expect. He had never been on a motorbike before and had serious doubts about his grandad's capabilities, but the rumbling bike moved smoothly out of the byre and onto the track to the road. Tom could feel the immense power of the engine as the bike pulled up the slope to the gate. It seemed to be just ticking over like a slumbering dinosaur.

When they reached the gate Bill simply looked down at Tom and pointed with a gauntleted hand. Tom leapt out of the sidecar and held the gate open for Bill and the bike and then back in again and they set off the three miles to the shop.

From his position in the sidecar the tarmac felt uncomfortably near but from this new perspective the countryside looked quite different from what he had seen on the way in. Everything was much more intimate and, despite the exhaust, he could smell the grass and the flowers that swayed on the verges in their wake. As they roared by, sheep and lambs ran away in panic, a family of hoodie crows scattered from a flattened rabbit just in front of them and delving oystercatchers cried out in complaint.

They seemed to be flying along and when Tom stuck his head out beyond the shelter of the wee opaque Perspex windscreen his eyes filled with tears. He laughed and shouted out "Geronimo … " Glancing up at his grandad he saw that he could not hear him above the barking of the exhaust, but was leaning forward with fierce concentration like a decrepit knight preparing to meet some immense challenge ahead. Tom lay back and watched the passing telephone poles, the swinging wires between them, blue sky and white clouds above and savoured the feeling of freedom and speed. He did not see the couple look up from their garden by the school and wave to his grandad as they swept by, or his answering salute.

It took them only five minutes to reach the shop, much too soon for Tom. It was like no other shop Tom had seen, a stone building among others looking over a little harbour from where a ferry ran twice a week to one of the smaller islands. Next to it was Magnus and Maisie's house. Across the length of the front of the shop, above the door and the two windows, ran a faded, brown wooden sign on which were painted the words *Herculeson and Sons Purveyors of Victuals and Flatcaps, Paraffin and Hardware*. Bill parked the bike by the front door. He stood up a little stiffly, peeled off his gauntlets, and pushed the goggles back over the helmet, which he then took off. These he placed casually on the windowsill of the shop behind him and then he struggled out of his coat, with Tom pulling down on the sleeves to help him. He threw the coat across the bike and Tom threw his yellow oilskin on top.

As Bill pressed the latch and swung open the door of the shop, a bell above it rang loudly. Inside the single large room Bill was greeted with a big hug and a kiss from Maisie. A little girl buying bread and tins of cat food stared at Tom until he realised he still had the hard-hat perched high on his head. He looked away and took it off as if he always wore it when he went shopping with his grandad.

"Tom, is it?" Maisie's broad, warm and smiling face looked down at him. She turned to Bill. "Du better stock up on mair dan a puckle of herring to feed dis growing bairn." Then she turned back to Tom. "Noo, if he does not feed dee properly, just du come over to wis. Mind dat, will du?"

Tom got the sense and nodded vigorously in reply.

Bill put a hand on his shoulder. "Why don't you explore around outside and me and Maisie will have a gossip while I get the supplies?"

Tom fished the shopping list out of his pocket and gave it to his grandfather then ran off out the door to the wee harbour, throwing the hard-hat into the sidecar as he passed.

There was an air of benign neglect around the shop and house. The harbour, though, had been recently repaired and on one of its arms sat a bright red-coloured crane, above a spanking new ferryboat that had just enough room to carry one car or maybe a tractor. Several wooden boats sat in the basin, moored between buoys and the harbour wall. Two lads sat on the end of the other arm that turned at right angles at its end to form some shelter for the boats. Their legs dangled over the edge and they concentrated on their fishing lines, twitching them up and down in the water. Tom wandered up the pier and stood behind them.

"What are you fishing for?"

They turned their heads and looked up at him. The older of the two pointed to a heap of small grey fish between them and returned his attention to his line.

"What are they?"

The younger one turned this time and said in a disparaging voice, "Sillocks."

"Oh," Tom answered, and acknowledging that neither was going to speak to him further muttered, "thanks," and turned away. Before he was out of earshot he heard them talking about him and laughing. He shrugged and wandered back to the shop where his grandad was loading several plastic shopping bags into the sidecar.

At the opposite end of the shop from the house was an older, roofless building with its gable end to the front and a flight of worn, stone steps leading up to what must once have been a door into the first floor. Tom walked up the steps and looked into the empty ruin.

"That was a böd," his grandad said, looking up at him as he pulled on his coat.

"What's a böd?"

"It's a kind of fishermen's store. Traders used to come to Shetland from northern Europe hundreds of years ago … every summer … to trade with the locals for fish."

"Must have been a smelly place," said Tom, turning up his nose.

Bill put his helmet on. "Not really … the fish were left on the beach until they were as dry as cardboard." He buckled the strap under his chin. "C'mon, time to go. I'm hungry … aren't you?"

Tom only thought for a moment. "Yes, I am," and he bounded down the steps.

The journey back was a little less comfortable for Tom, jammed as he was among all the shopping. He had almost forgotten about his grandad's story, so overwhelmed was he with his first experiences of Shetland. He could hardly believe he had only left home that morning. It seemed a world away.

After supper they sat around the stove and Bill tried to explain the family tree on his father's side to Tom: what relations they had and where they lived. Tom found it difficult to understand the finer points of second-cousins-once-removed. He yawned loudly.

"Who did you stay with when you came with your grandparents, then?"

"My grand uncle and grand aunt. Ina was my grandmother's sister."

"Did they live around here?"

"Oh no, they lived in the Ness … Dunrossness, to give it its proper name – the Ness of the roaring tide – at the south end of the island."

Tom pulled his feet up into the large armchair. "What was she like, your grandmother's sister?"

Using a taper from the mantelpiece, Bill lit his pipe from the open door of the stove and then threw on another peat. "She was a very elegant lady. There was something about her that one instantly respected. People, including myself, always wanted her approval. It seemed quite natural … and the only person who could pull her leg was grandfather. I think they had a fondness for one another. I can imagine she kept order in school by just a look or a phrase … nothing threatening … just to let you know you had let down her or yourself. I wish she had been my teacher."

He got up, rummaged on a shelf that still contained some books and papers and returned to his seat with a slim booklet. It was a little damp and he blew off some dust. "She was very different from uncle Bertie. He was an earthy man … a little rough in his ways … but straight, and I think he believed very much in the crofting ways of the time." He opened the booklet on his lap and flicked through the pages. "Aunt Ina was very bright and perceptive. She could have been stuck-up, as they say … snobby … you know what I mean. But she wasn't at all." He turned to Tom. "I think grandfather and grandma were looking to her to help them with me."

Tom stretched and looked across at his grandad. "How d'you mean?"

"Well, she was educated … and as I said perceptive … "

Tom screwed up his face. "Grandad!"

"I mean … well … you know how sometimes you can listen to someone and, despite what they are saying, you know that they are not telling the truth or that they actually believe something quite different. And yet if I asked you to tell me exactly why you did not believe them … …you would find it difficult to explain."

Tom was nodding vigorously.

"Well, perception is often more than that. I swear that sometimes when Aunt Ina was listening to me, besides knowing that I wasn't saying everything … she knew what I wasn't saying … *and* knew that *I* didn't know what I wasn't saying. If you can understand that!"

"I think so."

"She also had been an English teacher and she knew all the stories I had read and all about heroes and villains. Incidentally, she wrote some rather nice poems." He held the booklet open in front of him. "Want to hear one or two?" then added, "they're in English."

"Okay."

"Here's a bit of one about their horse, Flokki. Flokki was a thrawn beast that would never do what he was told. Aunt Ina said that Uncle Bertie once stood square in front of him when Flokki would not stand still to have his hooves cleaned. Uncle Bertie grabbed an ear in each hand and bellowed his anger at Flokki's forehead." He read from the book:

"Trying to get sense into a stubborn horse
Is like knocking on the hull
    of an abandoned ship.
The skull of a horse is designed
    to prevent all unnecessary communication
    and the ears are just for decoration."

Tom laughed. "I like that one."

"Ah, here's a slightly longer bit of one that I like. But to appreciate this one you have to realise that winter here in Shetland can seem very long, wet and windy. This one is about spring:

Today, the sun.
After weeks of grey in the sky,
Grey in the wind and grey in the faces
That moved to smiles with such economy.
And today, such stillness
That we crept from our beds
In fear of breaking it.
There was something in the movement of this day,
In the freedom of figures tarring a roof,
In their hesitation at doorways
And in the generosity of their greetings.
Suddenly, the landscape is alive with shadows,
Colour has crept back out of the stones.
Today is a day for taking stock,
A day for taking bearings,
A day for …… "

Bill glanced across at Tom as he came towards the end of Ina's poem, but his eyes were closed. "And I was going to tell you about Neil too … " He smiled at the sleeping boy, then, weary himself, closed the book, struggled to his feet and shuffled across to the armchair. "Tom," he shook him gently, "Tom, c'mon, time for bed."

Tom came half-awake, muttering to himself and stumbled with his grandfather guiding him, across to the ladder in the passageway. He climbed up. Bill threw up his pyjamas and left him pulling off his clothes with his eyes still closed.

Back in the kitchen Bill put on the wireless and found some music, it was something baroque that quite suited his mood. He opened the lower cupboard in the dresser, found a half-bottle of McCallan's, hesitated for a moment and then muttered "What the hell," under his breath.

He was sitting back in the armchair by the fire sipping his whisky when the phone rang.

Thinking it might be Magnus, Bill picked it up. "Hello."

"Dad. Is that you?"

He cursed inwardly. They must have come home early. He had hoped that it might be a few days before they discovered where they were.

"Hello, Alistair."

"I rang home and your message said you were in Shetland."

Alistair's voice sounded more worried than angry – that was a relief. Bill tried to make light of it. "Yes, that's right."

"What are you doing there?"

Not the truth quite yet, he thought. "Just seemed a good opportunity after Tom had finished his exams to show him where some of his family comes from and have a bit of a last look around myself."

"Is the cottage okay?"

"Yes, it's fine and dry. I'm afraid you've just missed Tom. I think he's fast asleep. How are things going with you?"

"We've finished early. Be flying back in a couple of days." There was a brief pause. "I wish you hadn't taken Tom away without asking."

Bill bit his lip. "Yeh … I'm sorry." But both knew that he probably would not have been allowed to take him on his own, had he asked beforehand.

"How long are you going to stay?"

Bill tried to think this one through quickly. It might be only a couple of weeks, but Alistair would come up if it were to be that long. "Oh … a week to ten days probably." He waited. Alistair was mulling it over.

"Okay. We'll give you a ring when we get home. Love to Tom. Take care, dad."

"Bye, Alistair. Don't worry, I'll look after him."

There was a short pause and then they were disconnected. He swore quietly to himself as he realised that he had not even asked Alistair about his work.

CHAPTER *11*

*'The book smelled new, the cover was marbled in blues
and its empty pages were lined in red.'*

*D*uring the next week, Bill took Tom on the motorbike all over the islands, along the way filling Tom's head with historical tales and the names of places and birds. They made up picnics out of Tom's favourite foods, from jam and peanut butter sandwiches to the strongest tasting crisps that stained the fingers like varnish. But first of all his grandad took him to the main town of Lerwick where he bought him a new sketchpad and pencils. Bill had a slightly ulterior motive for this, besides a genuine desire to encourage him. Every time he felt tired he found something for Tom to draw so that he could rest.

They went to the coast of Eshaness where the salt winds and the sheep had made a bowling green of the turf that abruptly ends where the black cliffs drop vertically to the sea. Tom found he could draw the cliffs after a manner but could not begin to capture the churning froth and spume that the rocks knocked out of the dashing waves. They went to St Ninian's Isle where a perfectly symmetrical bar of sand, scalloped by the sea on either side, links the island, with its ruins of a medieval chapel, to the Mainland. They went to the lonely peninsula of Fethaland where the ruins of 19th century fishermen's huts seemed to be waiting for their return while the sea's advances eroded their roots. There, Tom sketched the roofless buildings and the flat storm beach where the line-caught fish were dried. They had a picnic at Mavis Grind where the waist of Shetland is drawn so tightly by the sea that Tom attempted, unsuccessfully, to throw a stone from the North Sea into the Atlantic. Later, Tom drew a picture of the portage of a royal Viking ship across this rocky isthmus, en route from Norway to the King's farm on the island of Papa Stour. On about the sixth day, as they were sitting on a low wall in the old capital of Scalloway, while Tom was drawing the high and narrow Castle of Earl Patrick, a car passed pulling a trailer on which was a long, slim wooden boat.

They watched it pass and Tom asked, "Is that a racing boat?"

"Yes. It's beautiful, isn't it?" And suddenly he was reminded of a summer evening sixty years ago. "It's not a sailing boat though ... a yacht ... if you know what I mean?"

Tom put down his sketchpad. "How do they race them then?"

"They row ... tell you what."

"I know."

"What?"

"Let's go and get a cup of something ... "

"Good idea ... and then we'll go round to the marina and have a look at them."

They sat in a cafe overlooking the sea from where, across the bay, they could see people launching half a dozen boats in preparation for a race. Each boat was a different colour and one was varnished, otherwise, Tom saw, that each was exactly the same and they all sat low in the water.

"They're called yoals ... the boats ... Ness yoals."

"Ness yoals," Tom repeated, rolling his tongue and releasing the 'sss' slowly like a snake.

"The Ness, right at the south end of the island where the airport is, is where the yoals were traditionally used as fishing boats. There's a big tide-rip there and if the sea is running in the opposite direction to the tide it can be a nasty place to be. The yoal design, long, narrow and flexible with enough thwarts ... "

"Warts ... ?"

"Thwarts ... cross-benches ... seats. The boat is long enough to have enough thwarts for three pairs of rowers. Presumably to pull against the tide or to get out of danger quickly. Anyway, they are not much used today when you have big outboard motors and cheap fibreglass boats. Probably only a handful of the original yoals are left."

"These aren't?"

"No. They've been specially built ... along the same lines ... but for rowing for fun. They're much lighter and faster than the originals."

He put down his cup and began to fill his pipe. Tom put his hand on his grandad's arm and nodded to a 'no smoking' sign. Bill made a face and gestured to the door and as they got up he pointed with his pipe at the boats.

"My Uncle Bertie had one, but I'll tell you about his in the story."

"Don't forget to pay, grandad!"

Bill ruffled Tom's hair and settled up with the waitress. Then they walked along the road to a vantage point where they watched eight teams of six rowers and a coxswain, from different parts of the islands, compete against each other. There was a race for everyone: men, youths, women and even old men. The women were as skilled as the men and it was only sheer muscle that gave the latter the edge. Tom was impressed.

A day or two later, Bill took Tom on a little foot-passenger ferry for the short crossing to the uninhabited island of Mousa where they were dropped for the day with their rucksack and picnic. There they saw a colony of languid seals sleeping around the edge of a wide and shallow sea-pool; dodged diving terns and skuas; and, on the heather close to the shore, Bill gently lifted an eider duck from her nest, showed Tom the eggs and, as gently, put her back. At lunchtime Bill led Tom to a drystane dyke. Before they sat down he put a finger to his lips and motioned silently for Tom to put his head against the wall. Tom listened intently for a few moments and then he heard weird sounds from somewhere among the stones. He looked at his grandad.

Bill smiled. "It's a storm petrel. A seabird, the size of a swallow ... on its nest."

Tom wanted his grandad to take it out but Bill shook his head.

"It's so small," he whispered, "I could never get my hand in to where it is."

They ate their lunch silently, with their backs against the dyke, within a foot or so of the invisible birds as they chirred and purred in their eerie language.

In the afternoon they climbed forty feet up inside the walls of the two-thousand-year-old broch. Tom made several attempts to sketch it while his grandad told him the story of the young Viking, Erland, in the 12th century, who had eloped with Margaret, the mother of Earl Harold. They barricaded themselves within the broch and were able to hold off her irate son until he gave his consent to their marriage! Tom imagined himself, sword in hand, looking down from the top of the broch at an angry Viking.

At the end of the second week, Magnus' son Peter invited them to join him and his dad on a lobstering trip on his boat, the *Tystie*, which was moored in the bay by the cottage. The *Tystie* had an inboard engine, a forward cabin just large enough for three people and plenty of deck space aft for working the creels. Bill was not sure if he should go. He thought it might be too much for him but felt he couldn't disappoint Tom, who could hardly contain his excitement at the prospect of such a trip.

The forecast was good and the day dawned calm, dry and bright with a little swell running from the west. They left the narrow mouth of the rocky bay around noon and set off for Peter's creels that were laid around a small rugged island of red, volcanic rock, a couple of miles away. On the way across the sound, the stiff and narrow-winged fulmars, with their dark and gentle eyes, swept up on the boat effortlessly, then veered off on long tacks that brought them back again and again as if they had nothing better to do on such a lovely day. Weightless terns danced through the air and hovered just above, chiding them with their high-pitched calls. At one point they passed through a flock of feeding gannets that hurled themselves into the waves like a shower of black and white arrows. Tom was overwhelmed by all that was so new to him and Bill had to keep up a running commentary of explanations.

The coast of the island where the creels were laid had been eroded by Atlantic storms into an immense fretwork of stacks, arches, caves, shoals and skerries. Magnus worked his way unerringly around them, as if he were merely driving a car through city streets, while Peter caught up the floating leads with the boathook and pulled the pots on board with a little winch. Tom watched with respect as he whipped out lobsters and crabs with their great waving claws and threw them into a fishbox before they knew what was happening. He marvelled at the lobsters' long antennae and their medieval armour, the colour of the wet and cold, blue-black sea.

By the time they had pulled up and re-baited half the pots Bill was feeling the effects of the constant movement. Magnus, at the wheel, had been watching him out of the corner of his eye and got Tom to fetch a chair for him out of the cabin. They wedged it in the doorway so that Bill was sheltered and out of the breeze.

"Sit du dere, boy, so I can spaek ta dee," said Magnus, throwing an old jersey onto its seat.

Gratefully, Bill slumped into the chair. "Not used to this anymore, Magnus."

"Ach, let the bairns do the work. That's my motto!"

They laughed and cracked while Bill watched Peter give instructions to Tom on how to re-bait the creels. Warm and comfortable, Bill watched with pleasure as Tom manfully tried to keep up with Peter.

They stopped at lunchtime for a brew-up by the mouth of a cave from which occasionally came the mournful moan of seals. A big grey bull, with his head as scarred and wrinkled as an old Roman gladiator, surfaced to inspect them. Peter tossed a piece of fish towards him and he plunged after it with an almighty splash.

"Yon's the king o Vee Skerries," he said, "I see him most days I'm here." He turned to Bill and winked, "Except when he's wi his harem on the rocks!" They laughed, and Tom too, although he was not quite sure what he was laughing at.

The wind freshened in the afternoon as they came around the far side of the island and began their homeward leg. The sea was behind them and they bowled along at a nice pace, keeping ahead of the white breaking waves and matching the speed of the wind so that it was relatively warm and still behind the cabin.

Bill was tired and stiff by the time they got back to the jetty in the bay and he leaned heavily on Peter's arm as he climbed out of the *Tystie*. Tom hopped nimbly after him.

"Wid du laek a lobster, Bill?" Peter asked, as Bill stood above him on the jetty.

Bill shook his head with a regretful smile. "No ... thanks very much though. I used to love them ... but I don't have the appetite for them anymore."

Magnus leaned on the bulwark beside Peter, his huge hands lifting and slinging the fishbox full of lobsters at Tom's feet as if it were a box of tissues. "You boys be okay tonight?" His question was deliberately general, but Bill knew it was addressed to him.

"Sure," said Tom

Bill put his hand on Tom's shoulder. "We'll be fine, Magnus." He squeezed Tom's arm. "Thanks for a great day, Peter."

"Yeh ... that was cool," said Tom.

Behind Tom, Bill raised an eyebrow at the men in the boat and they all laughed. He turned Tom around with a mock shove of exasperation and they walked off across the shore to the cottage.

Back in the kitchen they peeled off several layers of clothing. Bill instructed Tom to make some tea while he surreptitiously took several pills with a glass of water. Then he raked the stove and laid and lit a new fire with driftwood and peat from the shed. Finally, he collapsed exhausted into one of the armchairs and greedily drank a mug of Tom's tea.

"I'll just have a nap before supper. You keep an eye on the fire, will you?"

Tom nodded from the table, where he was busy trying to sketch the *Tystie* among the cliffs and stacks while the image was still fresh in his memory.

Bill stretched himself out on the resting chair. "Oh ... by the way ... there are a few more pages of the story by the typewriter in my room. They're about Neil."

Tom glanced up. "Neil? Who's Neil?"

Bill closed his eyes. "Read the pages."

When Tom looked up again Bill was asleep.

For another ten minutes Tom worked on his drawing and by the time he put it down and went to get the story, his grandad's mouth was wide open and he was snoring loudly. Tom sat down in Bill's chair with several typescript pages, tucked his legs up under him, tried to ignore his grandad and began to read.

A day or two after we arrived I woke to the complete absence of sound and when I looked out of the window I could see absolutely nothing. Nothing, that is, except what seemed to be the inside of a cloud. It was as if the world had been taken away and the grey that was left was but its shadow or the formlessness before creation. The others were not up but I decided to get dressed and go out and have a look at this strange world.

The fog was so thick that I could not see the garden gate from the door of the croft and when I heard gulls crying and the neighbour's cockerel crowing the sounds were muffled as if someone's hand clamped their beaks. I needed the toilet and as it was just around the back of the byre, somewhere just in front of me, I decided I could not get lost. I crossed the track outside the garden and found the byre wall, then followed it around until I came to the little wooden building. It was so damp that by the time I reached it I was covered in droplets of moisture. I shook my head and it sprayed off me like water off a wet dog. The atmosphere was almost tangible.

When I was through with the toilet, I thought I would continue on and meet up with the track again. I had not counted on the thickness of the fog. I must have been daydreaming when I came out because I turned the wrong way, thinking I was setting off back to the garden. I had not gone many steps when I realised I had lost any sense of direction. I wandered over rough ground and past some old machinery. I came across another byre and another track. Maybe it was the same track as that in front of the house. Then I had an idea. I shouted for Uncle Bertie's dogs. They responded almost immediately but I could not tell exactly where the barks were coming from. So I stood in the middle of the track not knowing which way to turn. I just had to make a decision. I followed the track in one direction for several hundred yards, saw nothing at its edge I could recognise and decided therefore to retrace my steps. Once again I recognised nothing in the thick fog. Now I knew I was totally lost and I began to panic. I began shouting the dogs' names, staring blindly into the fog and listening intently.

It was then that I heard the faint crunch of feet on the track. I shouted, "Hello!" The feet stopped but there was no answer. Then they resumed their slow steps towards me, coming closer. I sensed that the person must be very close. Although I could not see him, I knew it was a man. The steps stopped again. He was listening and he was so close I heard him clear his throat. Why didn't he speak? Suddenly, I was very frightened. But before I could make a decision as to what to do the footsteps began again, and this time they stopped just as a young man appeared out of the murk, a yard in front of me. He looked down and smiled tentatively. His hands, hanging in front of him only inches from my face, clenched and unclenched nervously. Without speaking, he *looked around. I could see he was wondering either what to do with me, or which way to go. Then he looked down again, screwing up his face in concentration. He seemed to have made a decision. He put out his hand and my child's instinct recognised something in him that told me he was harmless.*

We walked silently along the track, hand in hand, turning several corners it seemed until we arrived at the front gate of the cottage. There, he simply let go my hand and, without speaking, turned away into the fog. I listened until I could no longer hear his retreating steps and then went back into the cottage. I decided not to tell anyone about my adventure in case I got into trouble.

I did not meet Neil again until several days later, to find that I was actually occupying his room, though I didn't know it at the time, and he was staying with a neighbour. Uncle Bertie had taken me and grandfather out to do some work on the croft. I felt very grown up walking between them, my hoe slung across my shoulder, just as their's, while they chatted away. We passed their black and white cow tethered in a circle of cropped grass at the top of the unfenced strips of fields. At the foot of the fields was a damp area of tall grasses, rushes and flowers and a slow burn full of bright yellow kingcups and monkey-flowers. The first strip was ungrazed, the next sown with oats and the third had rows of little green plants. Here, Uncle Bertie introduced me to the incredibly boring task of singling neeps – that is weeding out the rows of turnip seedlings with a hoe to leave the strong plants to grow on six inches apart. He had given me a small hoe but even then I struggled like only a spoilt child can! Neil joined us after a short while and Uncle Bertie, working on the row next to mine, stopped hoeing only long enough to introduce him to me and grandfather with a casual nod. "Neil, this is Jim and William … say hello." All I understood at that point was that Neil normally lived with Aunt Ina and Uncle Bertie.

Although he was a man in size and age, Neil seemed to me somehow childlike. He glanced shyly towards us without raising his eyes and there was no expression of acknowledgement on his face. He set to with the hoe on the row next to me with an almost manic concentration. There was something about him that was wrong but Uncle Bertie and grandfather seemed unaware of it. I lasted only another half an hour or so at the neeps before I was let off and I saw no more of Neil until we went out fishing later that evening.

How can I express the magic of that evening? Although being on the steamer with grandfather had brought me as close as I had been to my heroes, up to that time, that fishing trip set me right among them, the smugglers, the excise men and the pirates.

We did not set off from the house until very late in the evening when the sun was still in the sky. I was well wrapped up in extra jerseys and all of us were wearing rubber boots. Uncle Bertie, like his neighbours, had his boat pulled up above the shore. It seemed enormous to me then and was probably around 20 feet in length. It was kept, as several others lying adjacent to it, in its own boat-shaped cutting in the bank above the beach, which grandfather told me was called a 'noust'. In the winter this protected the boats from the wild storms. Grandfather also told me that the boat was a 'yoal' and that it was older than he was. In fact Uncle Bertie's grandfather had built it. I found that difficult to comprehend.

The boat was pointed at both ends, painted black on the outside and white on the inside and the hull was constructed of long, narrow wooden boards that swept like bird's wings from stem to stern. There were places for three pairs of rowers and tied lengthwise across the thwarts were six long oars; even I could see that she was a thoroughbred. Out of the corner of my eye, leaning against a flat-roofed shed at the top of the beach, I caught a glimpse of Silver whom I had almost forgotten about. There was envy on his face as he gave the yoal his expert eye and nodded his head at me.

There were five of us: Uncle Bertie who was in charge, grandfather, Neil, myself and another boy, much bigger than me but only a year or two older, called Magnus.

"Boys ... pit yon boards doon on the sand." Uncle Bertie pointed to some pieces of wood tucked by the side of the boat. "Neil, gie dem a haand."

I let Neil and Magnus go ahead of me and like them I picked a few boards that I could comfortably carry and followed them round to the sloping sand between the boat and the sea. They placed them at intervals, a few feet apart and I followed suit.

Uncle Bertie and grandfather untied a couple of ropes at either end that secured the boat to heavy stones and then hauled the lower one, which had a hole right through it, out of the way.

"Magnus, jump in and pit in the nile," Uncle Bertie said.

Magnus swung himself easily into the boat, pulled up a floorboard and pushed a cork firmly into a hole."

"Fine, boy. Noo bairns, I'll have Neil on my side and you boys help Jim on the idder."

We slid the boat down the beach over the pieces of wood and into the water. It was hard work keeping her upright but she slid over the boards surprisingly easily. Once there, shore-lapping waves slapped gently against her while grandfather held her and Uncle Bertie called the rest of us to help him throw the boards back up the beach and fetch the gear from the shed above the beach. Inside it, from hooks on the wall, he lifted down four fishing rods that were as long as the boat itself. He gave them to Neil and to me and Magnus he gave a couple of buckets, a board and a scoop for baling.

We loaded everything into the boat, including a couple of flasks and plastic cups which we had brought with us. Uncle Bertie ordered us all in, bar Neil. Magnus and I sat in the bow while grandfather and Uncle Bertie untied the oars. They took a pair each and slid them through rope-loops fastened to wooden pins on the gunwale.

"Right, Neil … shove off."

Neil put his weight to the boat and as she slid off the sand, with grandfather and Uncle Bertie pulling with the oars, he tumbled head first into the stern.

After about ten minutes Neil took over the oars from grandfather and he retired to the stern. For about half an hour Neil and Uncle Bertie rowed us out of the bay and round a little headland towards some cliffs. It was flat calm and the boat slid along as if the water were no impediment to her passage at all.

Apart from a few half-hearted calls from the handful of seagulls that lazily followed us, there were no other sounds except the slap of the sea against the stem, the squeak of the wooden oars against the pins, the gentle splash as they dipped into the water and a creak of complaint from the boat as she was pulled forward. Even when we rounded the headland and were in the open sea there was hardly any swell. The sky to the north-west was suffused with pink that shaded to a deeper red on row upon row of cotton-wool clouds. The coastline behind us with its little houses and fields was so sharply delineated, so still and so quiet, it seemed as if it was a cut-out, pasted on to the horizon. It must have been the most perfect evening of that summer.

I sat in the bow with my chin on my folded arms searching ahead. I felt Silver was somewhere in the boat behind me but I felt safe from him with grandfather and the others. A story began to form in my mind of a rescue and a race against death in a three-manned yoal: the wind ripping sails from the mast and freezing white waves crashing over the sides onto women and children huddled together on the floorboards.

"I tink this will be fine … eh, Neil?" I heard Uncle Bertie say.

"Let me row a wee bit and you can fish," said grandfather.

Gingerly, we all changed places in the boat. Magnus and I sat on the thwart facing the stern, grandfather took the forward pair of oars and between us sat Uncle Bertie and Neil. Uncle Bertie took a couple of rods, handed one to Magnus and then the other to me. He handed a third to Neil.

"Noo, dis is a waand," he demonstrated for my benefit, holding it vertically so that the line with the six white-feathered hooks, hung down into his lap. "It's maybe a wee bit on the heavy side for you, but if you balance it over the side of the boat that'll make it easier. Just watch Magnus."

The wand was one piece of bamboo, tapering from just over an inch thick at the handle to a quarter of an inch at the top, to which the line was tied. I watched Magnus put his wand out over one side of the stern with the result that the flies trailed in the water more than twenty feet astern. I put mine out on the other and Neil put his out to the side so that we should not get entangled. Meanwhile, grandfather, who had lit his pipe, commenced rowing quietly and slowly, taking the yoal along at a gentle pace parallel to the cliffs.

All the time Neil had said virtually nothing, but then neither had Magnus.

I was very excited and nervous and gripped the wand tightly in anticipation of it being pulled out of my hands.

"Relax, boy," said Uncle Bertie. "Just let it lie like a kitten in your haands."

We must have rowed along for about ten minutes before anything happened. Suddenly there was a sharp pull on the wand and my heart jumped. I yanked the wand up in the air and a dark grey, foot-long fish seemed to leap out of the water at the end of the line. It swung across the air towards me and dropped straight into my lap as the wand reached the vertical. Now I understood why the line was the same length as the wand! It flopped about until Neil, from behind, grabbed it, saying something unintelligible, and deftly twisted the hook from its mouth. He rapped its head hard against the edge of the thwart and dropped it into the fish box at my feet. It flexed a couple of times, its lower jaw, red with a touch of blood, hung open. It was not a beautiful fish, kind of fat in the middle and pointed at the ends.

Before I had time to congratulate myself, Magnus was swinging in his wand with four fish dangling from the hooks. I put my line back out as he tucked the wand between his legs and against his shoulder and proceeded to take off the fish, banging them against the thwart as Neil had done and chucking them into the fish box.

"What are they?" I asked.

"Piltock," said Magnus.

"Coalfish, or coley, to you and me," said grandfather, resting on the oars for a moment.

Then there were more tugs on my wand. I lifted it more slowly and managed to bring in two fish this time. They seemed to leap in all directions and if it had not been for Neil's help again my line would have got hopelessly tangled. One of the fish I managed to remove myself, but it slipped out of my hand as I tried to rap its head like Neil and it fell onto the boards where it thrashed about before Neil grabbed it and despatched it. After the first rush of excitement, when I pulled up my wand at the slightest nibble, I realised that Magnus was more patient, waiting until at least several fish were attached before he lifted his. So it became a friendly competition between us to see how many times we could catch six at once. Magnus was much more skilled than me and he easily won. By now the fish were coming aboard thick and fast and between the three of us we soon filled a couple of fish boxes. And then, quite suddenly, there were no fish. Grandfather moved back onto the forward thwart and called for the gutting board and knife. The board, knife and the fish boxes were moved up to him. Uncle Bertie and Neil took over the oars again and we moved to another spot a half mile to the west that Uncle Bertie chose with some precision after checking our position.

We lay there in the gentlest of swells and drank some hot, strong tea from a flask while grandfather began slitting the bellies of the piltocks and throwing the guts over the side. Immediately, the herring gulls, black-back gulls and maalies – as Magnus called the fulmars – appeared, and also a large and aggressive dark brown gull that was called a bonxie. Grandfather said it was a skua.

Up until the boat had stopped and my attention was no longer on fishing, I had not really thought of what we were doing or where we were. But the presence of the seagulls around us and the slow rise and fall of the boat suddenly reminded me that we were actually afloat on deep waters in a relatively small boat: the beach now seemed rather distant and the nearby cliffs rather forbidding. Our connection with the land felt rather tenuous and there seemed to be an awful lot of sea. The others, including grandfather, however, were chatting and joking and completely relaxed as if this was the most natural thing in the world. After a few moments I felt rather stupid that I had been afraid.

That was when the most magical thing happened: just when they were all sitting and chatting with each other.

In the direction I happened to be looking, an enormous fin, like a black sail, broke the surface of the water only a few hundred yards away. As silently and suddenly as it had appeared it disappeared, but in that moment I guessed it was on a course to pass quite close to us. Just as I opened my mouth, stuttered a kind of 'aaahhh', raised my hand and pointed, four other slightly smaller fins, and one much smaller, also broke the surface silently and rolled back under. The others turned in time to see them disappear.

"Killer whales," shouted Magnus, standing up excitedly, followed by Neil, for a better view.

"Sit doon, boys," said Uncle Bertie, grabbing Neil by the trousers and pulling him down. "Du'll coup the boat."

"Oh my," said grandfather, "I haven't seen one for years."

And then the first one with the huge stiff fin, as tall as me, surfaced again, closer this time and still heading towards the boat.

"Yon's the bull," said Uncle Bertie, "and I tink dere's a female an calf an maybe a couple of idder eens."

As if on cue the four other fins rolled out of the water in unison behind the bull, the small one tight against its mother, and then they were gone again.

"Oh boys, dere geng to be close," said Uncle Bertie.

Then he leaned over and put his hand on Neil's shoulder, saying as much for me as for him, "Noo, there's no need to worry. They'll no do us ony herm."

We waited with baited breath for what seemed an eternity. The sea was empty and quiet again, nothing disturbed its placid surface, but underneath we could feel the presence of those great animals travelling inexorably towards us. We waited and waited and then all gasped at once as the bull broke the surface only two oars' lengths away. He was easily as long as the boat and close enough for us to clearly see the scars on his head, his white chin and belly, and the white banding behind his fin.

Without thinking, I shouted, "Moby Dick!"

Uncle Bertie laughed. "Moby Dick was ten times bigger than yon!"

I heard grandfather whisper the word, 'Leviathan'. Then the bull was gone and the others emerged to take his place. Again they were so close I could clearly see the differences in their sizes and the fact that their fins were not like the straight-sided triangle of the mature bull, but curved on their trailing edges. Then they too were gone.

I was looking past the others and saw the expressions on their faces. That was a revelation, for both grandfather and Uncle Bertie had their mouths open, just as if they too were children. I could not help smiling at them and when grandfather turned towards me and saw my expression I could see that he was puzzled for a moment, before he returned my smile. Neil though, was clinging with both hands onto Uncle Bertie, looking into his face and chattering incoherently. Uncle Bertie patted his hands reassuringly. I was too excited to feel afraid.

"Just whales, Neil, just whales."

We watched to see where they would appear next but it was a surprising distance off and they were travelling swiftly away.

"I bet dere aff to Horse Holm to get dem a seal for supper," Uncle Bertie laughed. Then he turned to me. "Weel, boy, I doot du'll never see the laek o yon again. I'm never been as close as that afore and I couldna coont the number of times I'm been oot here."

Then I remembered the picture on the spine of Aunt Ina's copy of Moby Dick *and had an inspiration for a story. I couldn't wait to get back and write it down.*

At the time we were fishing and saw the whales I never questioned how Uncle Bertie knew exactly where we were. It was only a day or two later when grandfather and I were walking along the cliffs that he pointed out one or two landmarks and explained to me what fishing meids were and how Uncle Bertie lined them up as bearings.

When we had finished our tea, which had got cold in all the excitement, Uncle Bertie took up the oars once more and once again Magnus, Neil and I hung the wands over the stern and began to fish. It did not take long to find another shoal. But this time when the fish hit they were of another order of energy and nearly pulled the wand out of my hands. I lifted it and the fish that swung into my lap this time were ocean greyhounds compared to the piltock! They were shaped like torpedoes with thin crescent tails and their backs were striped with blue and silver.

"Noo, be careful wi yon mackerel," said Uncle Bertie to me, "dey hae a nesty, sharp spike by de ventral fin. Neil, gie him a haand."

I was grateful for Neil's help, for the slippery mackerel writhed with such strength that I could hardly hold them.

"Where's the spike?" I asked him.

He muttered, again unintelligibly, turned a mackerel in his hand on its back and pointed to a thorn-like spur.

"Is it poisonous?"

He looked at me vacantly.

"No, it's not," said Uncle Bertie, "just sharp."

Neil now looked at Uncle Bertie and it seemed to me to be for an explanation of my question. I wondered if he did not understand my accent. To my astonishment Uncle Bertie mimed being pricked by the spine and then being sick. Neil, the man, laughed like a child and repeated the pantomime to me as if it was a great joke.

Uncle Bertie spoke to him sharply, "Neil! Noo behave dee'self."

As quickly as he had burst into laughter, Neil was deflated and looked away, not so much in humiliation as fear. I wondered why he was over-reacting? Then Uncle Bertie patted him on the shoulder and he seemed to immediately forget the incident. I couldn't understand his sudden changes of behaviour, but the others took no notice.

We had caught about a couple of dozen mackerel when Uncle Bertie said that was enough and it was time for home.

By the time we were back at the beach I was beginning to feel the cold, but after sluicing out the boat, relaying the boards and taking my turn with Magnus to wind her back up the beach with what looked like a washing mangle that was cemented into the rock above the noust, I soon warmed up again. After putting everything back in the shed we set off home, back up the track to the croft, Uncle Bertie and Neil carrying the fish box between them. As we turned in at the gate Magnus and Neil continued on.

I felt like a real man, kicking my boots into a corner of the passageway along with grandfather's and Uncle Bertie's and hanging my jacket on a hook below theirs. We told Aunt Ina and grandma all about the whales and they listened in envy. Then they praised us for our catch and Aunt Ina took three mackerel that Uncle Bertie had brought in and began preparing them for the pot. She turned to us.

"Du'll hae a powerful hunger noo, nae doot?"

Grandfather smacked his lips, "A fresh mackerel would go down very nicely, thank you."

I was still in a high pitch of excitement and I hung around her to see what she did. After washing them under the tap she cut off the heads and tails, scored their sides deeply with a sharp knife and rubbed pepper and salt into the cuts with her fingers. Then she laid them in the frying pan with melted butter and put it on the stove. They sizzled and spat as they browned, giving off a rich fishy aroma. Grandma set the table, made a pot of tea and cut some bread and when everything was ready we were called to the table. Uncle Bertie pulled himself up from where he had been lying, full-length on the resting chair, his stockinged feet hanging over the end, and grandfather, with a hand from Aunt Ina, struggled out of the armchair by the stove.

"My, what a pair o aald men you are," she laughed.

We sat down to the table with a fish each and a large chunk of buttered bread. Grandfather lifted the skin off mine with the flat of his knife, parted the backbone from the flesh, lifted it out and dropped it in another plate. Then he took a lemon that grandma had split and squeezed it over the fish. The blue and silver torpedo had been transformed into one of the tastiest fish that I had eaten, even better than a herring!

The combination of a full stomach, the warmth of the kitchen and a wonderfully satisfying tiredness finally hit me at the end of the meal, just when I was beginning to think that I was nearly grown up. I was aware of grandma speaking to me and taking me by the hand, of 'goodnights' coming from different corners of the room. It was light enough to see but not to read and I think I fell asleep as soon as my head touched the pillow.

I dreamed of Silver and I in Uncle Bertie's yoal – now called the Piquod *– among the killer whales and woke early, as it seemed I did every morning that summer, with the sun in my face. The house was silent except for the sound of Uncle Bertie snoring. My head was full of my dream. Beside the bed, among the comics and books, was my old notebook. I propped myself up with a pillow and began to write, spurred on by Silver who sat on the end of the bed, sharing my adventure. Then I must have fallen asleep again for the next thing I knew was that it was broad daylight and Aunt Ina was by my bed.*

"Is du goin ta lie in bed aa day, den?"

I had slipped off the pillow and as I sat up my notebook fell off the bed and onto the floor. Aunt Ina picked it up and turned it over in her hand.

"That's my story."

"You're a writer, then?" she smiled. "Can I read it?"

She took it away with her and later in the day, when I was playing with the collies in the garden, she came up to me clutching something under her folded arms against her chest.

"William."

I pushed one of the collies aside and sat up as the other licked my face.

"I laeked your story."

"Did you?"

"Yes, and I hope du'll write some mair … for me."

I looked at her in astonishment.

"Will you?"

No one had ever asked me to write a story and I didn't know what to say. She unfolded her arms and produced my tatty notebook and a new hardback jotter.

"Why don't you write your new stories in dis book?" She passed it down to me. "It's a present fae me … ok?"

The book smelled new, the cover was marbled in blues and its empty pages were lined in red. There was not a mark on it. I opened the first page and in the cover Aunt Ina had written 'This book belongs to William'. I was pleased and very proud.

Bill awoke slowly and wondered for a moment where he was.

"Goodness me, what time is it Tom?"

Tom put down the manuscript noting that there were still several pages to go. He looked at his watch. "Eight o'clock, grandad."

Bill tried to rise from the chair but his limbs were heavy, his body exhausted and he felt nauseous. Tom was looking at him, so he tried to make light of it.

He grinned and slumped exaggeratedly back in the chair. "Am I tired!"

"You were snoring."

"Could be."

"No, you *were* snoring."

"Quite possibly."

"Grandad!" Tom said in exasperation.

"Okay, okay," Bill said throwing up his hands in surrender. Then he turned his head to the sideboard. "Do me a favour, Tom. Would you give me that bottle of pills and get me a glass of water?"

"Have you got a headache?"

He hesitated before he answered. "No … the boat trip has knocked the stuffing out of me and … I need those pills to get me going again."

Tom looked at him in a concerned way that touched Bill's heart. "Are you not well, grandad?"

"No, Tom, I'm not very well." He opened the bottle that Tom handed him and tipped a couple of pills into the palm of his left hand. Then he took the proffered glass of water. "Nothing to worry about though. Tell you what … can you make the supper tonight?"

"Right on!"

"Pardon?"

"I'll make the supper, grandad."

"Right. Well on the shelf in the porch you'll find the pan with the rest of yesterday's mince. Do you like curry?"

"I think so," Tom said, returning with the pan.

Under his grandad's instructions Tom stirred a teaspoonful of curry powder into the mince. Then he boiled up some water in another pan and added rice. They ate their meal on their laps by the fire.

Afterwards Tom asked Bill how he had got on with Neil.

"Ah," and he waved his hand in the direction of the manuscript on the table, "I think it's in there and you'll get all the rest when it's finished."

While Tom was washing up, feeling very competent after the success of his cooking, though the rice was a little soggy, Bill struggled to his feet, chucked a couple of peats in the stove, poured himself a dram and then sat down again.

"I think it's time we went down to Sumburgh."

"Where the yoals come from?"

"Yes," Bill answered, sipping his whisky and gazing at the fire, "where the yoals come from."

"Grandad."

"Yes."

"Is Magnus in the story, Magnus who drives the car?"

"Yes, he is."

"Grandad."

"Yes."

"Were you afraid of Silver?"

Bill took a sip of his whisky and gazed into the fire. "Not at first, but yes … he did begin to frighten me. Something had changed … I began to feel that I could not escape him … that he would always be there. I suppose that I now associated him with the incident on the ferry and was beginning to wonder if I should trust him anymore." Bill held his glass out to the fire and swirled the whisky around as if seeking something in its amber depths. "I think I was scared that he was going to lead me into something else and that I would not have the strength to turn back."

"Grandad."

"Yes."

"Could we see your Uncle Bertie's yoal?"

"What? Goodness! I don't know if … I doubt if … it may not be there."

"But we could have a look, couldn't we?"

"Yes," he raised his glass. "Yes, we will. To Uncle Bertie's yoal!"

CHAPTER 12

**'Realisation dawned that he had been afraid
but that now he was no longer.'**

It was Sunday and Tom awoke to the sound of the wind buffeting the cottage, not with the steady howl he had been half aware of in the night but with great concussive slaps that he felt as much as heard. The guttering under the eaves vibrated against the walls with a weird cry. The windows rattled in their frames and the rain lashed against them, running down the panes in sheets, so that searching through them he could barely see the boats straining on their moorings in the bay. Out front, over the shore, he could just make out gulls tacking into the blast that threatened to blow them out of the sky. They dipped and rose with a turn of their wings as if dodging unseen solidities of the air. On the skerry the terns crouched flat against the rocks and of the seals there were no signs. Sheets of water peeled off the sea and shredded into a fine driven spray so that it was almost impossible to see where water ended and the air above it began. Tom tightened the window catches, but even standing well back he could still feel the cold air fanning his face. In the passageway to the kitchen the inside front door whistled as the draught drove through the fine gaps between it and the jambs and there was a deep thrum from the stove chimney which had been turned into an eerie instrument of the wind. It was as if the cottage was perched on a rock in the middle of a wild ocean.

His grandad was not yet up so Tom put on the kettle to make him a cup of tea, opened the door of the stove and added some peat to the still smouldering ash. Then he went back up to his room and put on another sweater that he knew he would not have packed unless for his grandad's insistence.

With one hand he knocked loudly against the noise of the wind on the door of Bill's room, in the other was a mug of tea.

"Grandad! Would you like some tea?"

A muffled voice came from within. "Tea? Yes please, Tom."

A heavy curtain was pulled across the window and the room was almost dark. The air was faintly musty and stale, overlain with the familiar smell of his grandad's tobacco smoke. As Tom came in Bill propped himself upright with his arms and the loose pieces of his brass bed rattled with the movement.

Tom put the mug down on the desk by the window, picked up a large pillow from the floor by the bed and as Bill leaned forward he jammed it down behind him. Then he fetched the tea. In the morning light Tom saw an unshaven, tired old face. His grandad groped with one hand for the bottle of pills on the chair beside the bed. Tom gave it to him.

"Sounds wild out there this morning?" It was a statement rather than a question.

Tom turned to the window and opened the curtains as Bill took his pills and washed them down with the tea.

"I think it's a gale."

"And a half, I would say. Ah well, maybe we'll give church and Sumburgh a miss today," he joked, clutching the mug between two hands as if he needed its heat. "How's the stove?"

"Oh, I think it will be okay. I've put some peat on."

"*And* made my cup of tea. Well done, Tom. We'll make a housewife of you yet!"

"Dream on, grandad."

The bed rattled again as Bill laughed, shifting his weight and pulling the downy up around his chest. He pointed to a large red blanket folded over the bed end at his feet. "Hand me that will you, and could you give me my dressing gown from off that chair?"

Tom unfolded the blanket and spread it over the top of the downy, then he helped his grandad wrap the dressing gown around his shoulders.

"That's better."

Tom turned to go.

"Tom. If you look upstairs in the other room I think you'll find an electric heater. Could you bring it down here?"

"Sure."

"It plugs in behind the door."

Tom brought the heater down and switched it on. "Is there anything else you want, grandad?"

Bill handed back the mug. "You have some breakfast. You know where everything is, don't you?"

Tom nodded.

"Make sure the stove is going to stay in and then come back. I'm just going to stay here a wee while this morning since we can't really go out."

Tom was halfway through the door when Bill called out, "Oh yes ... could you bring me the wee transistor on the mantelpiece. It would be nice to listen to some music."

"Transistor?"

"Portable radio to you, Tom."

"Oh."

While Tom made his own breakfast of five weetabix, a spoonful of brown sugar and a half pint of milk, Bill fiddled with the radio and found a music programme. It was the end of a Beethoven piano concerto and he lay back against the pillows, pulled the dressing gown around his neck and closed his eyes. These concertos always cheered him up, they were so positive, so life-affirming. Now though, they seemed to speak of another world of which he felt he was no longer a paid-up member. The gale outside just seemed to emphasise his isolation. As he reflected on this the concerto ended.

The next item was Strauss' *Four Last Songs*, sung by the American soprano Jessye Norman. Now this was a language he recognised. It was as if they had been freshly written for him for just this moment, just as Strauss had written them near the end of his own life. The first song recalled life, without sentimentality or bitterness: a story now almost completed. The second spoke to him of companionship, of love, of the happiness of his time with Alice, of her fulfilment through painting, of their joy together. The dying notes of the horn at the end of that song seemed to be her voice calling to him from some peaceful place, not so far away. She seemed to call to him again through the third song, explaining and reassuring, as might his mother when he was a child, in preparation for some defining moment in his life. Jessye Norman's powerful voice filled him with confidence. The fourth was the most perfect psalm to death that he knew: the farewells to each other of lifelong lovers. It spoke without judgement, but with forgiveness and understanding. In another setting the violins might have seemed sentimental, but accompanied by that full and rich soprano voice they sounded like angels and she the hand that would take his and lead him to Alice.

The tears streamed silently down his face. He wished he had taken one of her paintings back with him. Realisation dawned that he had been afraid but that now he was not longer. As the last song ended he switched off the radio and lay back on the pillows listening to the wind and the rain beating relentlessly on the cottage: the chariots of death, restless and impatient. He wished Jessye Norman had also sung *Morgen* that Strauss had written for his bride in the beginning. For he and Alice had also walked the '*broad shore, blue with waves*' and looked '*into each other's eyes without a word*'. Despite his pain, Bill found himself smiling ironically, for Strauss, of course, had been referring to Mediterranean shores, not to those of Shetland, gale-ridden and only six degrees south of the Arctic Circle!

He pulled out a handkerchief from the pocket of his dressing gown and wiped away his tears. Above the wind, he heard Tom whistling in the kitchen.

"Tom!" he shouted hoarsely, "Tom!"

There was no reply but he could still hear the whistling.

"Tom!"

Still no response.

He leaned out of the bed with difficulty, picked up a shoe off the floor and threw it through the open doorway where it landed with a clatter in the passage.

Tom appeared a moment later wearing his iPod, with a dishtowel wrapped around his waist. "Yes, sir?"

"You could damage your ears with that," Bill said irritably. "And I could do with a cup of coffee."

Tom dismissed his concern with a shrug and then pretended to note the order with pad and pencil. "Would there be anything else, sir?"

"Yes, my man. D'you think you could bring that typewriter over here first?" He pointed to the desk.

Tom brought the typewriter and put it on his grandad's legs.

"Ow … that's heavy! Bring me a cushion to put under it and bring me some paper too."

When Tom returned with the coffee, Bill was busy typing away. He looked up.

"D'you mind if we don't go anywhere today?"

Tom shook his head, "No … "

"What'll you do?"

"Well … I haven't finished reading about Neil … and I want to finish some drawings."

"Would you have a quick look outside before you start? Check the byre doors and make sure nothing important is being blown away?"

"Okay."

"Wrap up well now and promise me you won't go further than just around the cottage? And use the back door."

"I promise."

"And be careful!"

When Tom opened and closed the back door Bill felt his ears pop as the air was sucked out by the gale. Shortly after, he appeared at the window wrapped up in the oilskins, staggering backwards and forwards with his eyes half-closed, leaning against the driving rain, but grinning broadly and unable to stay still in the blasts of wind. Bill waved him on and he disappeared again. Presently he returned through the back door, once again causing a mild explosion of air. From the kitchen he shouted, "Wow … that was great! I was almost blown off my feet. Everything's okay, grandad!"

"Thanks, Tom." Bill called back. "Hang your things over the pulley by the stove if they're wet." Then the phone rang.

"Answer that, will you, Tom?"

Tom ran through in his stockinged feet and picked up the phone.

"Hello. Yes, it's me." He turned and looked at Bill. "Fine … yes, he's fine … no, everything's okay. Yes, I will. Bye." He put the phone down.

"Who was that?"

"Magnus. He wanted to know if we were alright."

"Ahh … that was good of him. Now go and take that coat off and hang it up."

Tom did as he was told, then taking an apple from the bowl on the sideboard he settled down at the kitchen table with the rest of the manuscript he had been reading the previous evening. Apart from the muffled noise of the gale searching for an opening into the cottage the only sounds were the mechanical clacks of his grandad's typewriter.

> The next time I saw Neil after the fishing trip was when we went to the peats. I had never been on the hill before and I was really looking forward to it. Uncle Bertie had a wee grey Ferguson tractor and a green, wooden trailer with large tyres that he looked after with the same loving care that he gave to his car. We saw him off at the gate; the little tractor thrumming and hiccuping along the road like a living thing, almost bouncing Uncle Bertie off the seat. Aunt Ina explained to me that she had spoken to Neil and he and I were going to walk to the peat banks. It would only take an hour or so and I would enjoy it. The forecast was for rain but not until later in the day. She reassured me that I would be fine with Neil, though I didn't feel I needed it. The peat bank, she explained, was halfway up a heather-covered hill, at the end of a track that was dry and firm enough for the car, so she, grandfather and grandma were going to drive. I guessed they planned to do some of the work before we got there.
>
> The route Neil and I took went up through fields to the hill-dyke that marked the boundary between the arable and the moorland. Neil led the way, swinging his arms and striding out. He seemed so proud of the responsibility that he had been entrusted with. At first, I could hardly keep up and had to shout after him to slow down. When he turned and saw that I was lagging behind his face fell. Though I could not understand his words, it was clear that he was rebuking himself. I told him it was fine and he smiled again. We followed a narrow sheep

track on the moor that wound its way upward through the short heather and through a gap between two hillocks. As we got near the gap Neil became excited and pointed to two birds that were descending stiff-winged from the sky to some point just beyond the rising ground. He turned and chattered to me in his gobbledegook. I shrugged my shoulders and shook my head in response.

When we reached the gap Neil grasped my sleeve and pulled me to the ground behind him. He put a finger to his lips and made an exaggerated sign of quiet. I laughed at him. He smiled back and then tried to look serious, but that made me laugh all the more. He grew a little agitated and I controlled myself, nodding to him that I would behave. He crawled ahead on his hands and knees and I followed in like manner just behind. The ground was damp and by the time we stopped crawling, after a hundred yards or so, our hands and knees were black with peat. He motioned me to creep up beside him.

In front of us lay a small peaty loch whose water was dark, dark brown. Neil pointed to the far end, only thirty or forty yards away. Two large birds sat low in the water, their necks straight and their slim heads and long, narrow bills pointing slightly upwards. Nervously, they paddled back and forward, criss-crossing, one behind the other. I looked up at Neil beside me. He was totally absorbed, his eyes intense; leaning forward, his chin raised – just like the birds. Then we noticed that they were coming towards us.

Closer they came, silently over the still dark surface of the loch. Now I could see the identical dark plumage of their backs and the grey, corduroy striping from the crown of their heads to the nape of their necks. As one turned behind the other the sunlight lit up the blood-red triangle at its throat. All the time, as they approached us, weaving back and forward and compulsively dipping their heads into the water, they never made a sound. My left leg was uncomfortably bent below me but I held my breath and did not move. Eventually, they were so close I could see their ruby-red eyes. They were not the eyes of other birds, but tiny, piercing and perfectly round like the hard, glass eyes on a soft toy. They were the most mysterious and beautiful birds.

As if in agreement Neil and I turned our heads slowly towards each other. For one moment, something beyond words – Neil had none anyway – passed between us. Then it was gone as one of the birds lowered its head, stretched out its throat and gave an unearthly wail that raised the hairs on the back of my neck. That cry was so many things to me that I knew I would never fully understand. But I recognised a wail of anguish, a call from the dead and somehow the *language of that bleak landscape of unending moorland, lochs and sea. In unison, the birds turned away, raised their narrow wings and sped across the water. At the far end of the loch they rose again in unison and wheeled off into the air. We watched them until they were mere pinpoints, until they were just part of the sky, as if that was their real domain.*

After a few moments we got up and resumed our walk to the peat bank. The view from there, where we rejoined the others – and received sharp words for the state of our clothes – was breathtaking. Looking back down I could pick out the cottage among a cluster of others surrounded by the patchwork of fields, and beyond them I could see the sea and the beach with the boats. As most days, there was a little wind and large and scattered clouds were rushing across from west to east as if fleeing a dark and threatening line of cloud that crouched on the edge of the horizon. I lay on my back and watched the sky. For a moment everything was reversed. It was as if the sky was still and I was floating on the Earth, being carried off in the opposite direction.

"William!"

Uncle Bertie waved me over to help them to load the trailer. He was keen that we got the job done quickly.

We worked for more than an hour throwing the peat from a pile by the track into the trailer; grandma contenting herself with filling sacks with the smaller pieces. It was tiring work, especially for grandfather and grandma who were no longer used to such physical effort. To begin with, Neil worked as hard as anyone. Then he seemed to grow bored and began chucking the pieces of peat carelessly over the top of the trailer. Uncle Bertie remonstrated with him, but Neil just seemed to take it as a joke, laughing and chattering to himself. Then a lump of peat hit Uncle Bertie. He came around the trailer furious with Neil and was only stopped from hitting him with his cap by Aunt Ina. Instead therefore, he told Neil to fasten on the back gate of the trailer and to be sure to do it properly. It was just then, when the curtain of cloud reached the sun and the day suddenly darkened, that I understood why Uncle Bertie was in such a hurry.

Eventually, he declared that the trailer was full enough. While he roped the top the others set off down the track in the car. I remained, as I was allowed to return on the back of the tractor with Neil as far as the road. We stood on the bar hitch behind Uncle Bertie, clinging to the edge of the big rear mudguards. The tractor twisted and bucked as we came down the track as the first drops of rain began to fall.

Halfway down, one of the trailer wheels slipped off the track distorting the shape of the trailer. There was a loud bang and the back gate of the trailer must have swung open. I looked round and saw it dangling from its hinges on one side. Uncle Bertie cursed, stopped the tractor and we all got down and went around the back to see what had happened. We saw that half the peats had fallen out. Uncle Bertie looked at the catches on the gate and then turned to Neil, who was standing beside me hopping from one foot to the other. One of the catches could not have been securely fastened and the twisting movement of the trailer had worked it off. Much of the peat that we had spent so long loading now lay scattered on the track. We would have to load it all over again and now the rain, hanging like a grey sheet from the edge of the cloud, was fast approaching. Worse still, Uncle Bertie saw on inspection that the hinges of the gate were broken so that we would have to leave the scattered peat and trailer where they were until he could mend it.

He took off his cap, wiped his forehead with his sleeve and turned to Neil in frustration. "Doo's an idiot!" he shouted, taking a step towards him. Neil hung his head. "I telt dee." Neil said nothing. Uncle Bertie took another step and was now only a pace away from him. Neil was taller than Uncle Bertie by nearly a foot so that Uncle Bertie had to look up into his face. "Didna I tell dee to mak sure yon gate was secure? Didna I?"

Neil's eyes sought the ground to the left and right of Uncle Bertie to avoid catching his gaze. I could see he was frightened. I felt sympathy for him but could not understand his fear. The air turned cold and dark as we were enveloped in the shower that quickly turned into a downpour. Neil cowered and, as if in response, Uncle Bertie hit him across the face with his cap.

"Damn you, Neil!"

He turned away and Uncle Bertie swung his cap and hit him again and again on the head. "Damn you … damn you … damn you."

I just stood there not knowing what to do, not sure if I believed what was happening. The more Neil cowered, the harder Uncle Bertie hit him, until he was down on his knees and crying out unintelligibly. His black hair was plastered against his skull and rivulets ran down his face and neck. As it glanced off the top of Neil's head Uncle Bertie's cap flew out of his hand and skittered off the road into the ditch. He raised his arms and clenched his fists. "Du useless craitur at du is," he shouted down at Neil.

I watched him raise his leg and deliberately place the sole of his boot against Neil's shoulder as he squatted with his hands over his face. With a brutal shove he sent the grovelling boy-man rolling on his back on the dirty, wet track. They were both crying now: Neil in fear and Uncle Bertie in anger and frustration. I took a step towards them, but something held me back – it was Silver. He stood beside me, the collar of his coat turned up against the rain.

"No, matey. Ye got to take yer punishment like a man. Shiver me timbers ... if you don't discipline the crew ye get anarchy. And where would ye be then ... eh?"

"Whit am I going to do wi dee?" Uncle Bertie asked and began to kick Neil, half-heartedly, almost gently at first, then harder and harder. "Du'll be the daith o' me, Neil." Neil curled his body away from the blows, he was whimpering like a dog and his hands were clasped protectively around his head. "Why does du torment me like dis?" Uncle Bertie seemed to become an automaton. He cursed, kicked and cried as if releasing a frustration that had been pent up for years. The rain was coming down in sheets and we were soaked, most of all Neil, lying on the track in a river of water.

"Uncle Bertie! Uncle Bertie!" I found myself shouting above his curses and Neil's howls. He didn't hear. Despite Silver's words, I grabbed a sleeve. "Uncle Bertie ... stop ... stop it!" He flung me off. And then I saw the blood on the back of Neil's hand where Uncle Bertie's boot had split the skin. Silver was standing behind Neil, looking at me and shaking his head, the rain running off his hat and a brown burn swirling around his buckled shoe.

"Bertie!"

Neither of us had noticed that the car had come back up the track.

"Bertie!" Aunt Ina shouted, as she brushed past me and flung herself between him and the prostrate Neil. "Oh Bertie ... what has du done dis time?" She knelt down, oblivious of the wet ground, and cradled Neil in her arms, crooning to him softly.

Uncle Bertie stood above them both as if he was in a trance. Water dripped off his nose and chin, his eyes were blank, his chest heaved and his arms hung limply at his sides. He gave a kind of groan and turned his head away.

Then grandfather's hand was on my shoulder, leading me towards the car, and only then did I realise how violently I was shaking. I climbed in and sat beside grandma and began to cry. Neil was such a harmless person. How could Uncle Bertie have done such a thing? Beyond the trailer, I could just see him standing like a statue in the pouring rain. And beyond him, Silver glanced down at his wet foot with disgust then turned away with a shrug of dismissal. Still shaking his head he swung his crutch and set off with resigned steps back up the track.

"Why did Uncle Bertie bully him?" I asked grandma, through my sobs.

"Shush … shush."

"But … why?"

"He didn't mean to."

I pulled myself out of her arms. "But he did, grandma, he did!" I said vehemently, "And I didn't do anything … Silver didn't do anything."

Grandma's arms tightened around me. "There's nothing you or … there's nothing you could have done, William. It's not your fault."

I sat there in her arms, listening to the rain drumming on the roof of the car. A door opened and grandfather squeezed in beside us. Then Aunt Ina was helping Neil into the front seat. She closed the door behind him then sat in the driver's seat. Their clothes were sodden. Neil slumped against the door. As Aunt Ina turned the car I wiped the moisture off the window and looked out. Uncle Bertie was unhitching the trailer.

Later that day at tea there was a constrained silence. Aunt Ina had taken Neil to Magnus' house and I gathered that the doctor had been to check that he was alright. When the adults spoke to each other it seemed to be with exaggerated politeness. I avoided Uncle Bertie's eye and he seemed to be avoiding everyone else's. No one spoke about Neil and I knew enough to know that I should not raise the subject either. In the silence after the meal I fetched Moby Dick and my storybook and curled myself into a small chair in the corner of the kitchen until bedtime.

Years later, I learned from grandfather that there had been a family discussion that evening after I had gone to bed, for this had not been the first time that Uncle Bertie had hit Neil. Grandma had wanted to leave with me before anything worse happened. She had told the others how I had alluded to Silver in the car. Grandfather and Aunt Ina had persuaded her to wait a few more days to allow them to carry out a plan they had. Aunt Ina had also made Uncle Bertie promise them that he would not lift a finger against Neil again.

The day after the event at the peats we were all working out in the fields again, Neil included, as though nothing had happened. Except that Neil had red marks on his face, a bandage on his left hand and he *was very subdued. Uncle Bertie was turning hay and we were helping with long-handled rakes whose wooden teeth were thicker than my thumbs. At the bottom of the field where the ground was damp, the grass, which was full of different kinds of yellow, red and white flowers, had been left uncut. Grandfather said that soon the cows would be allowed into it to graze, but in the meantime, if I listened I would hear the corncrake that hid there. I never saw it but there was no mistaking its rasping call: it was like the sound of a key turning in a rusty old clock.*

Grandfather suggested we take a break and sit down by the fence, but first he sent me off to get the small milk pail of water and cup from the top of the field. When I returned he had spread his old jacket on the ground and was sitting on it, leaning against a fence post and filling his pipe. I sat down beside him and we shared some water between us. Then he lit his pipe, always the prelude to a story: it runs in the family.

He looked into the distance, rubbed the back of his neck with his free hand and then turned to me. "I don't know how much of this you will understand, but you ought to know it." He put his hand on my knee and shook my leg in a compassionate way, to emphasise a trust between us. "If you ever mention this to anyone, I want you to think very carefully first. In fact, I don't think Aunt Ina and Uncle Bertie, maybe even grandma, would want you to know." He drew on his pipe and let out a long stream of smoke.

"Before Uncle Bertie and Aunt Ina married, Uncle Bertie already had a child."

"Neil?"

"That's right. But it was a difficult birth, Neil ... was damaged ... and his mother died ... bringing him into this world."

Grandfather fiddled with his pipe and looked up towards the others who had also sat down for a rest. I could see that he was undecided as to what else he was going to tell me.

"You have to understand that Uncle Bertie and Neil's mother were not married."

I knew of no people who had children who were not married so I knew only that this was strange and possibly wrong. I nodded my head in response but it just seemed to make grandfather deliberate a little longer.

"Everyone was very critical of Uncle Bertie, but when he married Aunt Ina they raised Neil as their own." He looked at me and then over my head at the others again. I could tell that he was looking at Uncle

Bertie and Neil. "Imagine. Every time Uncle Bertie sees Neil … he is reminded of that tragedy."

I sensed that he was trying to explain to me why Uncle Bertie had beaten Neil. It was like the sky on the hill yesterday. I had imagined that good and bad were as distinct as the blue sky and the dark clouds; that the sky moved and the earth stood still, now suddenly, everything was confused. Uncle Bertie had done a terrible thing – and I didn't want to think that he had done it before or, worse still, might do it again – and yet he was loved by grandfather and grandma, and by such a special person as Aunt Ina.

"Neil's really a kind of uncle to you."

He ruffled my hair and stroked my head, his cheerful tone breaking my train of thought.

"Be good to him … and forgiving to Uncle Bertie."

A question suddenly entered my head from nowhere. "Did mummy and daddy know Neil?"

Grandfather's hand jumped off my head.

"What a question!" Then he put his arm around me and drew me against him. He smelled warm, a mixture of tobacco and the sweet scent of hay. "Yes, William … your dad played with Neil when we came here for summer holidays. The year they were married, he and your mummy stayed here and took Neil all over Shetland." I hadn't thought of my parents for such a long time, but thinking of them now made me feel safe and loved.

A narrow shadow fell across us. Involuntarily, I shivered, and grandfather tightened his embrace. It was like the shadow of a crutch, but when I turned to face it I saw it was the handle of a hay-rake. Grandma leaned on it and looked down on me with a smile on her face.

When I was on my own I tried to think about Uncle Bertie, Neil and Aunt Ina and about what had happened: how such a person as Aunt Ina could love a man like Uncle Bertie and how grandfather could be so forgiving? I was puzzled.

For the rest of that holiday I got on very well with Neil, we even had some laughs together, though he always went over the top. Poor Neil.

Bill got up in the afternoon and took his typewriter through to the kitchen where he sat down at the opposite end of the table to Tom, whose half-finished sketches littered its surface. Nausea and pain from near the base of his spine were gripping him in an embrace that he knew would never slacken. He had taken all the tablets that had been prescribed and even increased the dose as had been recommended if the pain got too much. The trouble was it made him drowsy and he knew that if he stayed in bed he would just fall asleep. He wanted to finish the story before he lost the desire and will to write. Tom would have to return home, perhaps tomorrow. Yes, he must arrange for Tom to leave tomorrow afternoon.

He shuffled back to the bedroom with the questioning eyes of Tom on his back and sat down by the telephone. He did not feel able to phone the airport himself so he phoned Magnus and asked him to book a seat for Tom. He also asked him if he would drive them to Sumburgh. Magnus queried if Bill was not going south himself? Bill said 'no, he wasn't'. But he asked Magnus if he would take them up to the lighthouse first, before Tom left.

Bill sat and waited by the phone. Fifteen minutes later Magnus phoned back and confirmed that he would pick them up at twelve o'clock: Tom's plane was not until four-thirty.

Next, Bill dialled Alistair's number. He did not yet know what he was going to say to him. But it was Cat who answered.

"Hello?"

Bill took a deep breath. "Hi, Catriona, it's Bill here."

"Bill! We were just wondering about you and Tom. When are you coming back … I'm missing my wee boy. How is he?"

"Fine … fine. Tom's going on the plane tomorrow."

"Going … ?"

"Well," he hesitated, "I'm staying on." And to try and forestall the question, "Can you meet him at the airport at six-thirty?"

"Yes, yes of course, but why aren't you coming back, Bill?"

He heard Alistair's voice in the background and the mouthpiece being muzzled while Cat relayed the message. He couldn't hear what she was saying. Then Alistair took the phone.

"Dad. What's this about you not coming back?"

He steeled himself. "Hello, Alistair. I was just saying to Cat that Tom will be on the plane tomorrow afternoon."

"I got that, dad. I'm asking why you are not coming back tomorrow?"

"Oh, I just fancy staying on for a wee bit longer." There was silence. "You don't mind do you?" He stared at the manuscript papers on his desk, unconsciously moving them around with his left hand and praying that Alistair would be satisfied. But he wasn't.

"How much longer, dad? You're not thinking of staying there now are you … after all the arrangements we have made? You know you would be better off here."

Bill pictured them in their living room. The questioning looks that were flying back and forwards between them. Typical of Alistair, he thought, to jump to a conclusion and the wrong one at that. He could hear Cat in the background now.

"No, Alistair, I'm not planning to stay here for good." Well, it wasn't exactly a lie, but he bit his tongue. He had so wanted to have a reasonable conversation with Alistair, but here they were winding each other up as usual. "I'm not quite sure though for how long." Another silence. He softened his voice. "You don't mind too much, do you?"

Alistair took a breath and responded in kind. "I suppose not. You do what you want and we'll look forward to seeing you back here when you are ready."

"Thanks," Bill said. He heard the tiredness in his own voice and knew instinctively that Alistair had heard it too.

"You alright, dad?"

In that fraction of a second as he formulated his reply, Bill knew that Alistair was not going to believe him, but neither was he going to press him for the truth. In that less-than-moment a trust was established between them.

"Fine … fine … got a bit of a cold that's all."

Alistair spoke very quietly. "Well … you just let us know if there is anything you want … anything we can do."

"Of course, of course."

Then they returned to safer ground.

"What time did you say Thomas would be at Edinburgh?"

"Six-thirty. It's the direct flight. I'll make sure he's looked after."

"Okay, dad. Give our love to Thomas and tell him we're looking forward to seeing him and hearing all about his holiday."

"I will, I will. By the way … Tom has been doing a lot drawing here. Did you know he's quite good at it?"

"Thomas … drawing?"

"Yes."

"I didn't know Thomas could draw." Alistair turned to Cat and Bill could just hear him, "Did you know Thomas drew?" he asked her. There was a muffled casual affirmation.

"You should encourage him, Alistair. I think he has inherited his grandmother's talent."

"D'you think so?"

"I do." Bill waited for a real sign of interest.

"Well, maybe we should do something about it."

"I think you should, Alistair. He needs some proper tuition." Bill closed his eyes and made a silent prayer.

"Okay, dad … I got the message."

"Promise?"

"Promise?"

"Yes, promise!"

"Okay, I promise."

He turned his eyes to the ceiling. "Thanks, Alistair, thanks. Well I'd better get Tom packed, he'll be excited. Goodbye just now, son."

"Goodbye, dad."

Bill sat for a long time with his hand on the telephone as if reluctant to finally break the contact with his son. He turned in the chair and looked out of the window. The gale had passed on, the wind had dropped and the rain almost ceased. Some sheep emerged tentatively around the corner of the house, checking the exposure. Beyond them there were breaks in the clouds on the horizon promising an end to the grey sky. In the absence of the wind, the rolling surge of the swell rinsing the shingle beach now resumed its place as the dominant background sound.

At last he took his hand away from the phone and to ease the pain called out to his grandson. "Tom!"

Tom strolled through from the kitchen. "Yes."

"What about a … "

"… Cup of coffee?"

"Right on."

He leaned against the door. "Grandpa, that's ancient!"

"Oh," he muttered, disappointedly.

"Who were you talking to?"

Bill stood up with difficulty and stretched. "You make the coffee and I'll tell you."

They went back to the kitchen and Bill sat at the table while Tom put on the kettle. A shaft of sunlight burst through the window bringing a feeling of warmth back into the room.

Bill tried to make himself comfortable on the hard kitchen chair. "I was speaking to your dad."

Tom turned quickly. "Oh … I wanted to speak to him."

Bill acknowledged his error. "I'm sorry … of course you did." He stretched out an arm towards Tom. "But you'll see him tomorrow anyway."

Tom's face lit up. "Tomorrow … wicked! Is he coming up, then?"

"No … actually, you're going home."

Tom's face fell and then he looked perplexed. "But why?"

"Well, you can't stay up here all the time … and anyway, your mum and dad want to see you."

But Tom knew those weren't the reasons.

"Are you not coming, grandad?"

The kettle boiled and he turned away and poured the hot water into the cafetière. Once again Bill did not know how much to say, this time to Tom.

"No. I'm staying, Tom."

Tom was stirring the coffee with a wooden spoon, his head was bent and he spoke as if it was unimportant. "Aren't you coming back?" They both knew he meant 'at all'?

"No … no, Tom, I'm not coming back." There, he had said it.

Tom carried the cafetière over to the table, put it down and, as he turned to fetch a mug, threw out another oblique question. "What did dad say?"

Bill sighed, folded his arms as if he was cold, and stroked his chin. He waited until Tom was standing by the table in front of him, had poured out his coffee and until he lifted his eyes from the mug and looked at him. He put out a hand, covered one of Tom's that was flat on the table in front of him and looked up into his face. "Tom. Your dad doesn't know that I won't be coming back. Can we keep that a secret … between us?"

Tom gave the briefest of nods.

"You're ill, grandad, aren't you?"

This time Bill nodded in reply and tried to smile.

"I'm old, Tom … its natural."

"No it's not!" He turned away with tears in his eyes at the unfairness of it.

"Tom … Tom, come here." And he held out his arms.

Tom stumbled into his grandad's embrace. "It's not fair … it's not fair, grandad."

Bill stroked Tom's head. Hot tears fell freely onto his neck. "Things aren't always fair, Tom."

For several moments, with tightly closed eyes, Tom held his grandad fiercely as his body shook with sobs then abruptly he pulled himself free. "I'll stay with you."

Bill held him at arm's length, gripping him above the elbows, his hands encompassing Tom's thin arms. He squeezed the small muscles to emphasise the finality of the decision. "You can't, Tom … you can't." He smiled proudly. "But thanks for the offer. That means a lot to me. Thank you." Bill kept smiling at his grandson until he was forced to smile in return. "Listen … we've got quite a few things to do before tomorrow and then Magnus is going to take us to the lighthouse at Sumburgh … where the story ends and … "

"We've got to look for Uncle Bertie's yoal." Tom interrupted.

"Yes, yes of course," Bill answered, "and then you have to catch your plane. But right now," he said, changing the subject, "I want to see your sketches."

Tom was relieved to be diverted from thoughts of his grandad's mortality and eagerly pulled together the sketches scattered on the far end of the kitchen table and brought them around to Bill.

"Here's one of the broch on Mousa, but I'm not very good at drawing ponies."

"Well, life drawing is particularly difficult … it will take time."

"This one of Peter's boat I like. I don't think I've got the shape of it quite right?"

"Not bad at all. I think you should give it to him."

"Would he want it d'you think?"

"I think he would be proud to have it," said Bill, holding it up and turning it so that the light from the window fell on it.

"Would you like one?" Tom asked tentatively.

"Yes, I would."

"Which?"

Bill sorted through the small pile of sketches. There was one of the cottage drawn from the same perspective as his favourite by Alice.

"Can I have this one?"

"Yes."

They left the connection unspoken but understood.

"I want it signed, of course."

Tom took his pencil and, with an exaggerated flourish, scribbled his signature on the bottom of the drawing.

"And the date," added his grandad.

He wrote the date and handed the sketch to Bill, who accepted it graciously.

"Now you'd better tidy the rest away in your folder."

As Tom tidied up, Bill casually said, "By the way, when I spoke to your mum and dad I mentioned your drawing."

Tom looked up. "And … ?"

"I think, just maybe, that your dad may help you."

"Really?"

"Yes … really, but remember what I said … "

"Be patient?"

Bill nodded his head. "Just let him get used to the idea and give him a reason to trust you. Don't neglect your other studies … will you?"

"Thanks, grandad, oh, thanks a billion." And he turned for the door with a skip in his step, threw up an arm and shouted, "Yes … yes … yes!"

"Tom!"

There was something else. He turned.

"D'you remember when we sat in the garden at home and you asked me to call you Tom and not Thomas?"

"Yes … "

"Do *me* a favour, will you? Call me Bill."

Tom grinned in the doorway and in his best grown-up manner said, "Okay … Bill." Then he turned and climbed the stairs to the bedroom, clutching his folder of drawings and practising under his breath. "Bill … Bill … Bill."

"And pack your clothes!" his grandad shouted.

"Right, Bill."

Bill laughed and it set him coughing for a moment. Then he picked up his typewriter and made for his bedroom.

"I'm going back to bed, Tom. You can heat a tin of soup for supper if you want."

Later, after supper, when Tom came through to say goodnight, he found Bill propped up in bed with the typewriter on his lap and his yellow woolly hat on his head to keep himself warm.

"I hope I won't keep you awake, but I want to finish the story tonight."

Tom shrugged, "I've got a book to read anyway."

"Goodnight, Tom."

"Goodnight, Bill."

CHAPTER *13*

'Somehow I knew that I was destined to be here.'

*M*agnus drove with his usual slow deliberation through a landscape that was emerging from under a rising mist like a living, breathing thing, still and exhausted from the gales of yesterday. To Tom it suddenly seemed as if he had been here forever. Everything that had been so strange and new when he had arrived was now friendly and familiar. Now he anticipated the scene around every corner of the narrow winding road through fields and over moorland hills; now he looked for the figures to wave to; now he recognised the bobbing redshank in the ditch and the mellifluous call of the whimbrel over the heather. He felt his chest tighten with longing, as, from a vantage point in the road, they looked over bare and rolling hills pocketed with lochs of every size and shape, at the long fingers of sea that penetrated deep into the land, at distant cliffs and islands and at the line of the horizon where the sky met the ocean. Sitting in the back seat with his rucksack and bag, and clutching his folder, or portfolio as his grandad insisted he called it, he pressed his face against the window and vowed to come back.

They had the best part of the afternoon before the plane left so Magnus took them first to Longdale where he was born and where Bill's great-aunt and uncle, and of course Neil, had lived. It seemed to Tom as if this was where he had come in, as Bill and Magnus once again regretted the changes that had transformed the traditional strip-fields of barley, oats, potatoes, rye grass and neeps, tethered cows and ponies, into a monoculture of silage, or grass grazed to the quick by too many sheep and strewn with the litter of their discarded wool.

Magnus parked the car above the beach and they made their way past the flat-roofed shed and through a tired old wooden gate tied to its supports at both ends by blue, sea-bleached ropes. Unlike the sheltered and circular bay at

Sandness, this was a short and narrow geo, the tiny beach protected only by the red shoulders of ancient granite cliffs. The burn that filtered through the wetland at the foot of the fields debouched here, wide and shallow, dashing and dancing over the pebbles in its eagerness to reach the sea.

Magnus led the way, untying and lifting the gate aside as if by his little finger and Bill followed clumsily, leaning with his hand on Tom's shoulder.

"I've no been doon here for a peerie while." Magnus pointed to a little concrete slipway on the edge of the beach. "Somebody's been making some improvements."

Above the slip, propped upright on a couple of triangular wooden frames, sat a Shetland-model boat with a modified transom to take an outboard. But when they looked to the top of the beach beyond that, to where the ground rose into a sheltering bank, cut back to form the boat nousts, there was only one occupied. Silently they approached it.

It was a yoal alright, but one that would never float on the sea again, except as driftwood.

"Is this it?" asked Tom

Magnus ran his huge hands along the gunwale. "No." He turned to Bill. "Does du mind aald Jimmie … Jimmie o' da Brake?"

Bill shook his head.

"Dis was his boat." He pointed to the first of the five other empty nousts, "Dat's where Bertie's boat used to bide."

Above the empty noust, silhouetted against the sky was a rusty iron frame, as tall as Tom, with rollers and a large wheel with four curved spokes.

"Well, well," said Bill, as he turned to Tom, "I remember me and Magnus trying to turn that wheel to pull the boat up … the night we saw the killer whales."

"Du minds dat?" said Magnus, recalling the massive bodies and fins of the whales so close to the boat.

"Mind it! I will never forget it."

For a moment the pair of them relived the excitement of that childhood boat trip and then Tom reminded them of one of the others in the boat that evening.

"Bill, what happened to Neil? You never told me."

Magnus couldn't help but smile at Tom's familiarity and raised an eyebrow at Bill who gave the faintest of shrugs. Then his smile slowly dissolved as Bill searched for words. The question seemed to take some of the remaining strength out of him. He half-turned and leaned his weight against the flaking stem of the ruined boat. His head bowed. He brought it up with an effort and looked squarely at Tom.

"There was a terrible accident … on the cliffs." His hands clutched the gunwale and he gesticulated with his head towards the mouth of the geo. "Apparently a sheep got stuck. Bertie took some rope and Neil to help him." Bill looked at Magnus and Tom saw that it was not for assistance in recalling the event nor for confirmation of the truth, but for some other reason that he could not put his finger on.

"Something happened, we don't know what, but Bertie fell off the cliff and was killed." He continued to look at Magnus, who held his eye. "Nobody could get any sense out of Neil, not even Ina. His mind seemed to have broken down completely and they had to put him in an institution."

Tom struggled to understand. "Poor Neil."

Bill pushed himself upright again and Tom watched him and Magnus closely for clues. "Yes, poor Neil," Bill said, "but it was Ina who really suffered." He looked again at Magnus. "It broke her spirit." Magnus nodded. "She was never the same woman again." He stared at the empty noust.

"Bairns," said Magnus, breaking the uncomfortable silence. "If we're geng to Sumburgh Head afore Tom checks in at the airport, we'd better get a move on." He strode off towards the gate leaving no opening for further discussion. Bill and Tom followed.

> "Wid du laek to see inside a lighthouse?"
>
> I thought of the light above my bed at home and of the Bell Rock. "Yes, oh, yes please."
>
> Ina exchanged a glance with grandfather that I just caught but could not interpret, and between them for a fleeting moment was Silver, rubbing his chin. "I'm sure cousin Wullie at Sumburgh will let us in. I'll give him a phone and maybe we can go later today."
>
> It was the early evening of a couple of days later, however, before cousin Wullie, one of the lightkeepers at Sumburgh, was free to take us around. Uncle Bertie was busy that day, grandma did not want to come for some reason but grandfather did. It all seemed very casual, but I knew from something in their behaviour that this was all rehearsed and arranged between them. Aunt Ina drove with grandfather in the front and I sat in the back holding onto the cord to prevent myself sliding all over the seat. It was the first time I had watched her drive and she drove just as she did everything – upright and formal, but she was not very good at the gears and they made an awful noise. I could see that grandfather was deliberately staring out of his window each time she changed as if he was totally absorbed in something else … only the regular stiffening of his neck betrayed his discomfort. Aunt Ina, on the other hand, made no comment other than her general announcement as

we left the cottage – "I'm maybe no mechanically minded Jim, but be assured that I am a safe driver."

Magnus drove them past the airport to the end of the public road, across a cattle-grid and up the unfenced road towards the lighthouse on Sumburgh Head. Bill would have liked to have walked up to the lighthouse with Tom, as he had done fifty years ago with grandfather and Aunt Ina, but he knew that was no longer possible. He was curious to find that there was now a car park where they had once stopped. It was very busy and groups of people were looking at information boards and over the cliffs at the seabird colonies.

> *Ina drove a couple of miles over rough roads until they reached the main tarmacadamed road to the south end of Shetland. The last piece of the road climbed a hill so that when they reached its summit they overlooked the sandy isthmus which was the runway of the airport and the link to Sumburgh Head. This southernmost headland, crowned by the white buildings and tower of the lighthouse itself, rose about two miles ahead of them to the south-east. At a similar distance to the south-west, the land swept up over 800 feet to form a mile long ridge that hid a huge cliff on its seaward side.*
>
> *They descended the hill to Sumburgh and followed the road across the isthmus before beginning the climb up to the headland as the setting sun dropped below the level of the great cliffs to the west. The sandy pastures behind the dunes were full of the mauves and yellows of vetches and trefoils, but as the road wound its way up the headland these were replaced by scattered carpets of fading sea-pinks. As they reached the midway point in the climb the low rays of the sun reappeared creating a faint blush on the white walls of the lighthouse.*
>
> *Ina pulled off the road onto the grass and switched off the engine, it shuddered for a moment and then was silent. We gazed at the red ball of the dying sun and at the enormously long shadows on the landscape that the low light threw towards us. The door handle on the driver's door clunked loudly and Aunt Ina stepped out. She beckoned to me through the open door.*
>
> *"William. I've got something to show you."*
>
> *Grandfather, with his arm around the back of his seat, gestured to me to get out. I pulled the door lever in the wooden frame below the window, stepped out and stood beside Aunt Ina looking down on the isthmus of sand from the opposite end to which I had first seen it from the hill on the road. Aunt Ina pointed to the roofless ruins of a house set among other older ruins that we must have passed on the way but which I had not noticed.*

"*Jarlshof.*"

I stared at it for a moment before I remembered ... of course. "*Magnus Troil's house?*"

"*The very one,*" *she answered in the sombre tone of Sir Walter Scott's* The Pirate. "*Now, what else might we see from that novel?*"

I looked up and she smiled encouragingly at me before scanning the horizon as if searching for something. She seemed very tall so close beside me. I looked around too but it was my memory I was searching. The headland ...

"*Captain Cleveland was rescued by M ... Mor ... Oh, I can never remember his name.*"

"*Mordaunt Mertoun.*" *She put her hand up to her mouth and exclaimed,* "*Or was it the other way round – Mertoun Mordaunt? I can never remember.*" *She put her hand on my shoulder and laughed quietly.* "*It's such a silly name onyway.*"

I had never heard an adult speak of Scott so lightly and looked up at her in disbelief. Then I saw her, and something else in her face that I could not quite understand, in a new light. It was as if I was looking at something that I had, as yet, no name for.

"*And that,*" *she pointed at the long, high cliff behind which the sun was setting,* "*is Fitful Head, where Norna lived.*"

She swung me round and pointed to the cliffs beyond the lighthouse. "*Over there, somewhere, was where Captain Cleveland's ship was wrecked.*" *Her hands slipped off my shoulder and around my arms, drawing me close to her as she stood behind me.* "*You know ... I always found Captain Cleveland far mair interesting than Mr Mertoun. Noo, if I had been the heroine I know which one I wid hae chosen!*"

My jaw dropped and I looked at her open-mouthed.

"*It's often the dubious characters that are mair exciting ... don't you think? And mair human too.*"

I didn't know what to say, but I was thinking of Silver and Alan Breck and suddenly realising that they were a little like Captain Cleveland. Did that mean Aunt Ina preferred them ... like me ... it was almost unthinkable. I looked at her tentatively. She gave me a long stare in return. Her lips were clamped together as if she was struggling with inner thought, but her eyes told me that her full attention was turned on me. It was nice but a little scary!

"*What do you mean ... more human?*"

She glanced over my head at grandfather and then back at me and when she spoke I knew that she was choosing her words very carefully.

"Sometimes the heroes of stories are just too good to be true." She searched the sky above my head. "In reality we all have weaknesses … we all make mistakes." Her eyes held me again. "That's why we can't really believe in characters laek Mordaunt Mertoun and therefore the whole story." She paused. "He's too good to be true. But we can believe in … and love … characters laek …"

The answer emerged from me unbidden, as a whisper, "Long John Silver."

"Exactly!"

My mind was in a whirl trying to tease out the meaning of her words and my reply.

Then she spoke again, this time in a much more light-hearted manner. "Did du know that Robert Louis Stevenson read The Pirate when he was a boy but dat he never finished it?"

I shook my head.

He called it an 'ill-written, ragged book'.

I looked at grandfather still sitting in the car. He made a face, shrugged and smiled. We were all smiling at each other now. A burst of laughter welled out of me and Aunt Ina and grandfather joined in. Behind Aunt Ina in the gathering darkness I was suddenly aware of the light blinking from the lighthouse.

We left the car where Aunt Ina had stopped, as the last part of the road up to the top of Sumburgh Head and the lighthouse was steep, narrow and winding, and she did not feel confident of getting the car up. We walked slowly, stopping every now and again for grandfather and to look over the wall that was built on the very edge of the cliffs, to watch the sad and comical puffins and the noisy kittiwakes. Eventually, we reached the lighthouse buildings. They were all painted white, squat and flat-roofed – to collect water I learned later – and I was a little disappointed to find that the lighthouse itself was no higher than the one on the Isle of May. But it was still like the living thing that had lit my bedroom wall for as long as I could remember and I wanted to see the heart of it.

As Bill had requested, Magnus dropped them right up by the lighthouse buildings and promised to return in an hour to take them back to the airport. The light was automatic and unmanned, but to Tom's surprise there were lots of people there, many with binoculars. A woman grabbed Bill's arm as he and Tom made for a viewpoint. She had a rucksack on her back and a baseball hat on her head. In her free hand she held a tiny pair of binoculars. She whispered to them, sotto voce. "D'you mind going round?" She pointed to a flock of small, green, parrot-like birds that were eating seed scattered on the ground ahead of them.

"Oh ... what are they?" Tom whispered back.

"Crossbills ... from Scandinavia ... they had an irruption this year."

"Eruption?" exclaimed Tom.

Bill nodded to the woman and guided Tom away. "Irruption ... probably an exceptional breeding year and therefore lots of young birds. They've had to move on to find food." He bent down to Tom's eye level and pointed to one that was close enough for them to be able to see its crossed bill.

"Wow, poor thing."

"No, you idiot ... their bills have evolved into that shape ... to pick the seeds out of pine cones."

Tom made a face, grinning at his mistake. Then he turned to Bill. "What're they doing here, then?"

"Well, they were probably making their way south in Norway and got blown across the North Sea ... happens quite a lot."

"What'll they do now?"

Bill pointed to the birdseed that had been spread on the ground. "When they've finished that they'll have to move on south and find some pine seed. Anyway," he said leading Tom to the viewpoint, "I want to show you some things."

"If you ever read *The Pirate* by Sir Walter Scott ... and I don't recommend it ... you'll find that some of the action takes place here." He put an arm around Tom's shoulder and explained the significance of Jarlshof and Fitful Head. Then he took him to the very end of the headland where the lighthouse, like a white exclamation mark, rose to mark the southernmost tip of the Shetland mainland. Finding a convenient flat stone by the retaining wall, Bill lowered himself onto it and leaned against the wall. He turned his face away from Tom to hide a grimace of pain. He gestured for Tom to sit beside him. They sat there in the sunshine with their backs to the view and the seabirds, and stared up at the lighthouse. A man turned from watching the seabirds to follow their gaze. He searched the top of the lighthouse with his binoculars, looked at the old man and the boy briefly and turned back to watch a bonxie sprinting across the waves after a fleeing puffin.

> Cousin Wullie met us at the door and took us in. Everything was painted and shiny, even the floor. Cousin Wullie was round like Uncle Bertie and wore blue trousers and a blue jersey with the letters N.L.B. stitched in white on his chest. He had a rag in one hand. For a few moments we stood in a circle while I was introduced and grandfather and cousin Wullie got reacquainted. I gazed at the iron stairway that circled

up the wall and disappeared through the ceiling. It drew me so strongly that I found myself ascending it before asking anyone's permission.

The steps took me up to the next floor which was bare. From there a second iron staircase took me up to another floor, the centre of which was taken up by the enclosed machinery of the light. At this level there was a short wooden ladder that led through the thick wall to a door to the outside and a steep iron ladder inside that led upwards. Climbing the ladder I emerged onto the floor of the light itself. It sat in the middle and there was just enough room for me to walk around it, between it and the glass wall. It was like nothing I had ever seen or imagined. I circled the light, astonished at its fragility and the silent manner in which the whole structure slowly revolved. The shell of the structure was four vertical lenses as tall as myself and enclosed within these were myriads of glass crystals. I had expected that this close I would be blinded by the light. It was a wonder to me that the insignificant looking bulb at the very centre could possibly send a beam of light for miles across the sea. I could hardly believe that the light that lit up my bedroom nightly had a source so complicated and yet so benign as this, but it was somehow comforting that it did.

"'Tis a wonderful thing, lad." He stood on the other side of the light looking through it at me and scratching his head. "Beyond me, matey. If I were to try and explain this to me poor old mother, bless her, she would think I had been marooned too long among the savages."

"Silver."

"Aye, lad?" He shuffled uncomfortably towards me around the narrow space between the light and the outer circular glass walls.

I was still thinking of Aunt Ina's remark about Captain Cleveland. He was a wicked pirate like Silver … and yet … she seemed to like him, just as I liked, and rather feared, Silver. Were neither as bad as I thought? If not, how bad was I? Maybe I wasn't bad after all. I knew I wanted to ask Silver something, but I didn't know what it was. I sniffed hard as unbidden tears began to form in my eyes, and then Silver was down on his knee beside me pulling out a large red handkerchief from his coat pocket and wiping my eyes.

"Hey, matey … only old pirates cry."

Then we heard the footsteps of the others ringing on the iron steps.

"Time for me to stow me gear with another crew, I think." He winked, struggled to his foot, patted me on the head and vanished.

"Ah, there du is, William," said cousin Wullie as he emerged at the top. He was followed by Aunt Ina who gave me a concerned glance and then by grandfather who was breathing hard from the climb and seemed a little apprehensive.

Aunt Ina's head turned this way and that as she stared out of the windows rapturously. "What a grand view du has here, Wullie ... and to think dat du keeps it all to yourself."

"Widna be room to move if I telt everybody, Ina." The three stood looking out, ignoring the light itself, and I realised then that I hadn't looked outside at all.

Grandfather leaned on the rail around the glass. "You know, I've seen lighthouses all over the world, but I think this is the very first time I have ever been inside one."

Their attention swung from the view to the light while mine took the other direction. I could hear cousin Wullie explaining the mechanism to the others but I was now as entranced with the view as Aunt Ina. The sun was setting and daylight was fading. I could just discern the beam of light from behind me as it swept across the sea on three quadrants, and over Fitful Head and the South Mainland of Shetland on the fourth. It was the nearest thing I could imagine to being in the crowsnest. The world was spread out around me, unimpeded. The line of the horizon, where the roof of puffy pink clouds met the sea, stretched in a long arc some thirty miles away. The swell was coming from the south towards the headland so that I had the impression of the lighthouse and myself advancing through it towards the horizon. I felt I could stretch my wings and fly from there.

"Did du hear dat?" Aunt Ina's voice broke into my thoughts.

I shook my head and looked at cousin Wullie who had been speaking.

"I wis just saying to your Aunt Ina dat we are probably standing on the very spot where Sir Walter Scott once stood."

"He was here, in the lighthouse?"

"Yes, he cam as a guest on the Lighthouse Yacht wi the Lighthouse Commissioners. Dey hed aboot ten o a crew and cerried six guns." He pointed through the glass to the bay on the western side of the sandy isthmus that now lay in deep shadow. "Dey anchored doon dere an climbed up here to inspect the light."

"Dat was when he collected the information that he used in The Pirate," interrupted Aunt Ina.

So, Sir Walter Scott had stood here.

"And," interjected grandfather, "they had with them the Chief Engineer to the Commissioners, the man who built this lighthouse and the Bell Rock and ... " he turned to me " ... the same man who built the Isle of May light!"

"*So he would have stood on this spot many times too,*" added Aunt Ina.

I looked from one to the other trying to see what they were getting at, for they were surely getting at something. It was a strange feeling to know that the man who had constructed the Isle of May light – the nightly light above my bed that had come to mean so much to me – had built this too and that I could almost be standing in his shoes. But there was more to this, I knew there was.

Cousin Wullie excused himself and moved off down the ladder to attend to his duties while grandfather and Aunt Ina looked at each other and me, as if for clues.

Grandfather looked out through the glass. "*The chief engineer's name was Robert Stevenson and he was the first of three generations of Stevensons who devoted their lives to building lighthouses throughout Scotland.*" *He turned from the window and looked down at me.* "*He was Robert Louis' grandfather.*"

I felt a curious tingle of excitement as I looked at my grandfather and felt the distant but very real connection with Robert Louis.

Grandfather continued. "*Not only that, William, but Robert Stevenson's son … and Robert Louis' father … Thomas Stevenson, was also a lighthouse engineer employed by the Lighthouse Commissioners and Robert Louis sometimes accompanied him on his inspections. In fact we know he accompanied his father to Shetland … so Robert Louis himself … has stood on this very spot!*"

He was watching me for a reaction but no prompting was needed. My heart hesitated and then thumped so hard in my chest I thought it would burst. So the creator of my best hero had stood here. Had walked up these stairs, touched this light and looked out on this scene just as I was doing. Unconsciously my fingers caressed the rail in front of me as a welter of thoughts and sensations passed through my mind like shooting stars. Somehow I knew that I was destined to be here … maybe I could really be a writer too … Robert Louis had said he *had never been able to finish* The Pirate *… Silver was not above breaking the law but he was also a loyal friend … what had Aunt Ina said … that such characters were human … we all have weaknesses?*

I stared out of the lighthouse over the sea. Only a narrow pink band remained on the horizon and there was just enough light to see the tops of the waves almost all the way to it. I was aware of grandfather and Aunt Ina leaving me and descending the ladder.

Then it hit me. Grandfather … and Aunt Ina … knew all about my … stupid acts … mistakes … whatever they were … and my pain … and didn't hold them against me. I was just the same as everyone else. All the guilt that had accumulated in me that I had carried around and that had shaped my every move, hindered my every step, could be discarded. I felt as if a huge weight was being lifted off me.

I watched the beam of light sweep from the end of the Sumburgh rocks across the greying sea towards Fitful Head. For the briefest of moments it illuminated a little boat with a sail and a figure in the stern with his hand on the tiller. He turned towards me as the sail filled, bearing him away. The other hand was in the air holding a tri-cornered hat, waving.

The next time the beam came round he was gone.

"Are you okay?"

It was the woman with the baseball hat. Her face was very close to his. Bill looked around and saw the figure of a small boy with his back to him peering over the wall. He was familiar.

"I said, are you okay, sir?"

She had an American accent that he hadn't noticed earlier, and that unnerving and disarming American politeness.

He took a deep breath as he regained his senses. "Must have fallen asleep. Thank you, I'm fine."

"You don't look very well, sir."

"Ah … well … it's just a touch of vertigo." Then, added as an afterthought, "Had it for years." He smiled weakly at her and held out his hand to request a help up.

"Maybe you shouldn't have come up here?"

"No, no … it was the making of me."

"Pardon me?"

"I'm okay, really." He pointed to Tom. "I'm with my grandson. He'll look after me."

"Well … if you … "

But he broke away from her and walked over to Tom. "Hey, how long was I asleep for?"

Tom turned. "Not very long. You looked so tired I just left you." He took Bill's arm and made him look out over the wall. "It's a great view … a man told me that sometimes you can see whales from here."

They stood side by side looking out over the wide expanse of sea.

"Grandad … Bill … you said this is where the story ended."

"I did." And as he spoke he turned his head and saw Magnus by the car waving to him. "But here's Magnus, we've got to go."

"Aren't you going to tell me?"

"Yes." He took Tom's hand. "C'mon. I'll tell you, I promise." But he was tired, so tired. He urged himself on. Just get him onto the plane, he thought.

In ten minutes they were at the airport and checking Tom in for his flight. The booking clerk politely informed them that Tom would have to go with the stewardess, but Bill requested a few minutes to say goodbye. It was so much more difficult, he thought, to say goodbye to children than to adults. Their feelings were so transparent and it was not possible to pretend they were any less than they obviously were.

"It's been good having you here, Tom. I'll miss you." He gave him a great hug and then released him again.

Tom bit his lip to stop the tears. "Me too."

Bill turned to Magnus standing beside him and held out his hand. Magnus produced the brown paper parcel from behind his back and gave it to Bill. Bill handed it on to Tom.

"That's the story, all the bits you have and haven't read. I promised you."

Tom put it by his feet so that he could open his small rucksack. He took out his old Walkman and after searching in the side pockets, a tape. Shyly he offered them to Bill.

"D'you remember after Christmas when you gave me a list of the music you liked?"

Bill nodded.

"Well, I didn't forget. I copied them from your records when you were out ... you can have them now."

Bill looked at the Walkman in his hand. "But ... "

"You can keep it." He grinned. "I have my iPod now."

"That was very thoughtful, Tom. Thank you. And," he handed Tom a scruffy piece of paper, "by way of return, this note will tell you how to play Ina's pianola." Understanding dawned on Tom's face. "Yes, it's the one in my room. It's yours."

To Bill's relief the stewardess approached them. She put a hand on Tom's shoulder and smiled brightly at them both.

"Time to go ... if you're to get a good seat."

"Bye, Tom," said Magnus. "Du must come hame again soon and bring dy dad and mum."

Tom nodded to Magnus and then turned to meet Bill's eyes.

"Bye, Tom."

"Bye, Bill."

They hugged each other tightly and then Bill gently disengaged Tom's arms and pushed him in the direction of the stewardess.

As he walked away Bill called out.

"Keep up your drawing and remember … have … "

Tom looked back over his shoulder. "I know … patience."

Then he was gone behind the desk and into security, clutching the brown paper parcel close to his chest.

$\mathcal{P}$OSTSCRIPT

$\mathcal{T}$om put down the manuscript on his grandfather's couch. Tears had fallen on the pages and he wiped them away with the back of his hand. Closing the file, he remembered his grandad's last words to him. He pulled his head up, sniffling loudly, glanced around the room, saw his grandmother's paintings, then a framed sketch that had not been there before caught his eye. It was his first drawing of his grandfather that he had given to Bill as a present.

Biting his lip he got up and searched in the music cabinet for the cylinder. He found the one he wanted, loaded it, carefully following Bill's instructions and sat down at the keyboard. He took a deep breath and pumped the pedals with his feet. The opening bars of Paderewski's Minuet filled the room and filtered down to the kitchen where Alistair put a restraining hand on Cat's arm as she turned to make for the stairs.

****

In Shetland not many days later, Bill listened to the same piece of music on Tom's Walkman. It was late evening and he was sitting on a chair outside the front of the cottage wrapped up in a blanket with his yellow woolly hat perched on his head watching the colour of the sky slowly deepen after sunset. Magnus and Maisie had been in earlier, stoked up the stove and left some hot soup in a flask. Magnus promised to return around midnight despite Bill's weak protestations.

Away to the north Bill could just pick out the flash and faint beam of the Eshaness lighthouse, yet another Stevenson light. He pulled the blanket around himself, wincing with the effort. After Tom had left he had stopped taking the pills: it was only prolonging the agony. Instead, he had stepped up his consumption of whisky. There was a bottle by his feet and a glass clutched in his gloved hands. God, he felt cold … not enough blood to heat the body.

His ears filled with those oh-so-familiar chords that had the power to stop time and take him back to his earliest memories. Not a great piece of music, he granted, but it contained all of his formative life – that minuet. He closed his eyes and tried to imagine his parents but all he could conjure up were the few photographs that grandma had kept for him, so static, so lifeless. How could they be his mum and dad? His grandma he could picture at the piano, his grandfather listening and drawing on his pipe. He thought of Alistair. He thought of Tom with it all to come. He thought of Alice, dear Alice.

Then he thought of Silver, and the faintest of wry smiles crossed his face. Strange, how lighthouses, Scott, and Stevenson, had played such a large part in his early life. All these stories he had written as a child and yet he never wrote or published one when he grew up. He wondered if Tom would like the story he had written for him ... and Alistair? He fantasised for a moment that they might publish it, but under his breath muttered Tom's favourite expression, "Dream on."